AT THE SCENE OF THE CRIME

© 2008 by Tekno Books and Dana Stabenow
(Individual stories copyrighted as per page 4.)
All rights reserved under the Pan-American and International Copyright Conventions
Printed in the United States

9 8 7 6 5 4 3 2 1
Digit on the right indicates the number of this printing

Library of Congress Control Number: 2008928969

ISBN 978-0-7867-2055-2 *3928 6181* *11/08*

Cover design by Mark Cohen
Interior design by Amanda Richmond
Typography: Minion and Trade Gothic

Running Press Book Publishers
2300 Chestnut Street
Philadelphia, PA 19103-4371

Visit us on the web!
www.runningpress.com

AT THE SCENE OF THE CRIME

FORENSIC MYSTERIES FROM TODAY'S BEST WRITERS

EDITED BY DANA STABENOW

RUNNING PRESS
PHILADELPHIA · LONDON

COPYRIGHTS

Introduction by Dana Stabenow

TABLE OF CONTENTS

INTRODUCTION

BY DANA STABENOW

A COUPLE OF YEARS BACK MARTY GREENBERG, the Anthology King, poked his head up and noticed how popular an obscure little television series called *CSI* was. He wondered if perhaps a book of short stories involving criminal cases that turn on hard evidence found at the scene might be equally popular. He wondered further if I would edit such a collection, and I replied, as to my cost I often do to Marty, why, sure. He and John Helfers rounded up a stellar cast of writers and found a publisher, and the result is the book you hold in your hand.

So here, for your enjoyment, thirteen investigations into means, motive, and opportunity that together prove the law of unintended consequences can trip up even the most masterminded criminal, so long as the investigator on the scene is on the ball. I find that kind of comforting.

The scenes of crime are all over the American map, from Brendan DuBois' story set in a coastal fishing village in New Hampshire, to Julie Hyzy's in a retirement home in Florida, to Kristin Katherine Rusch's in a suburb in Oregon, to mine in a wilderness in Alaska. Anything is grist for the investigator's mill, from forensic dentistry to the rate of nuclear decay. John Lutz uses satellite imagery as part of his crime scene equipment to solve the murder of a retired major league baseball player.

Loren Estleman writes about twins separated at birth reunited by murder, Jeremiah Healy sets his story in a McMansion in an Everygated community, and Edward Hoch writes about an arsonist who may or may not be retired. Maynard F. Thomson tells of a retired medical examiner's memories of his first murder. Max Allan Collins and Matthew V. Clemens write about high life in the heartland, and Michael Black's hero takes a bite out of crime in the Arizona desert. N.J. Ayres writes a haunted memoir set in rural Pennsylvania, and Jeanne C. Stein sets a tough urban narrative in the rare book room of a Denver university.

And then I, just to be contrary, wrote a Liam and Wy story that proves that sometimes it isn't all about the evidence. Sometimes it isn't; sometimes it's all about the hunch, whatever that is, wherever it comes from, and whatever you call it, at the scene of the crime.

Pull on your rubber gloves and your paper booties and come on in.

SMART ALECK

BY LOREN D. ESTLEMAN

"WHO CUT HER DOWN?" HENRY ASKED.

Coopersmith, the young medical examiner who'd replaced old Doc Wingate, never looked up from the gizmo that looked like a Game Boy he was manipulating. "Neighbor from across the hall. Door wasn't on the latch and she went in to warn her about that for like the thousandth time."

"Too bad it didn't take after nine hundred and ninety-nine."

The dead woman was identified as Angela Kaybee. She'd worked as a receptionist for a local optometrist, a job that called for a certain amount of good looks, but her protruding eyes and tongue marred the effect. She'd strangled, as most hanging victims did; snapping the neck was a professional's game.

"Suicide?"

Coopersmith didn't respond, absorbed as he was with his gadget, which seemed to be designed for measuring body temperature, but apparently it wasn't working. Sergeant Henry left him, stepping over and around earnest young technicians taking digital photographs and collecting lint in Ziploc bags. Mac Davidoff, his partner, stood out of the way bobbing a tea bag up and down in a cardboard cup.

"Suicide," Davidoff said in greeting. "I heard you, even if he didn't. No ligature marks on the wrists. She tied herself to the ceiling fan and kicked over the chair. Sorry we couldn't come up with something more stimulating, Aleck. This could be your last case."

Henry bent to look at the body sprawled in its taped outline on the floor. "Wears her watch on her right wrist."

"I didn't notice. So you going to travel or what?"

"I thought I'd come down to headquarters every day and sit and tell stories, then drive home real slow in a big car with a hat on my head. Where's the neighbor?"

"In the kitchen. I was about to send her home."

"I'm not retired yet, Mac. Let me finish the job."

"Okay. Don't get testy."

"It's not you, it's these techno-poops. They didn't used to be such pains in the butt."

"That TV show spoiled 'em."

"What TV show?"

"You're kidding. How could you miss it? It's either that or funny home videos on every channel."

"I think I saw one once. The CSIs all carried guns and badges and went around interrogating suspects. Makes you wonder what all the real cops are doing."

Alexander Henry had been with the department thirty years, twenty-two of them with the detective division. He had a reputation among his contemporaries as a wizard who connected scattered leads into working theories when logic alone failed. They called him "Smart Aleck," with varying degrees of affection.

"Hey!"

Trying to avoid a hefty young woman on her knees with an aerosol can, Henry bumped into Coopersmith, still thumbing buttons on his handheld device. "Sorry."

"I wish you gumshoes would go out and get a doughnut or something until we're finished here."

The sergeant found a middle-aged woman worrying her hands at the table in the apartment kitchen. He introduced himself. "You were right to cut her down. A lot of people assume they're dead already."

"I watch TV. I used a knife from the kitchen." She shuddered.

"Did you know Miss Kaybee well?"

"No. She wasn't that sort of neighbor. But we've had some burglaries here. Some of the younger residents don't lock their doors and it gets around that the building's an easy mark. When I saw her door wasn't even closed—"

"Was she right- or left-handed?"

"I—I don't know. I don't notice that kind of thing."

He smiled. His warm, weary smile was his best interview technique. "That's because you're right-handed. We lefties have to mess with tools designed for the other hand several times a day, so we're sensitive to a thing like that."

"How did you know I'm right-handed?"

"You wear your watch on your left wrist. People tend to wear it on the one they don't use as much, to avoid banging it against things. Miss Kaybee has hers on her right wrist."

"I didn't see her all that much. She was rude the last time I told her she should lock her door. I don't think she was a nice person. Is it important what hand she favored?"

"Probably not. I'm supposed to ask these things is all."

"Well, if it is, I'm sure the criminalists will figure it out. They're so dedicated."

"Yeah, we're lucky to have 'em."

Back at headquarters, Davidoff rapped on Henry's desk. The sergeant was staring at a safety poster that had been on the same wall for ten years. "You're not retired yet, you said. Plenty of time to daydream when you're out fishing every day."

"I don't like fish."

"There's always catch and release."

"What's the point?"

Davidoff shook his head. "We got a positive ID on Angela Kaybee from her boss, the optometrist. Of course, that's just for the paperwork. Her DNA matches the hair and skin cells all over the apartment."

"Prints?"

"She had no criminal record in this state, so there's nothing on file, but we printed her postmortem. They matched with the partials all over the apartment and a honey of a full set on a bathroom glass. Pretty soon we won't have to take civilians down to the morgue anymore. I won't miss that part of the job."

"Pretty soon there won't be a job. The wonks will vacuum up everything we need and spin it in a dish and e-mail the results straight to the prosecutor. Department'll gut all the interview rooms and put in handball courts."

"What do you care? You'll be living on your pension."

"Did you ask the optometrist if she was left-handed?"

"How could I forget? You've been obsessing over it. He said she was a rightie. He's a southpaw himself, so he noticed."

"Any chance someone else dressed her after she was dead and put the watch on the wrong wrist?"

"CSIs would've reported that, but you can ask."

"Did you play the despondent card with the optometrist?"

Davidoff smiled. "Did you ever notice live people aren't ever despondent, only sad or depressed? They're only despondent after they clock themselves." He shook his head. "He was too preoccupied to judge. He was working up his nerve to fire her. She was rude to patients and he suspected her of dipping into petty cash."

"Her neighbor said she was rude too. It'd be a nicer world if people hanged themselves because they were rotten human beings. If she was a thief, she might have a criminal record in another state."

"We're doing a search, that's routine. It won't matter to the investigation. We know who she is without having to check any prints she might have on file, and the techs says all the evidence is consistent with suicide."

"Toxicity report?"

"You'll have it when we get it."

Henry looked at the safety poster. "Don't we usually compare DNA with samples from blood relatives, just to plug all the holes in ID?"

"No relatives yet. Prescription medicines in her cabinet gave us her doctor. Family history in her records lists a mother, deceased. Nothing on her father. She wrote down Düsseldorf, Germany, under place of birth."

"No one said anything about a German accent."

"We're doing a computer search on the mother. That ought to clear up plenty."

"Computers and test tubes," Henry said. "Maybe this time next year we'll all be fishing."

"And the techno-poops shall inherit the earth."

"Now I'm despondent."

The morgue was all stainless steel and Coopersmith, the medical examiner, all starched white cotton. He got out his cell phone to check the time; Henry seemed to be taking too much of it from the first minute. The young man drew the sheet down from the victim's naked corpse so the sergeant could examine her left wrist.

"Doesn't look like she ever wore a watch there," Henry said.

"She didn't. There are old pressure marks and a tan line on the right, where she wore it all the time."

"I'm working on the theory she was left-handed."

Coopersmith lifted a sheet on a metal clipboard. "Greater muscle and bone density in the left biceps, humerus, radius, and ulna, indicating more frequent use. Theory checks." He sounded reluctant to surrender the point.

"Her boss said she was a rightie."

"Witnesses are human. Trust science."

Henry straightened. "This isn't Angela Kaybee."

"Based on what, some kind of hunch? Those went out when DNA came in. It's her. No two people have the same."

"That's what they said about fingerprints."

"They said that because it's true. It's like snowflakes."

"I saw a snowflake last winter that looked just like one I saw in 1963. Nobody's taken a close look at all of them. If you printed everyone who ever lived and everyone who ever will, the law of averages says there has to be a duplicate set somewhere, sometime."

"But not in the same place or time. Odds against it are ridiculous. This is Angela Kaybee." The M.E. slid the sheet back up over her head as if to seal off any more discussion.

The mother's name was Kaybee as well. The computer search established her as a natural-born U.S. citizen who had married a German national named Oskar Bern and accompanied him when he returned to Düsseldorf. Hospitals in that area found no birth records connected with either name.

"Home delivery," Henry told Davidoff. "Spread the search to include individual doctors and midwives."

"New faith in technology?"

"It has its advantages when you know where to look. What about that toxicity report?"

"Next item on the list." Davidoff turned a page in the folder he'd carried to Henry's desk. "Barbiturates in her system. Checks with the prescription bottle in the bathroom. Her doctor was treating her for insomnia. That can lead to depression, you know."

"Did she take enough to kill her?"

"No."

"Why use a rope when sleeping pills are so much easier?"

"Let's ask her. Oh, wait, we can't. She killed herself!"

"What effect would the amount she took have on her?"

"I asked. I'm a detective too, don't forget. Depends on level of resistance. She'd been taking the pills for a year. Trace amount could put a beginner out for the count or just make a chronic user pleasantly drowsy."

"What I hate about science," Henry said. "It isn't an exact science. Somebody slipped her a mickey, then strung her up."

"I gotta say she was a possible candidate for murder. So far everyone we've talked to—coworkers, neighbors, her boss, even her doctor—wouldn't nominate her for Miss Congeniality. Money seemed to come up missing from purses when she was around. That doesn't mean they hated her enough to go to any more trouble than just bonk her with a rock."

"You're forgetting it isn't her in the morgue."

Worry lines accordioned his partner's forehead. "Aleck, you're running full-tilt into a brick wall of evidence, all because a couple of people who knew her said she was right-handed."

"Three so far. It isn't her. What's holding up that out-of-state record?"

"You'll have to look into it yourself." His partner spoke coldly. "The brass want this one closed so we can get through the rest of the pile sometime this year. You can afford to be a dinosaur. I've got three years till retirement."

"Okay, Mac."

Davidoff snapped shut the folder. "Oh, hell, I'll get you what I can. You realize if it turns out she's wanted for something it's just another motive for suicide."

"I'm okay with suicide, if that's what it is. I just can't go fishing until I find out who it was who committed it."

It came to him next morning when he was brushing his teeth.

The evidence clerk didn't recognize Sergeant Henry at first. A careful dresser, he had his coat buttoned wrong today and the skinny part of his necktie hung down longer than the wide part in front. It was plain he'd thrown everything on at a run.

"Kaybee case," Henry said. "I need her driver's license."

He drove with it to the airport, where he showed the clerks at the airline counters Angela Kaybee's picture on her license with his thumb covering her name. Northwest and American were no help, but as he was turning away from Delta a baggage handler spotted the photo and remembered her as the woman who'd tipped him a quarter to push a half-dozen bags up to the counter. The clerk who'd checked her through was drinking coffee in the break room. She nodded when Henry showed her the picture, shook her head when he moved his thumb away from the name.

The police in Düsseldorf arrested Angela Kaybee when she stepped off the plane. She was traveling on a passport in the name of Andrea Bern.

"Twin sister." Mac Davidoff shook his head over the fax from Europe. "Separated in infancy when the parents divorced. The mother returned to America with Angela, Andrea stayed in Germany with her father. How did you know?"

Henry sat on the corner of his partner's desk. "I heard somewhere that identical twins have identical DNA. Techs overlook that; untidy. It made Andrea a likely candidate for the woman in the morgue. They were mirror twins. In a case like that, one is left-handed, the other right. Sometimes they even have their organs on opposite sides, but not this time."

"They don't have the same fingerprints."

"Not exactly, but there were enough points of similarity not to clash with the partials we got from Angela's apartment. She gave us the only complete set we got when she pressed Andrea's fingers around the bathroom glass. By then the barbiturates had made Andrea pliable enough for anything. They were Angela's prescription, remember; she was the one with the resistance."

Davidoff glanced through the rest of the communications on his desk and slid them over. "Angela dipped into the till of every business she ever worked for in three states. She'd've done forty years easy when it all caught up with her. Her sister picked a hell of a time to visit."

Henry read. The recent death of Andrea's father had placed his documents in her hands. When she found out she had a twin sister in the U.S., she'd looked her up on the Internet.

"It was a gift to Angela," Henry said. "Andrea's record was clean and she had their father's trust fund. Angela even had a sample of her sister's signature on her passport for practice."

"She needed it. She had a one-day layover in Germany, just long enough to transfer the fund to a Swiss account before she skedaddled to Amsterdam. She couldn't risk slipping up in front of her sister's friends in Germany."

"I knew she'd be moving fast. She'd need the cash to fight extradition once we got the official fingerprint file and found out it wasn't Angela in the morgue."

Davidoff grinned. "Congratulations, Aleck. You proved all the scientific bells and whistles in the world are no match for old-fashioned detective work."

"I'm not knocking the bells and whistles today. They'll help make the conviction."

"You can afford to be generous; you're legend now. What was the name of that old-time railroad worker who beat a steam engine?"

"John Henry."

"Any relation?"

Alexander Henry glanced at the watch on his right wrist. He'd been retired six minutes. "We'll have to compare DNA to find out."

BETTER LUCKY THAN GOOD

BY JEANNE C. STEIN

DETECTIVE PATRICK MCDUFF WAS ON A TEAR.

"We can thank television for this. Not a thing goes on anywhere in the world that we aren't privy to. We've become inured to the horrible atrocities inflicted every day upon the most vulnerable in places whose names we can't pronounce. Terrorists and tornadoes wipe out entire villages in third world countries and we don't give them a second thought. Wars are waged, but unless they affect the price of oil, we yawn and click the remote."

I had to stifle a yawn myself. I agreed with everything he said, not that it bore the faintest relevance to what we were here to investigate. At best, he was making an ass of himself in front of strangers. At worst, his pontificating in the middle of a case confirmed what some of my colleagues long suspected: my partner was losing it.

We're standing in the middle of the Rare Book Room at a major Denver university. McDuff, me—Detective Lorna Fitzgerald of the Felony Theft Squad—and the forensic team. It's 9:30 a.m. on a Tuesday in late October. The call came in to dispatch two hours ago. The head librarian reported to work and found the door ajar. At first, she thought it was the cleaning team. Again.

Until she opened the Rare Book Room. Six volumes were missing. Books worth a cool $3.2 million.

Standing right outside the room now are two hand-wringing librarians: the head librarian who discovered and reported the crime, and her assistant, who arrived moments after we did. Members of the forensic team have taken photographs and are now at work processing the scene.

The Rare Book Room is a room in name only—in actuality, it's a vault. About ten feet by ten feet in size. Two walls with floor-to-ceiling glass-fronted bookcases fitted with key locks. Tempered glass, according to the librarians. The vault door is six-inch tempered steel with a combination lock. There is no sign that it was tampered with. The interior is temperature controlled, with a security camera in the upper right-hand corner. A six-foot steel work table and two metal chairs with padded seats and backs are against the third wall. The only items on the table are a computer monitor and a box of latex gloves.

All my observations. McDuff doesn't seem interested in anything except continuing his diatribe.

"The one area we seem to be paying close attention to," he says, "is crime—specifically how to commit it and get away with it. We have here a perfect example."

He draws a breath, poised to rage on.

I put a hand on his arm. "I think calling this a good example of a perfect crime is disturbing the natives." I keep my voice low and surreptitiously jerk a thumb toward the librarians. "They're upset enough without giving them the idea we'll never recover their books."

McDuff pauses at that, looking down at me as he always does, making me feel like a kid who wandered into the adult's corner by mistake. He's fifty-something to my twenty-nine, six feet to my five-two and built like a square-bodied wrestler, all planes and angles. He has six months to go until retirement and he's determined to spend those last six months letting everyone know how he feels about everything.

He does, however, stop long enough to follow my gaze to the two outside the door. The librarian closest to us has stopped her hand wringing and is frowning. "You don't think you'll catch whoever stole our books?"

Thick, horn-rimmed glasses perched on a thin nose magnify the concern in her owlish eyes. Even with those glasses, she's pretty in an efficient sort of way. Her short, sun-touched brown hair frames a heart-shaped face. She's wearing a nicely tailored suit, good shoes. She's in her forties, and, according to her statement, the head librarian.

"Not at all, Ms. Simmons," I reply before McDuff can. He'd probably advise her to file the insurance claim. Now. "We're giving this case our full attention. These books, besides their monetary value, have immense historical value as well. They are irreplaceable and we intend to get them back."

She doesn't look reassured.

Probably because McDuff is shaking his head in a way that suggests I have no idea what I'm talking about.

As usual. The fact that we've been partners for a year and have the best record in the major crimes department for closing cases is eternally and irrevocably lost on him.

Laura Givens, one of the forensic investigators, catches my eye. I excuse myself and step over to where Laura has been swirling fingerprint powder over the glass doors that until a few hours ago held six rare art books. She inclines her head in a curt nod toward McDuff.

"He's in fine form today."

"Let's shut him up. Got anything?"

Givens nods and points to a set of fingerprints caught by the magnetic powder above the catch on the cabinet door. "Clean as a whistle except for this. One full, several partials. Of course, we won't know if these belong to our thief until I compare them with Ms. Simmons and her assistant. According to her, they're the only two allowed access to the books."

"Run them as soon as you can and let me know."

I've turned back to Ms. Simmons, now speaking with quiet urgency to the woman introduced earlier as her assistant, Melanie Byers. Byers is a little shorter than Ms. Simmons, heavier, plainer. Ten years older. She's dressed in tan slacks and a white shirt over which she's draped a worn cardigan of muddy brown. She's looking up at Simmons with an expression bordering on hysteria. I step closer to hear the exchange.

Simmons: "Why did you come back last night?"

Byers: "I didn't."

"Don't lie. I saw you. You were spying on me."

"Why would I?"

An eyebrow rises. "Because you wanted something to use against me? You've been trying to get in his good graces since I came on board. This must have looked like your best chance."

"Use what against whom?" I interject myself into the conversation.

They jerk away from each other and turn toward me.

Simmons speaks first. "No one."

Byers: "We weren't talking about the robbery. We were talking about— something else."

And I'm the tooth fairy.

I'm going to let it go. For now. "The security camera. I need the tape."

Simmons nods, regaining composure. "Of course. Come with me."

We leave the vault and I follow her to the back of the library, through a door she opens with a key, into a small room. Six by six. Barely bigger than a broom closet. Nothing but a console in here and a computer monitor. Green blinking lights on the console board indicate tapes running. Simmons points to one of them.

"That's the camera in the vault. The two next to it are focused on the main reading rooms. The others are cameras above the entrance outside, my office and the stairwell."

"I'll need them all."

She reaches to eject the tapes.

I stop her, slipping gloves on my own hands. "Just show me."

She does, pointing to the eject buttons below each tape well. I take each tape as it slides out of the machine, bag and tag, watch as she slips new tapes into the slots and reactivates the system.

"Are you the only one with access to this room?"

"Yes. No. My assistant has a key. She's not very computer savvy so I'm the one who checks the tapes each morning to be sure the system is running. I change the tapes once a week. On Monday morning."

Today is Tuesday. The robbery took place last night. Only twenty-four hours to examine. Very efficient, considering most businesses change their tapes once a month. Or once a year, making the tapes worthless as constant rerecording deteriorates the images until they become unrecognizable.

"What do you do with the old tapes?"

"We keep them for a year. In a storage area below the administration building."

"I'll want our tech to dust for fingerprints in here."

Simmons nods and I speak into my radio, asking Givens to join us. She does and I let her work her magic while Simmons and I return to the vault.

The forensic team is finishing up. They've dusted the surface of the table, the chairs, the area up around the security camera. The supervisor, Will Lahey, a tall, lean black man with hawkish eyes, is speaking to McDuff when I return.

"Nothing. Whoever broke in probably used the latex gloves so obligingly available on that table. Didn't even have to bring his own."

Simmons catches the undertone of sarcasm and bristles. "The books in this vault are priceless. Some are hundreds of years old. The gloves are used to protect the paper and ink from oils on the human hand that would destroy them over time. Without gloves, we'd have no access to the books at all. We couldn't touch them."

McDuff is listening, a thoughtful rather than abrasive expression on his face. For once.

"Who is allowed access to the books?" he asks.

Simmons ticks them off on her fingers as she replies. "Professors, some grad students, occasionally members of the public if they're doing research and are vouched for by a staff member. Everyone signs in and either Byers or I remain with them while they are using the books. They are allowed one book at a time. They can work two hours at a time. They must make an appointment in advance." She's shaking her head. "With all our safeguards, I don't understand how this could have happened."

McDuff says, "Can I see the sign-in book?"

Simmons leads him over to her desk. Byers, who I've almost forgotten about, follows behind.

I turn to Lahey, consulting my notes. "Simmons said she's the only one with the combination to this door. She and Byers each have keys to the cabinet, but without access to the combination, the keys aren't worth much."

Lahey smiles. "A real locked door mystery. Maybe the prints on the cabinet will give us a clue. I wouldn't count on it, though." He takes the bagged tapes out of my hand and holds them up. "I'll get these back to the lab. Do you feel lucky?"

"Unfortunately, no." McDuff was right. Anyone who has watched *Law & Order* would know how to disable or cover a security camera lens.

"Jenkins and Taylor will stay behind to finish up in the outer office," Lahey says. "I'll see you back at headquarters."

McDuff comes back just as Lahey is leaving. He hands him the sign-in book, also in a plastic evidence bag. Simmons watches Lahey depart; a frown of concern pulls at the corners of her mouth.

"Ms. Simmons."

She drags her eyes off the departing Lahey and refocuses on me. "Yes?"

"You are the only one with the combination to the vault, is that correct?"

A nod.

"You can't be here every hour of every day. What happens when you're on vacation? Or have a day off?"

"Access to the books is restricted by my schedule. If I'm not here, no one goes into the vault. Period."

"But the combination must be kept somewhere. What if there was an emergency? A fire? Or something happened to you?"

"The vault is fireproof. If something happened to me, there is one other person with access to the combination. The president of the university. He keeps it in a safe in his office."

Givens rejoins us, giving me a furtive shake of her head. Nothing in the security room either.

She heads off in the same direction as Lahey had moments before.

McDuff looks around the vault. "I think we've done all we can for now, Ms. Simmons," he says. "The president of the university is waiting for us downstairs. No one is to have access to the vault until we give the okay. We'll have to secure the outer office, too. I'm sorry for the inconvenience."

McDuff apologizing? He actually sounds sincere. Unbelievable. Could he be on to something?

Simmons looks as if she's about to object. I follow McDuff's lead. "We can't risk missing something that might lead us to the thieves. You want to get those books back, right?"

That's something she can't argue. McDuff motions to Simmons and starts for the door. He casts a backward glance at me and then to Byers, still standing beside the desk that held the sign-in book. Her posture is rigid, her expression drawn and frightened.

I let McDuff escort Simmons out of the room before I approach Byers.

"I'm sorry about all this," I tell her. "It must be very upsetting. I don't suppose there's a place we could get coffee, is there? The forensic team needs to finish up in here and it would be easier if they didn't have to work around us."

She shrugs. "There's a staff lounge down the hall."

"Do you mind showing me?"

She casts an uneasy glance toward the open vault. "What about that?"

Interesting. Simmons didn't make that inquiry. She just left with McDuff. "There are two policeman stationed right outside. I'll ask them to come in and stand guard until we get back. Will that be all right?"

She reluctantly agrees, I bring the uniforms in, tell them not to let anyone except the forensic team in or out, and we head for the lounge.

It's a typical faculty setup. Coffee bar, refrigerator, a few vending machines, utilitarian tables and chairs. Doors marked "women" and "men" against the back wall. There's no one else in the room. We had moved everyone outside as soon as we began to process the scene. The coffee machine is making gurgling noises, though. It had been started before we arrived.

I gesture to the coffee machine but Byers shakes her head.

I motion to a chair and she sinks into it. I perch my butt on the corner of the table. "Have you worked here long?"

"Twelve years."

She's staring down at her hands. "She's going to blame me for this," she says quietly.

"Who? Simmons? Why would you say that?"

She doesn't look up. "Because she wants to get rid of me. She's wanted to since the day she arrived."

"Which was?"

"Six months ago."

I feign surprise. "She's only been here six months? And she's your supervisor?"

Her shoulders draw up. "She has the advanced degree. It's the way academia works. I trained her. I know more about rare books than anyone else in the state. In the country, probably. But she has the advanced degree so she gets the title."

I shake my head sympathetically. "It's the same with police work. Some kid comes off the street with a college degree and he's promoted to detective over street cops with ten years' experience. It's a bitch."

"You're pretty young to be a detective," she says, eyeing me warily. "You one of those kids, too?"

I grimace. "You caught me. But I did my time on the street before I got my degree. And I work hard to prove myself. Have to with a partner like McDuff."

I get a half-smile at that. "He's a character. He doesn't think we'll get those books back, does he?"

"He's been wrong before." I let a few heartbeats of silence stretch between us. "What did Simmons mean about your coming back last night?"

She flinches. "It's nothing."

"I don't think it's nothing, Ms. Byers. And if you want to keep Simmons from accusing you of complicity in the theft, maybe even of being an accessory, you should tell me your story before Simmons tells hers to McDuff."

Byers's eyes widen. "Could that happen? Could I be charged with being an accessory?"

"Depends on what you did."

Color floods her cheeks. "She told me I could have the night off even though it was my turn to close. She's never done that before. I don't know why I was suspicious, but I was."

"Simmons said she saw you. What did you see?"

The color deepens. She hesitates, then, "This is too embarrassing."

"For whom? You?"

At that question, her reticence evaporates. Words tumble out. "No. Not for me. For Simmons. I might have been wrong to sneak back but what she was doing was certainly worse. She was having sex."

Byers spits out the word like it tastes bad. It's such a visceral reaction, I have to keep from smiling. She doesn't notice though, because she's still caught up in her story.

"It was the most shameful thing I've ever seen. They were doing it on a chair. She was straddling the guy. That's how she saw me. Of course, as soon as I realized what was happening, I got out of there."

I'm visualizing the layout of the office. The vault. The outer office. The outside door opens directly into the office space. The vault door is in the back, out of sight. For Byers to approach unnoticed, Simmons must have been having sex—

"They were in the vault?"

Byers nods. "Awful, isn't it?"

"Could you see who she was having sex with?"

She shakes her head. "No. They were on one of the chairs. She was facing the door. He had his back to me. She didn't even stop when she saw me. Just gave me a look and I left."

The chairs in the vault are metal but the seats and backs are cushioned. "Excuse me a minute," I tell Byers. "I need to check in with headquarters."

She nods and I step into the hall. I dial one of the CSIs still working the office. Don't want to risk walking down there and having Byers follow. I keep my voice low.

"Jenkins? Check for DNA evidence in the vault. The chairs, specifically.

There might have been some extracurricular activity there last night. Thanks. Let me know what you find."

Byers doesn't look as if she's moved a muscle since I left the room. Is she even breathing?

"Sorry for the interruption. Let's get back to what you saw last night. Can you tell me anything at all about the man with Simmons?"

Byers draws a breath. "Not much. I only saw him from behind. He had short brown hair. He was wearing a red plaid flannel shirt. Jeans." She frowns in distaste. "I know because I could see them bunched around his ankles. And he wore glasses."

"Glasses?"

She looks pleased that I picked up on that. "They were on the table. Horn-rimmed frames. Tinted lenses."

"Wow. That's very observant of you. Anything else?"

She shakes her head. "No. I'm sorry."

"Was there anything about him that you found familiar? Do you think you may have seen him before?"

She considers the question a minute before answering. "You know, there was something about him. I'm just not sure what. Can I think about that awhile?"

"Of course. While you do that, I'll go back down to the office to check on the crime scene techs. See if they've come up with anything to help us."

She nods.

"Would you like a cup of coffee or some water before I go?"

A smile. "Water would be nice. There are some bottles in the refrigerator."

I fetch one for her. I leave her sipping from the bottle, her expression veiled and serious, anxious, I'm sure, to dredge up anything to identify Simmons' lover.

I'm just at the door when she snaps her fingers. "Wait. The security camera. It would have caught them. Have you checked it?"

I shake my head. "The tape is at the lab. I'm sure as soon as a technician examines it, he'll let me know if it can help us." I pause again. "But Simmons knows the vault has a camera. I doubt she'd let herself be caught on tape."

A cloud darkens Byers's eyes. "And she knows how to manipulate the tapes, too. I'll bet she's erased everything that happened last night."

"If she has, we'll know."

This time when I start out the door, she doesn't stop me.

Jenkins is working the vault when I come in. He's using an LED lamp on the chair cushions. He slips off orange UV glasses and hands them to me.

"Bingo."

I look through the lenses. Semen is naturally fluorescent and under the lamp, the sample glows. "And the other chair?"

Smith nods. On the table rests a plastic tube containing a pad stained orange-red. He takes a second from his kit, opens the cardboard cap, and moistens the pad with distilled water. He runs the pad over the chair seat and slips it back into the tube. He crushes a vial, squeezes, and this pad, too, turns color.

"Who knew rare books were such a turn-on?" he says.

Not me. Of course, none of this brings us any closer to knowing who stole the books. Consensual sex is not a crime.

Smith is putting his toys away. "I'll get the samples back to the lab. Any idea who the donors are?"

"Not sure. For now, run them through CODIS. Maybe we'll get lucky."

Smith grins and holds up the tubes. "Somebody did."

Byers is right where I left her when I head back to the lounge. She's finished the water, is rolling the empty bottle nervously between her hands. She looks up when I appear in the doorway. "I haven't remembered anything else yet," she says with a sigh. "I'm sorry."

I shake my head. "Nothing to be sorry about. You're doing your best. Why don't you join Ms. Simmons and my partner downstairs? I'll finish up here and join you in a minute."

I stand aside for her to precede me out of the lounge door. She tosses the empty water bottle into the trash can to the right of the door on her way out. It's a natural, reflexive thing to do.

Just as it's a natural, reflexive thing for me to pick it out of the trash and take it to Jenkins.

McDuff is standing in the foyer of the library with Simmons and Byers and a tall, lean, graying man in a well-tailored suit and Gucci loafers. Outside, there's a knot of about thirty or so students and a half dozen faculty members either drawn by curiosity because of the police cars parked around the entrance, or waiting for the library to open. They've been corralled by uniforms and moved to the side.

McDuff spies me coming out of the elevator and calls me over.

"Detective Fitzgerald, this is Arthur Nichols, president of the university. Dr. Nichols, my partner."

We shake hands, briefly because he drops mine at the moment of contact, and says, "Are you finished with the library yet?"

The question catches me off guard. I would have expected his first inquiry would be whether or not I had any idea who stole the school's most valuable books. I frown. "We'll finish up as soon as possible. We have a team checking the entire building as well as investigators working the Rare Book Room and the outer office. I must tell you, though, it may be tomorrow before we can allow general access to the library and longer for the Rare Book Room. We'll have to seal that area until our investigation is done."

He isn't happy with my answer. He has the kind of face that you see featured on ads for retirement villages—distinguished, tan, comfortably well off. However, the vibe he's throwing off—abrupt, aggressive, almost hostile—is at odds with the image.

We've been together long enough for McDuff to pick up on my vibes and right now, he reads my negative impression of Dr. Nichols. "We'll hurry things along as much as we can," he says to him in a placating tone. "You must realize, though, that our first priority is getting the books back. I'm sure it's your first priority, as well."

Nichols grumbles that of course, it's important to find the books. He throws Simmons and Byers a look that suggests regardless of the outcome, their tenure at the university is in serious jeopardy. Then he's charging back through the door, avoiding questions thrown at him by the milling crowd outside.

McDuff follows. Simmons said Nichols had the only copy of the combination in his safe. McDuff will be on his way to see if it's still where it's supposed to be.

Simmons and Byers look shocked at Nichols' attitude. Simmons breaks the silence first. "He thinks it's my fault."

Byers opens her mouth as if to respond, then abruptly closes it. After a moment, she says, "He blames me, too. How could he blame me? You're the only one with the combination to the vault. Did you forget to lock it last night? After all, you were distracted."

Simmons's eyes flash. She looks at me, then back to Byers. "You told her?"

Byers' jaw tightens, her shoulders tense. "What the hell," she snaps. "What do I have to lose? I'm probably going to be fired, too. At least I'll have the satisfaction of taking you down with me."

My own shoulders are tensing as well. Am I going to have to break up a catfight? "Ladies, ladies." I motion to a uniform standing a few feet away. "Ms. Byers, will you go with this officer? Just for a few minutes. I need to talk to Ms. Simmons."

She doesn't argue. She has the self-satisfied look of one who is about to witness something wonderful.

Simmons, on the other hand, is exhibiting great concern.

I take her into an alcove and she leans against the wall. She covers her face with her hands.

"It was stupid," she says. "I shouldn't have done it."

"Shouldn't have had sex at work or shouldn't have stolen the books?"

She straightens up. "I didn't steal the books."

"What about your boyfriend?"

"Boyfriend? God. He's not a boyfriend. Exactly."

"He have a name?"

"Jeffrey Talbot."

"Did Jeffrey steal the books?"

"No. The cabinet was locked when we were—" she blanches, "when we were having sex."

"Why the vault?"

A shrug. "It was different. It's a game. We take turns coming up with inventive places to have sex."

"You've only been with the university for six months. How long have you and Jeffrey been playing this game?"

"We've known each other since I moved to Denver. Almost two years. It's not what you think. He's married to my cousin. We get together once a month or so. None of this makes me sound like a very nice person, or a smart one, but having an affair is not against the law."

Her tone is becoming defensive. Her bearing is, too: she's leaning toward me, hands in fists at her side.

"If you want a suspect, look at Byers. She's jealous of me. She wants my job. She may have the combination to the vault for all I know. She's been undercutting me with the president since the day I arrived."

"What about the security camera in the vault? What am I going to see when I look at it?"

That deflates the aggressiveness. She sinks back against the wall. "I rewound the tape when we finished. There will be a time lapse of about forty minutes." Her voice drops, then brightens. "But doesn't that prove I had nothing to do with the burglary? You'll be able to see the cabinet and the books inside. I closed the vault at ten. The books were there."

My cell phone chirps. I excuse myself, telling Simmons to stay put until I come back.

When I'm out of earshot, I open the connection. "Fitzgerald."

"It's Laura. Ran the fingerprints on the cabinet. They belong to Byers. Found tiny particles of something foreign in the prints. I'm running tests on that now. Lahey is processing the DNA from the chairs. Any chance you can get samples from Byers and Simmons for comparison?"

"I'll ask. I gave Jenkins a water bottle. Start with that. In the meantime, I'll call for a warrant. Just in case I can't persuade the librarians to volunteer."

Laura signs off and I call an assistant DA to request a warrant. When I return to the lobby, Simmons is no longer where I left her.

She's squaring off with Byers.

"You bitch. You're not going to get what you want. You saw Dr. Nichols. He'll fire both of us as soon as this is sorted out. I won't have any trouble getting another job. What are you going to do?"

Byers isn't rising to the bait. "I can take care of myself," she says. "But I wouldn't be too sure about finding another job if I were you. With the Internet these days, you never know what's going to show up."

Simmons's face darkens. "You post anything defamatory about me and I'll sue you."

Once again, Byers opens her mouth as if she's going to fire back, then stops herself, takes a deep breath, remains silent.

I touch Simmons's arm. She turns toward me, her expression angry, combative. This time, I tell the uniform to escort her to the other side of the lobby. She looks like she wants to resist, but doesn't, casting one last, fury-filled frown Byers' way.

"She's something, isn't she?" Byers says to me. "I'll bet she and her boyfriend plan to sell the books and run off to Tahiti. She doesn't care about the loss to the university. She only cares about herself."

My cell phone chirps. I shake a finger at Byers. "Stay here."

She nods and I walk away to take the call.

"It's Lahey. I've got two interesting bits for you. First, the stains from the chairs in the vault. Semen and vaginal fluids in one. The other—just vaginal fluids. The combination we can't match. Not until we get samples from Simmons and her boyfriend. The vaginal fluids, though, are Byers's. We were able to match it from the water bottle."

"No semen in that one?"

"Not a trace. And nothing to indicate a condom was used. No lubricant, no spermicide, no residuals of any kind. I'd guess it was a party of one. Second, the substance in Byers's fingerprints? Coal dust. Minute particles."

I snap my phone shut. Coal dust?

I look around the building. The university is one of the oldest in Denver. It's been retrofitted many times with new heating and air conditioning systems. Originally, though, I'd bet there was a combustion heating system of some kind. I dial McDuff.

He picks up on the first ring. "Yes?"

"Are you still with Nichols?"

"In his office as we speak. The combination was in the safe in an envelope with a notarized stamp across the seal. Doesn't look as if it has been tampered with."

"Ask him if the library had a coal-burning heating system at one time. And if there's an old furnace room somewhere in the building."

I hear him put the question to Nichols. And I hear Nichols' answer. When McDuff comes back on the line, I ask, "When was the last retrofit?"

Nichols answer comes through.

Ten years ago.

McDuff says he's on his way back to the library and I sign off.

The next call I put through is to the search team making a sweep of the building. They'd started on the top floor of the five-story building and were making their way down. I tell them to send a team to the basement and look for an old furnace room.

Byers has been watching me. Not out of concern. Her expression is detached, more curious than anxious. I'm about to start back to her when my cell phone rings again.

"Fitzgerald? This is Dan Lowrey from the computer lab. Ran through the tape you sent us of the vault. Had no idea librarians were so frisky."

"Meaning?"

"The tape from last night? Twenty-two minutes of nonstop sex in glorious color. Followed by ten minutes of black screen. Then, the camera is back on and the books are missing."

Whoa. Not what I expected to hear. "Have the tapes been doctored in any way?"

"It's possible. We'll look at that next. Just thought you might want a preliminary report."

I snap my phone shut. Simmons thought she'd erased the tape. I look over at her. She's talking to the uniform, gesturing toward Byers, her posture tense, angry, incredulous. She admitted to erasing the tape. Obviously, the tape she erased was not the one she expected it to be. That tape must have been removed before she got to it.

I cross the room and tell the uniform he can go back to Byers. Simmons's expression is wary.

"Ms. Simmons, I just heard from the computer lab. The tape we took from the player isn't missing any time. At least, not the time you were with Talbot in the vault."

Color drains from her face. "That's not possible. I took careful note of the time. I erased ten minutes before and ten minutes after . . . after what we did."

"Did you watch the tape before you erased it?"

"Of course not. Why would I? I used the time indicator on the control. I was very precise."

I feel Byers's eyes on me. When I glance over, she's watching us.

Simmons's voice is tipping quickly to hysteria. "Do you mean what we did is on the tape?" She looks past me to Byers. "She did that, didn't she? She must have stayed behind and switched out the tape before I got to it. That's what she meant by something showing up on the Internet. She copied it." She stops. Suspicion flashes in her eyes. "What else? What else did she do to the tape?"

"We're not sure she did anything, Ms. Simmons. But I will tell you that there was a ten-minute blackout on the tape and when taping resumed, the books were missing from the case."

Simmons jaw tightens. "She's setting me up."

"I thought you said she wasn't very computer savvy."

"That's what she's always told me." Another flash of sudden awareness narrows her eyes. "Do I need a lawyer?"

"Up to you. Of course, if you deal with us, tell us where the books are, you stand a much better chance of making a deal down the road."

Her jaw tightens. "I want a lawyer."

I shrug and gesture to a telephone on a nearby desk. "Your call."

McDuff has entered the lobby and we step off to the side. "Simmons has lawyered up."

He peers down at me. "You don't look convinced she did it."

Once again, I feel Byers's eyes on me. When I turn around, she's watching with the same detached expression. I don't acknowledge her, but focus again on McDuff.

"What was up with Nichols? He acted more put out than concerned over the loss of such valuable university property."

McDuff shrugs. "The university is just recovering from a football sex scandal involving the entire offensive line and a call girl operation. It seriously impacted alumni funding. He's afraid the bad publicity this is going to generate will exacerbate things."

Money. It always comes down to money.

McDuff is looking over my shoulder. "Here comes the search team. Looks like they've found something."

Byers has been listening to our conversation. Her eyes snap from McDuff to the three uniforms approaching. Rather than turn myself, I watch her. Emotions flash across her face like a fast-forward slide show: disbelief, denial, frustration. She catches me watching her and her expression morphs instantly into polite curiosity.

Too late. I saw what I needed to.

I join McDuff in the middle of the room. One of the uniforms is holding a bundle, a heavy bundle by the way he's hefting it. It's large and square and covered by a blanket stained with coal dust. He lays it on the desk and starts unwrapping.

"Found it in the bottom of the boiler in the old furnace room."

Under the blanket is an oilskin tarp. Under the tarp are the books.

Simmons rushes to join us. "My God. You found them. They were here all the time? How did you know?"

McDuff is looking at me. I'm looking at Byers.

She joins us, too. "So," she says. "You found the books. I guess you weren't as clever as you thought you were, Simmons. What were you planning to do? Produce the books later to collect the reward?"

Simmons stares at her. "What are you talking about?"

"Oh come on. You know the university would offer a reward. A substantial one, I'd bet. That's why you weren't worried about finding another job."

Simmons turns to me. "You don't believe her, do you? I swear I had nothing to do with stealing the books. I didn't even know there was a furnace room, let alone how to find it."

I gesture to one of the uniforms. "Take her outside."

The officer takes her arm and steers her away. McDuff hasn't said a word, but his expression as he looks down at me is questioning.

"Why don't you go with them?" I say, jabbing a thumb toward Simmons and the uniform as they head for the door. "I've got a few questions for Ms. Byers to wrap things up."

He nods, his eyes narrowing as he tries to fathom where I'm headed with this. He knows if I was convinced Simmons was the thief, I'd have told the uniform to read her her rights. After a moment, he gives up.

"Okay, Fitzgerald, see you outside."

Byers watches him cross the room. "That was good work, Detective." Her tone is calm, confident. "Do you solve all your cases this fast?"

I laugh. "I wish. I do have a couple more questions for you, though, if you don't mind." There is a stone bench beside the library entrance. I point at it. "Shall we have a seat?"

She lets me lead her to the bench and we both sit. I lean in toward her. "There are just one or two things I'd like you to clear up for me. You know, I've seen a lot of crime scenes and I must admit, I've never come across one as clean as this one. That cabinet in the vault? What do you do, wipe it down every night?"

She smiles, relaxed, cat-like. "Actually, yes. The former librarian insisted on it and I do it now out of habit."

"And the security room, too? The forensic people tell me there wasn't a print on that console. Strange, don't you think?"

"I don't know about that. I never go in there. Simmons probably wiped it down after she doctored the tape."

"Well, that's another strange thing. The tape doesn't appear to be doctored. Doesn't make sense, does it? She tells me she erased forty minutes of the tape and yet, it's all there. In fact, the only doctoring seems to have occurred after she and her partner finished their sex game. There's ten minutes of dead time and then the camera shows an empty bookcase. How could she have made a mistake like that?"

Byers shakes her head. "You'll have to ask her. Besides, don't criminals make dumb mistakes all the time? Isn't that how you catch them?"

"Yes, it is. In fact, I have a hunch that I'm about to catch another criminal right now. Want to know how?"

The tone of my voice, suddenly harsher and accusatory, makes Byers' eyes widen. "What criminal?"

"Well, let's see. You know when I mentioned the cabinet had been wiped down? Well, you didn't do such a thorough job this time. Our investigators found prints. Yours. Above the lock on the cabinet door."

"How do you know it's mine?"

"Good question. All employees of school systems are fingerprinted when hired. Yours was on file. Not tough to match."

"But that means nothing. I told you I wipe down the cabinets every night. I just missed a spot last night."

"But there were particles found in these prints."

"Particles?"

"Coal dust." I glance behind me to the desk where the books were still laid out. "I'll bet we match it to the stuff on that blanket. And I'll also bet when we search your house, we find shoes with the same dust on them. You've been here long enough to know this building. Simmons hasn't. If someone were going to hide stolen property, what better place than an unused furnace room. No one ever goes down there, right? The books would be safe and you could produce them to collect that reward you were sure Dr. Nichols would offer when the time was right. In the meantime, Simmons would be in jail."

Byers' gaze slides away. Her jaws are clamped so tight the muscles at the corners of her mouth twitch.

"I think Simmons underestimated your resourcefulness, didn't she? It was pretty smart of you to keep her in the dark about your knowledge of the security system. What was it at first? A way to get out of an irksome housekeeping chore? She didn't think you knew anything at all about a computer surveillance system, let alone how to dub and substitute tapes. But that's what you did, isn't it? You waited until Simmons and her boyfriend were getting their clothes back on, then you snatched the tape before they left the vault."

She shifts on the bench, squeezes her hands together. She still doesn't say a word or look at me.

I sigh. "You got a lucky break when she didn't look at the tape before erasing it. Our forensic people are examining the tape you left now. I'm sure they'll find something to link you with it. By the way, did you film your little celebratory masturbation act? Was that a way of thumbing your nose at Simmons?"

She sits up straight, her eyes dark with anger. "What are you talking about?"

"You know what I'm talking about. You left evidence on the chair seat."

"What evidence?"

"Come on. You must know. Bodily fluids are detectable. We found your DNA."

"How do you know it's mine and not hers?"

"We matched it."

"How did you get a sample of my DNA?"

"From your water bottle."

"Is that legal?"

"You bet."

She gets quiet again.

"You know, you have an opportunity here to help yourself. We have the books. We can work something out with the DA. Make it easy on yourself. No trial. No messy publicity."

She looks at me a long moment, then smiles. "How did I get into the vault? I don't have the combination."

I've been waiting for that. It's the one thing I don't know. "I can't answer that. Yet. But if I ask Simmons, what are the chances she'll say you could have been looking over her shoulder any of a dozen times she's opened the vault in your presence? Or when we contact the former librarian, will she tell us she trusted you with it for one reason or another? I don't think that's going to be a problem for us. I think it's far more likely to be a problem for you."

Another long minute of silence. Then she says, "I want a lawyer."

McDuff is waiting with Simmons when the uniform leads a handcuffed Byers down the steps and to a waiting cruiser. I hang behind a minute to order a search warrant for Byers' home. I'm hoping we'll find more than coal dust. I'm hoping we'll find the missing tape.

When I join them, Simmons's face is pale with shock. "She stole the books? How—"

I shake my head. "We'll fill you in downtown. We're going to need to get a statement from you. This officer will take you now and we'll be along in a few minutes."

McDuff stands beside me, watches the cars pull away.

"Good guess, Fitzgerald," he says. "It's just like I always say. Better to be lucky than good."

I think about fingerprints and DNA and a computer team poring over evidence in a lab downtown.

"No, McDuff," I reply. "It's better to be both."

THE HIGH LIFE
A HEARTLAND HOMICIDE STORY

BY MAX ALLAN COLLINS AND MATTHEW V. CLEMENS

SUMMER INVADED IOWA IN JUNE LIKE A HORDE OF HUNS, and kept up the looting and pillaging on through July and most of August. With each week the heat grew more intense, the crops suffering in the rural areas, everybody in the cities turning sour, then angry, then just plain pissed.

Now, with Labor Day only a couple of weeks away, the nighttime temperatures in the high eighties and equal humidity made for heat indexes over ninety and a crime rate that rose exponentially with the temperature. The city's crime lab was so overtaxed that the state Bureau of Criminal Investigation just up the road in Ankeny had been forced to pitch in most nights.

Des Moines had become so testy that two citizens had been shot to death at the scenes of separate fender-benders in the last two days—one not even involved in the crash, merely an onlooker who'd spoken up at the wrong time. The sprawling but usually welcoming city had this summer morphed into an unfriendly, hotheaded place where suspicious glances took the place of ready smiles, paranoia pushed out hospitality, and violence had its way with tolerance.

As the hateful cauldron simmered, the concrete buildings of downtown worked like a giant oven. One such downtown building, the Crossroads Towers—a new high-rise apartment complex—had been open less than a year, "paradise in the heart of the city," the brochures said, complete with a full-service mini-mall on the ground floor, including grocery store, sparing its well-heeled residents from ever having to re-enter the real world, if they could work from home, anyway.

Tonight, though, with heat lightning cracking the sky, the real world had entered the Crossroads Towers, where even the twenty-fifth floor didn't seem high enough to avoid the rage that gripped the city.

Pulling up to the guard shack at the entrance to the building's underground parking facility, BCI crime scene supervisor Dale Hawkins—"Hawk" to friends and subordinates alike—was loathe to roll down the window to speak to the guard, and sacrifice air-conditioning for the blast of heat. Fiftyish, with dark hair graying at the temples, Hawkins wore a black short-sleeved shirt with BCI-CSA embroidered inside a badge over the left pocket, the word "SUPERVISOR" embroidered beneath the emblem. Black slacks and black Rocky oxfords completed the outfit.

Cops only wore two brands of shoes, Rockys or Bates. Hawkins had always been a Rocky man. His only accessory was a Glock 21 .45 automatic that dug into his right hip under the seat belt. Slim, rectangular black-framed glasses perched on a nose that might just as easily have been the source of Hawkins's nickname as his surname.

In the passenger seat, willowy brunette Krysti Raines tried not to look as nervous as Hawkins knew she must feel. Porcelain-skinned with wide-set brown eyes almost as dark as the chestnut locks clipped into a short bob, Raines was riding into her first crime scene as a CSA. After four years on patrol with the Des Moines PD, and presumably on the road to detective, Raines had gotten gridlocked by the seemingly endless supply of gold shields in front of her who never retired or took better jobs. Hawkins, seeing the young woman's potential wasting away as she became more and more frustrated, had lured her away to the BCI.

He had practically watched her grow up with the PD. Hell, he'd even instructed her fingerprint class. She'd excelled in several other classes, too, and Hawkins knew she had the skills to handle the tough, demanding job of Crime Scene Analyst.

Now, they would both find out if he was right.

Reluctantly, Hawkins pushed the button on the electric window. The glass hummed down, the heat pouring in like an oven door opening. The guard stepped closer, his thin mouth a straight-line frown that told Hawkins he didn't want to be out in the heat any more than the CSA supervisor. Pushing sixty, the guard could easily be a retired cop, but Hawkins didn't recognize him. His name tag read STUART, and Hawkins, displaying his credentials, briefly wondered if that was a first or a last name.

"What about her?" Stuart asked, his voice obviously ravaged by years of cigarettes.

"She's with me," Hawkins said.

Raines held her own credentials toward the driver's side so the guard could lean in for a better look.

Finally, Stuart nodded them through. "Take the elevator to the twenty-fifth. . . ."

Hawkins pulled away before the guard finished. He knew where the crime scene was and the guard knew he knew. This had just been Stuart trying to exercise his minimal authority. Hawkins hoped the guard had been this diligent all evening, and would make sure the detectives questioned the man about people coming in and out.

As Hawkins wound the SUV through the aisles of the parking garage, Raines remained conspicuously silent.

At this hour, nearly two in the morning, no parking places presented themselves anywhere near the elevator doors. Hawkins turned into a parking place clear across the garage diagonally from the elevators. The two CSAs climbed out of the black Chevy Suburban and marched to the back to unload.

Raines's attire mirrored Hawkins's: black Rockys, black slacks, and black Polo with the embroidered BCI badge on the breast pocket, but her shirt was a Small where his was Extra Large. She gave up six or seven inches to his six-foot-two and weighed half his two-twenty. His new assistant was roughly the age of his oldest daughter, and he figured he was allowed paternal feelings for his recruit.

They each grabbed a silver metallic crime scene valise out of the back, Hawkins chivalrous enough to also lug the camera case.

"Hey, I can get that," Raines said, hand snaking toward the case.

"I'll get it. If you're as good at this job as I think you'll be, you'll have twenty-five more years to lug this stuff around."

"Something to look forward to," Raines said, as Hawkins closed and locked the Suburban's rear doors.

"Long hours, low pay, no gratitude from the bosses or the clients, and on top of all that, if you make a mistake, you lose your certification and your job. What's not to love?"

He was referring to the position Raines strove for: Certified Latent Print Examiner. In the state of Iowa, only a dozen people, including Hawkins, held that certification, and only a couple of hundred nationwide had attained the status conferred by the International Association for Identification.

The price for a single error was indeed the loss of certification. Every member of the small fraternity knew the price of a mistake, and it wasn't just their job at stake. Their screwup could mean an innocent person went to prison, or in some states, on a homicide, to death—chiefly based on an ident they'd made.

"You left some of that out of your recruitment pitch," Raines said as they crossed the garage, their footsteps echoing off cement walls.

Hawkins grinned at her. "Maybe I'm just teaching you not to accept anything at face value."

They got to the elevators and Raines touched the UP button. They had to wait for only a moment before the doors whispered open. The pair got in with their gear and Hawkins hit 25.

"The penthouse?" she asked.

"One of them," Hawkins said. "My understanding is there's four, two on each of the top two floors."

"That must cost a pretty penny."

"A lot of them—those pads are a cool one-point-five million a piece."

"Money's always a good murder motive," Raines said.

"Let's not get ahead of ourselves," Hawkins said.

The twenty-fifth floor bustled with people and noise. The small foyer shared by the two apartments was jammed with two uniformed officers, two EMTs, a guy from the coroner's office, two civilians, a man and woman who might be neighbors, and Detective Ron Stark, a short, skinny guy with longish, dark hair parted on the left. In his early thirties, Stark wore a dark suit too big for him and had inquisitive gray eyes and a straight, thin nose that bisected his face like a sun dial.

"Been a while, Hawk," Stark said, his voice quiet but friendly.

Hawkins nodded. "What was it, the gang thing over by Drake in April?"

"Yeah," Stark said, and shook his head. "That was a rough one." He looked to Raines. "Hey, Krysti, how's the new job treating you?"

She smiled at the detective. "We'll find out."

Hawkins asked, "So what's up, Ron?"

Stark nodded toward the open door on the right. "You might as well just ask Yack. Ain't no point in you hearing the same spiel twice."

"Yack's here?" Hawkins asked. "Middle of the night?"

Stark nodded. "High-profile crime, high-profile detective. These rich people start killing each other, you just know Chief Anderson's going to demand his best man. And you also know Yack can't hardly wait to tell you CSAs how he's already solved the case."

Yack—Phil Yackowski—was, by his own admission, Des Moines' top crime-solving detective. He had the stats and the scrapbooks to prove it. Hawkins had known Yackowski for the better part of twenty years and, unlike the general public, knew the detective had made his bones by stealing the credit on a murder case from a beat cop who had turned up the vital clue.

Gesturing vaguely toward the man and woman huddled in front of the door at left, Stark said, "Roger and Angela Triplett. They're the tenants across the hall."

Hawkins, who made the husband and wife as both in their early forties, was struck by the incongruity of their attire. Mrs. Triplett, an auburn-haired beauty with piercing green eyes in a heart-shaped face, wore a gold evening gown cut just low enough to create an interest in what lay beneath the flimsy fabric.

Husband Roger, his dark hair cut in a flattop, wore jeans, a white Polo, and tennis shoes, expensive ones, but tennis shoes nonetheless. His brown eyes seemed dazed by the crowd and the activity. He kept a protective arm around his wife's shoulders and Hawkins noticed a tiny burn on the man's forearm.

"What's their story?" Hawkins asked. He was content to get this from Stark, not Yack.

"Mrs. Triplett was downstairs," Stark said. "She was hosting a charity function in the second floor ballroom. Her husband said he wasn't feeling well, so he's been up in their apartment all night. He heard the shots, called us."

"Can I talk to Mr. Triplett for a second?"

"Sure."

They approached the couple and Stark made the introductions.

"Mr. Triplett," Hawkins said, after they had shaken hands. "You said you heard the shots?"

"Yeah."

"I would think these apartments would be well soundproofed."

"Yeah," Triplett said, "they really are. The sound was very faint, but I do know a gunshot when I hear one. I served in Iraq."

Given the man's age, Hawkins was a little surprised.

"Not this time," Triplett said, reading Hawkins. "Desert Storm, back in ninety-one. No matter how muffled, I know gunshots when I hear them."

Hawkins nodded. "Mrs. Triplett, you weren't around when your husband heard the gunfire?"

The woman seemed to shrink further into her husband's embrace at the mention of her name.

"No, I was downstairs until Roger called my cell," she said, a quaver in her voice, "and told me."

Hawkins wondered where she kept a cell phone on that dress, but for now didn't push it.

"What about your neighbors?"

"The Hoffs?" Triplett asked.

Before Hawkins could respond, Mrs. Triplett spoke up, surprising him.

"I knew Carl had a vindictive streak," she said, "but I never imagined he was capable of anything like this."

"So, the Hoffs were having trouble?"

"They were separated," Triplett said. "Caroline was living here, Carl spent most of his time away on business."

"What kind of business?"

"He's a commercial real estate developer. He had deals going on all over the country."

"Did he have any history of violence that you know of?"

Triplett shook his head. "I had no idea either of them even had a gun."

"Thank you," Hawkins said. "I'm sure Detective Stark explained that we might have more questions later."

They both nodded.

As Hawkins and Raines moved away, Hawkins turned his attention to Stark.

"Yack's already inside?" Hawkins asked.

Stark nodded. "You and Raines better get in there before Yack decides it was a double suicide and sends everybody home."

Hawkins moved toward the open door of the other apartment, Raines just behind him. They stopped outside the doorway long enough to don latex gloves and plastic shoe covers with the word "POLICE" stenciled in the bottom, so they could tell their own footprints from any they lifted. One thing Hawkins knew for sure: unless the perp was Superman and flew in and out of the crime scene, he'd have left footprints.

The living room was bigger than any two rooms in Hawkins's house. The floor was a light-hued hardwood. The wall opposite the door was at least nine feet high and all glass, letting in the night and the lights of the city.

Raines said, "That's a lot of windows. Could we have a witness in another building?"

"This is the tallest structure in Des Moines," Hawkins said. "Short of having somebody passing by in a low-flying plane, I don't think we're gonna have an eyewitness."

The right-hand wall was mostly bookshelves that ran floor to ceiling, filled with leather-bound books that looked shelved more for their appearance than their content. A large cut-out center section held a big-screen plasma television. The surrounding living room was furnished with a long, wide sofa, two huge chairs with ottomans, and a glass coffee table on a white area rug. The furniture was white leather. At the near end of the shelves, a dark corridor led back to what Hawkins assumed would be bedrooms and the bathroom.

On the left the large room was bisected by a stone wall that contained a gas-driven fireplace. Hawkins estimated the large openings on either side of the fireplace wall were about eight feet wide, figuring the far opening led to the kitchen while the near one revealed a full bar (and another uniformed cop, who waved).

Before Hawkins could say or do anything, Raines stepped up. "C.J., what's up?"

"Hey, Krysti," the uniform said. He was a tall, broad-shouldered kid with a blond crew cut and an easy smile.

"Jacobsen," a voice growled from the adjacent room. Hawkins recognized the cantankerous tone of Phil Yackowski.

The blond uniform turned away from them.

"Does you opening your mouth mean the crime scene crew is finally here?"

Hawkins chuckled to himself. What a jackass. He stepped forward and peered around the stone fireplace to see Yackowski standing next to a white piano, directly between two bodies sprawled on the floor, one male, one female, a small puddle of blood near the man, relatively little blood around the woman.

The female wore only a revealing negligee, her breasts clearly visible through the gauzy material. She lay on her back, a small, neat entry wound in her forehead. The male victim lay on his stomach at almost a ninety degree angle from the woman, his head resting on the left cheek, his eyes open, staring at nothing. He wore a tan Polo shirt, khakis, and expensive brown loafers with no socks. A nine millimeter automatic lay on the floor near his right hand. He had an entrance wound on the right side of his head.

"Yackowski," Hawkins said easily. "What brings you out in the dark?"

The detective was a muscle-bound weightlifter whose biceps bulged beneath the polyester of his navy blue suit jacket. His florid face included a nose that had been broken at least twice and a forehead wide enough to serve as a solar panel.

"Hawk," the detective said noncommitally. Then he grinned and added, "What can I say? The chief wanted the best on this one."

"Where's Dearden, then?"

"What's that, a dig? Dearden didn't get the call, did he?"

"What call? The one advising the detective in charge to tromp through a crime scene before my team had a chance to process it?"

Yackowski's already ruddy face turned crimson as he looked down to see where he was standing. "I took care, damn it. I was studying the evidence."

"You were contaminating the evidence, Yack. You think you can get out of there without messing it up any more than you already have?"

The detective fumed, but carefully walked over until he was in front of Hawkins, the BCI supervisor at least three inches taller than the detective.

"Don't make no nevermind, anyhow," Yackowski said. "This fucker's open and shut."

"Always nice to hear a professional opinion," Hawkins said. "Care to tell me how you arrived at it?"

"The woman," Yackowski said, gesturing vaguely in the direction of the female victim, "Caroline Hoff—this is her place."

"Well-off lady," Hawkins said.

"Not so much. She was married to decedent number two, Carl Hoff. Rich guy with a pretty little trophy wife. Problem was, they fought all the time, and maybe Caroline ran around on him some. So he was divorcing her, only the prenup gave her the condo—she could hump the doorman and the UPS guy and still wind up with the fancy digs. Seems Carl had second thoughts, about losing the apartment anyway, so he comes over, they argue, one thing leads to another, bing, bang, boom, murder-suicide."

"You must have witnesses," Hawkins said, "to have it all laid out like this."

"Just the neighbor across the hall, who heard the shots. He was the one that called it in. Besides, what do you care? Who needs witnesses? It's all about the evidence, right, Hawk?"

Hawkins moved closer to the two bodies. Squatting next to the male victim, he examined the entrance wound in the man's head, near the back of his right ear. There was a small, neat hole, not unlike the woman's wound, with a smear of blood around the wound.

"Yack, nothing would give me more pleasure than to let you go to Chief Anderson with your half-assed theory. . . ."

"Half-assed how?" Yackowski bellowed.

"This is a double murder."

Yackowski wanted to argue, but he hesitated. "Not a murder-suicide?"

"If he shot himself, where are the powder burns around the wound? There'd probably be a starburst wound from a contact or near contact wound, too. That's not here, either. And to top it off, unless Hoff was double-jointed, I'm not sure how he shot himself from this angle. The wound was delivered from almost behind him. Tough shot if you're holding the gun yourself."

Yackowski just stood there.

"Only person shooting himself tonight, Yack," Hawkins said, "will be you, in the foot, if you take this to Anderson."

"All right, all right," Yackowski said. "I get it. You do the crime scene, then we'll go talk to the neighbor again. Maybe he heard more than shots. He might have heard the killer."

"Good. And we'll start with you taking off your shoes and giving them to CSA Raines."

"What the hell?"

"You don't have on shoe covers. You want us to be able to tell your prints from the killer's, or would you just like to give a statement as to your whereabouts at the time of the crime?"

Grumbling the entire time, Yackowski slipped off his shoes and handed them to Raines, who bagged them and somehow managed not to smile.

Yackowski shuffled out on the hardwood floor in his stocking feet, grumbling the whole way, Jacobsen trailing him as far as the door.

When the others were out of earshot, Raines said, "You two have a nice rapport."

"See, already you're analyzing."

"Thanks," Raines said. "Where do you want to start?"

"You do the bodies and the immediate scene. I'm going to poke around a little. Want to make sure we can rule out robbery as a motive."

The rookie looked hesitant. "Are you sure you don't want to do the bodies yourself?"

Hawkins took a couple of steps toward her. "You're going to have to do it sooner or later. Sooner's better."

"This is an important murder—"

"Are there unimportant ones? You're as natural at this as anyone I've seen, and you've had good training, Krysti. Trust it."

She took a deep breath and let it out. "Yes, sir."

In the living room, Hawkins looked around. Knickknacks on the coffee table were untouched, magazines stacked neatly. On a side table next to the front door, a small basket held envelopes that proved to be the day's mail and a set of keys, presumably Mrs. Hoff's. Everything seemed to be in order.

He went down the hall. On the left, he peeked into a small bedroom that had been turned into an office. Again, nothing seemed disturbed.

On the right side of the corridor, he entered a bathroom that felt like stepping onto the flight deck of the starship *Enterprise*. Two glass sinks perched on twin black columns beneath two stainless steel plates with no visible faucets. Beyond those, a small cubicle housed the toilet. Against the opposite wall was a deep, two-person tub outfitted with water jets. Dominating the center of the far wall was a glass-enclosed shower with four brass heads aimed at various angles. The glass walls still showed beads of water. In front of the shower a huge, furry, lavender rug covered most of the Mexican tile floor. It felt damp, but not wet. Someone had taken a shower earlier in the evening. He looked at the towel rack on the wall next to the shower—empty. Maybe Mrs. Hoff had taken the towel, or towels, into the bedroom with her.

Getting his face down in the rug, Hawkins peered at the footprints pressed into the nap. They were already fading away, with no way to preserve them, but Hawkins was sure he could see the outlines of at least two different size feet in the damp rug.

Mrs. Hoff had been wearing a negligee, but Mr. Hoff had been fully dressed. Could they have had a short-term reconciliation that went bad later?

Maybe.

Hawkins pulled a short, unfolding ruler from his pants pocket. Normally he used it to give scale to evidence he was photographing, but tonight he measured the disappearing footprints in the rug. The first print was almost exactly eight inches long, the length of the ruler. The second print was at least two inches longer than the first and much wider.

Again, he wondered where the bath towels were. Looking at a second towel rack between the sinks, he noticed two lavender hand towels matching the rug. He rose and considered trying to photograph the footprints, but he knew by that time he could get the lighting right they would have long since disappeared.

He left the bathroom and returned to the corridor, where he checked two doors, both on the left side. The first door led into a small bedroom that had been turned into an immaculate office, apparently undisturbed. A computer desk occupied one corner, the monitor on top in sleep mode with the power on.

The second door led to the master bedroom. He flipped the light on and found this room immaculate, too. A tall armoire stood immediately to the right of the doorway. A king-size bed took most of the right-hand wall along with two night stands. In the corner in front of him, a flat-screen television and DVD player occupied the top of a dresser. Nearer to him, on the left-hand wall, a double-door closet was closed. After opening it carefully, he pushed back both doors all the way without touching any areas that might contain fingerprints. A wicker laundry hamper stood against the right-hand wall. He used his Mini Maglite to see inside. There were no towels. Where the hell had they gone?

He knew that someone, probably two people, had showered earlier in the evening. Why weren't the towels here?

Hawkins turned away from the closet and let his eyes wander the room as if the towels would suddenly appear before him. He was staring emptily at the bed when he realized a wrinkle stood out on the floral bedspread just where it disappeared beneath the pillows.

Hawkins was no OCD type who needed everything just so, but the obsessive-compulsive who lived here was. That meant that even this tiny wrinkle, something Yackowski probably would have overlooked if he had even bothered to come into the room, yapped at Hawkins like an angry little dog.

No way Mrs. Hoff would have been able to tolerate this affront to her neatness.

Raines appeared in the doorway. "Something's not right."

He looked at her. "What's not right?"

"No shell casings."

Hawkins considered that. "There have to be. The pistol's an automatic. The ejected shells are somewhere."

"Agreed," Raines said. "Just not in this apartment."

"Don't get ahead of yourself."

"Well, they're not in the room where the crime happened, anyway."

"Better," he said. "You've moved the furniture?"

She nodded.

"The bodies?"

Another nod.

First the towels disappeared, now the shell casings. Some murder-suicide. He still had a hunch about the wrinkle in the bed. "What do you see here?" he said.

She took in the room for several long moments, before pointing at the closet. "I see the same thing in here that I saw in the rest of the apartment, somebody with serious obsessive-compulsive issues. The hangers all face the same direction. The clothes are divided by her good clothes, her work clothes, and her casual clothes, and within those sections, subdivided by style and color. Everything has a place and everything is in its place."

Hawkins nodded. "Anything else?"

Raines looked around again, Hawkins watching her. Hawkins was about to tell her his theory when she suddenly said, "The bedspread is wrinkled."

Smiling, he said, "It sure is."

"But what does it mean?"

Hawkins shrugged. "Maybe something, maybe nothing, but the small out-of-place things can sometimes be the most important. Do you have a forceps with you?"

Nodding, she pulled the ten-inch stainless steel tool off a loop on her belt and handed it to Hawkins.

He took it, opened the serrated jaws, got the end of the bedspread between them and locked the jaws, then pulled back, revealing the pink blanket beneath.

It, too, was wrinkled. Releasing the jaws of the forceps, the bedspread fell away and he repeated the action with the forceps on the blanket and top sheet. Beneath that, on the pink satin bottom sheet, was a wet spot the size of a half-dollar near the middle of the bed.

"Looks like someone had sex recently," Raines said.

"Swab that."

But Raines was already moving in, buccal swab at the ready.

She pushed the swab up out of its protective plastic sleeve and gently wiped it over the spot on the bed. Next, she pulled the paper handle so the swab disappeared back into the sleeve. She snapped the small lid on it, then held it carefully as she handed Hawkins a roll of an adhesive tag from her pocket.

Using his Sharpie, Hawkins dated the tag, initialed it, then pulled off the backing and handed it to Raines, who placed it over the lid of the swab sleeve, sealing it.

"What have we got?" Hawkins asked.

Raines took a deep breath, then let it out. Holding up the swab, she said, "We have evidence that someone, probably Mrs. Hoff and a partner, had sex in this room."

"Her ex?"

Raines considered that, then shook her head. "Doubtful. I used the electrostatic print lifter and got footprints off the wood floor. I think we have a third person present. Another man, this one wearing sneakers."

Hawkins told her his theory about the towels and the wet rug in the bathroom.

"So," she said, "there were three people here."

"I think Carl Hoff definitely interrupted something. Tell me about the shootings."

"Both were shot from a distance of about six feet. It looks like they were both shot with the same gun, about the same caliber anyway, judging from the entry wounds, and the shell casings have disappeared from Hoff's automatic."

"Anything else?"

"The footprints indicate a struggle between the man wearing the tennis shoes and Hoff, who was trying to get away when the man shot him. The killer wiped the gun clean of fingerprints, then put it on the floor near Hoff."

"Which one of them shot Mrs. Hoff?" Hawkins asked.

"Hoff tested positive for gunshot residue. It looks like he shot his wife, wrestled with her lover, lost the fight for the gun, then tried to get away but got shot in the head."

"What's the first rule about witnesses?" Hawkins asked.

Raines gave him a sharp look. "First on the scene, first suspect."

"Good. Now, who called in the crime?"

"The neighbor, Roger Triplett."

"Right. What kind of shoes was he wearing?"

"Tennis shoes."

"Did you notice the burn on his arm?"

"Yeah. It wasn't very big."

"About the size of an ejected shell casing?" Hawkins asked.

"Oh hell."

"Go get Yackowski and Stark."

"Right away," she said, and turned toward the door.

"Krysti."

She stopped and looked back.

"If Triplett's still in the hall, don't let him know you know. If we're going to convict him, we're going to want the towels and casings. He didn't have time to leave the building, so they've got to be here somewhere. We can only hope he was dumb enough to hide them in his own apartment."

She gave him a quick nod and headed down the hall. Hawkins pulled out his cell phone and woke Judge Jonathon Maynard from a sound sleep. The judge was, naturally, livid, but once Hawkins explained the situation, Maynard agreed to sign a search warrant and fax it to the security office of Crossroads Towers.

Hawkins went out to the primary crime scene where Raines and the two detectives waited for him.

"You got something?" Yackowski asked.

Hawkins had Raines explain their findings to the detectives.

When she finished, Yackowski said, "I'm supposed to believe that shit?"

"If Triplett got the gun," Stark said, "why shoot Hoff?"

Hawkins said, "For one thing, Hoff now had a witness to him killing his wife. Triplett would never be safe. At some point, Triplett's going to claim self-defense."

Stark shrugged. "Could it have been?"

"This is a far-fetched bunch of bullshit," Yack said.

"If it was self-defense," Hawkins said, answering Stark and ignoring the older detective, "what exactly was Triplett protecting himself from? Hoff was disarmed and running away. Self-defense is not shooting a man in the back of the head from six feet away."

Raines asked, "And in the case of self-defense, why steal the evidence? What we have here is two separate homicides. Hoff shot his ex-wife, then Triplett shot Hoff. The crimes just happened to have been committed with the same weapon."

Starting to buy in, Yackowski said, "And you're sure the lab will find what you say they'll find?"

"They'll do all the tests," Hawkins said, "but I'm betting we'll get a DNA match to Triplett from the bed, match his shoes to the prints in the dining room, and we can probably get a positive GSR test with the warrant. If we find the towels and shell casings, we'll have a slam dunk."

Turning to Stark, Yackowski asked, "Where's Triplett now?"

Shrugging, Stark said, "We released them. I think he and his wife went to bed. I know they went into their apartment. Hell, it couldn't have been ten minutes ago."

Without another word, the quartet moved through the apartment and into the corridor.

A security guard in a Crossroads Towers suit jacket and black slacks waited for them. He held out a small sheaf of papers. "Which one of you is Mr. Hawkins?"

Hawkins accepted the papers. They had their search warrant.

Yackowski knocked on the Tripletts' door.

No answer.

Turning to the security guard, Hawkins asked, "How many elevators are running at this hour?"

The guard said, "Just the one. Security. We lock down the others."

Yackowski pounded on the door again.

"Was anyone in the elevator when you got on?" Hawkins asked.

The guard shook his head.

The apartment door opened and a teary Angela Triplett opened the door.

"We need to speak to your husband," Yackowski snapped.

She took an involuntary step backward. "He . . . he's not here."

"Where is he?"

The woman was crying again now. "The stress was getting to him. He went out for a pack of smokes. He knows I hate it when he smokes, so he won't do it in here."

Yackowski headed for the elevator.

Hawkins stepped forward. "Mrs. Triplett, how long ago did he leave?"

"Not even five minutes ago," she managed through ragged breaths.

"Was he carrying anything?"

The woman looked puzzled, her handkerchief now twisting between her hands. "How did you know that?"

Ignoring her question, Hawkins asked his own: "What was it?"

"He said he was going to drop the garbage down the chute," she said pointing at a small door recessed in the wall between the apartments.

Yackowski was already punching the elevator button, but Hawkins yelled, "He's in the stairwell!"

Yack stood frozen for a second, but Stark hit the stairway door and started down. The burly detective came out of his trance and tossed a walkie-talkie to Hawkins. "Stay in touch," he said as he went through the door behind his partner.

"Follow them," Hawkins said to Raines. "Triplett might just be dumb enough to ditch the evidence in the building's trash bin."

With a curt nod, Raines disappeared after the two detectives and the suspect.

The elevator dinged and the door slid open. Hawkins stepped in.

"You want me to come with you?" the security guard asked.

"No," Hawkins said, holding the door open. "You stay here. Are you armed?"

The guard nodded and held up a small can of pepper spray.

"You stay with Mrs. Triplett. Make sure she doesn't warn her husband by cell or otherwise."

"Yes, sir."

"If Triplett comes back, you don't hesitate, you don't warn him, you just spray the hell out of him and call 911. You understand?"

"Yes, sir," the guard said.

Hawkins half expected the guy to salute and snap his heels, but, thankfully, the doors whispered shut and the elevator started its descent. Hawkins had pressed the button for the parking garage, figuring that was where Triplett was headed. As he rode, Hawkins withdrew his nine mil and clicked off the safety. Triplett had left Hoff's gun at the crime scene, but that didn't mean Triplett didn't have one of his own.

As the elevator eased to a stop, Hawkins dropped into a shooter's stance. He knew he was ahead of Raines and the detectives, but he probably wasn't ahead of Triplett—

The doors silently slid open and Hawkins arced the gun across the opening.

He saw nothing in the darkness. He stepped out and waited a few seconds as his eyes adjusted to the dim light of the garage. He listened carefully in the silence for a sound, any sound, the scraping of a shoe on concrete, the click of the safety of a gun, the clunk of a car door, anything that would tell him where Triplett was.

Creeping forward, pistol at the ready, Hawkins strained to see into the cars on either side of him as he moved down the middle of the aisle. He wished he had thought to ask Mrs. Triplett where their parking place was. This was slow going, one car at a time, first on the left, then on the right, then back on the left . . .

Sweat ran down Hawkins's back; his hair matted to his forehead as he inched forward. The garage was cooler than outside but only a little and the heat pressed in on Hawkins as he searched the Lexus, then the BMW, then the Jaguar.

Still no sign of Triplett.

To his left and behind him, Hawkins heard the scraping of a door and it occurred to him that maybe he had beaten Triplett to the garage and the killer was now behind him. Hawkins spun and trained his pistol on the doorway and saw a nine millimeter Glock coming through the door first. He increased the pressure on the trigger. Just as he was about to squeeze off a round, Hawkins saw the burly frame of Yackowski follow his pistol into the garage.

Then a car roared to life and Hawkins whirled as a gray Lexus lunged out of a parking place, tires squealing as it charged toward him.

Steadying himself, even as he heard Raines shout behind him, Hawkins took aim and squeezed the trigger, once, twice, three times. The car continued toward him even as the first shot punched through the windshield. The other two bullets followed the leader through the spiderwebbing glass as Hawkins dove for cover between two cars.

The Lexus heeled to the left, scraping against a concrete pillar, sparks flying as the car smashed into a parked Cadillac. Even before the sound of the crash had fully died away, Hawkins was on his feet, running toward the smashed Lexus, his gun poised to shoot. The air bag had deployed and Triplett was trying to get out from under it as Hawkins aimed his pistol through the shattered passenger-side window.

Triplett saw Hawkins and the weapon and stopped battling the bag and raised his hands. Yackowski, Stark, and Raines came running up.

The detectives yanked the suspect out of the car and cuffed him. Raines reached a latex-gloved hand through the window, picked up a white garbage bag, and carefully shook the broken glass off it. She set the bag on the concrete floor. Inside were two lavender bath towels that Hawkins recognized as a match to the ones in the Hoff apartment.

Two shell casings fell out of the towels.

Stark read Triplett his rights, but the suspect shouted over them: "Carl shot Caroline! I was just defending myself."

Hawkins pointed to the garbage bag. "And this?"

"I panicked. I didn't think anybody would believe me."

"You're a smart man," Yackowski said. "'Cause we don't."

Triplett's eyes widened.

"He was running away from you," Yackowski said. "You didn't have to shoot him. You had the gun. Why didn't you just call 911 and bust his ass?"

Triplett's gaze fell and he said nothing.

Hawkins stepped forward. "Because Hoff knew. That's it, isn't it, Roger?"

Triplett kept his eyes on the cement.

Yackowski asked, "Knew what?"

Hawkins's eyes bored into Triplett until the suspect finally met his eyes.

His voice barely above a whisper, Triplett said, "He knew about Caroline and me."

Yackowski, incredulous, said, "You witnessed a man kill your lover, his ex-wife . . . and then you shot him because he found out about your affair?"

"Our money's all Angela's. If she found out about Caroline and me, she'd have divorced me, whether Caroline was alive or dead."

Yackowski was shaking his head now. He looked over at his young partner, who shrugged and rolled his eyes.

Hawkins laid a hand on Triplett's shoulder. "Why pick up the shell casings, and take them with you?"

Triplett didn't answer.

Hawkins pointed at the burn on the man's arm. "The ejected shell casing was hot and burned you—you figured we could get DNA from that. You didn't know which casing burned you, so you took 'em both, right? To avoid DNA testing?"

Triplett swallowed, then nodded.

"Just so you know? We couldn't have got a damn thing off those casings."

At his side, Raines whispered, "He'll go away forever. All to cover up an affair with a dead woman."

"I guess the lowlife just didn't want to risk it."

"Risk what?"

"Losing the high life."

RUST

BY N. J. AYRES

You have to keep the dark voice away. It does no good.
Life breaks every man, didn't Hemingway say?

TROOPER ERIN FLANNERY, OUT OF BETHLEHEM, PENNSYLVANIA: Five-six. One-twelve, brown over brown. Red-brown over brown. Over hazel, make it, a kind of green. At her funeral, speakers said she was a loyal friend, good at her job, full of zip, had a beautiful smile. Everyone loved her, they said.

When she came aboard Troop M, even I thought of asking her out. But dating people from work—no good. The day our Commander, Paul Ooten, told us a female was joining us he warned not to engage in excessive swearing and crude remarks to see how she'd take it or to show she was one of the boys. He'd seen it before, and it was comical and juvenile, and nothing more than bias in the guise of jokes. He reminded us of the word "respect" used in the state police motto, and that our training includes the concept of military courtesy applied to civilians, peers, and superiors, whatever the gender. Unless some miscreant pissed us off while breaking the law, and then you can beat the shit out of him, he said. We laughed. Commander Paul Ooten. A lot like my dad. Upright, ethical, fair. Firm, yet fun when the time called for it. He also reminded me of my dad in the way he talked and in some of his mannerisms, like swiping a knuckle under his nose after he delivered a punch line. My father died when I was twelve. Heart attack in his police cruiser.

Everything changed.

My mother was okay for a while. Then she slowly took to drinking. By the time I was fourteen, she was into it full throttle. She dated, and each time it hardened me more. The idea of her wanting anyone but Dad sickened me.

It wasn't like she brought guys home, but she might as well have.

As soon as I was out of school and found someone to share rent with, I moved out, enrolled in community college, and later, with my AA degree in hand, applied to the Pennsylvania State Police Academy. What I really wanted was to go to Missoula where my uncle lived, study writing and film, and then wind up in California or New York, doing that scene. But I needed money from a job. I more than satisfied the physical training, aced the written and orals. Bingo, I are a cop.

Within seven years I earned a couple of medals for distinction in service. The last recognition was from the community, the "DUI Top Gun Award" for nailing forty-nine intelligent people who got behind the wheel while drunk.

Once, when I was ten, I alerted some neighbors across the street that their house was on fire. They called me a hero. I wasn't a hero. I was an ordinary kid who knew enough to realize a ton of smoke was not coming from a leaf pile in the backyard. My dad was the hero. He ran to the house with a ladder to get Mrs. Salvatore from the second floor.

I'm twenty-eight today. Today, like when you go to the doctor and the assistants ask and even the doctor asks how old are you today? Uh, yesterday I was twenty-eight, and today I'm twenty-eight also, thank you. And I'm single after a two-year marriage to a girl who couldn't dig someone who always thought he was right. I tried, really did, to see more gray instead of black and white. The marriage just wasn't meant to be. She went back to Alabama, teaches elementary school there. I wonder how she'd view me now.

How old are you today? A hundred inside.

When Officer Flannery transferred over she was required to put in her time on reception. Nobody likes that duty, but there aren't enough civilians for it even though our governor is high on recruiting them. Right away the guys started testing her, seeing how available she might be. Married, unmarried, didn't matter. It's a thing guys do. I should say here I never saw our commander flirt or kid in any way that made it seem Erin was anything but another trooper.

Commander Paul Ooten's a real family man. That's what I heard all the time. I'd seen him with his family at a state patrol picnic once. Pretty wife. Two kids, about eight, ten.

And I saw him one night, behind a motel near Tannersville, coming down the stairs from the second floor, Trooper Flannery in front of him.

I had just gotten in my car after coming out of a restaurant. Parked perpendicular to the restaurant, nose in to the motel, I went to wipe moisture off the side mirror and then looked up. At first I thought my eyes were playing tricks on me. The light over the staircase and landing was fuzzy from moist air. The couple had long coats on. I watched them walk over patchy snow to her car. She got in, and a different light, coming from the motel sign near the street, hit her face, brighter, paler. Paul shut her door. She rolled down the window, and he leaned over and kissed her, then stood watching as she pulled away.

The next day I had a hard time looking at him.

A couple of weeks later, I was at my desk on a weekend. I had off, but my review was coming up and I had to get some overdue paperwork in. Ooten's door was open. Half of him was visible through the doorway, cut vertically, or I'd see him when he'd get up to go to his file cabinet.

Bill Buttons was in too. He's a kiss-up. Buttons thinks he's Bruce Willis. Shaves his head, swaggers around, crinks his mouth to smile. Sometimes when Ooten is around, Buttons makes like Bruce Willis making like John Wayne, saying, Wal, pardner, let's get 'er done. The effect: ridiculous.

That day, Paul Ooten came out of his office a couple of times, said something to Buttons, something to me. I tried forcing my feelings, tried to look at him the way I did before the night outside the motel with Erin. But I kept picturing him on her, her doing stuff to him.

When Buttons left for lunch, Paul—it's hard to call him Commander Ooten anymore—came into Room 5 where there are mail slots against the wall, a supply cabinet, a small refrigerator, the coffee machine. I was pouring coffee for myself. Ooten put a memo in a slot and then took some time to mention the weather, the Eagles game, and how he'd been thinking of taking a course in Excel. I couldn't hide my lack of interest, but I guess because I had recently lost my mother to cancer, he said, "If you need to talk about it, Justin, my door's always open."

I said something like Thanks, I'm fine. His manner, the kindness behind it, touched me. And I resolved to put what I saw at the motel out of my mind.

What's bitter is that Erin Flannery didn't die from a car accident or a long-hidden disease. She died from brain trauma in her own home.

Detectives interviewed the civilians in her life: family, friends, neighbors. They interviewed us at Troop M too, in due time. I wondered what Paul Ooten had told them. I wondered if the strained expression I saw each day was worry about his secret being outed, or if the tightness in his face was the shame he knew he brought to the badge. I'll say this: for some guys, if they learned the commander was boning Erin he'd only be more of a hero in their eyes.

No boyfriend turned up in the investigation. Bill Buttons said that's sure hard to believe, a piece like that.

A crime of opportunity, we concluded. It happens. Even to cops.

Kleinsfeldt said he overheard there was something odd about the evidence in her case, he didn't know what. We asked who he heard it from. He wouldn't say.

I reminded the guys that Flannery had been an LEO, a Liquor Enforcement Officer up in Harrisburg. It sounds like soft duty, but not necessarily. You go undercover to nab idiots who sell to minors. You look for cheats who avoid taxes by importing liquor from other states. You bust speakeasies. Yes, they still call them that, those enterprises too un-enter-prising to get a liquor license. The Bureau of Liquor Control Enforcement also goes after illegal video gambling machines, looking for operations sus-pected as hooked to corrupt organizations. Maybe she found one and was afraid she'd get cashed out because of it. Patrol sees our fair share of action, I don't mean we don't. It's more than spotting violations of the vehicle code. When your number's up you can get killed responding to a distur-bance call as well as by some desperate speakeasy owner.

One time Erin found a note on the seat of her desk chair. It said he wished he were her seat cushion. She told me about it only because I was walking through the lobby and saw the look of disgust on her face as she studied the paper still in her hands. "Some jerk," she said. Said it quietly, almost with sadness. I don't know why that particular note would bother someone so much, but then I've never been a woman. I told her maybe it could be the computer guy, Steve Gress. He was in every week, supposedly upgrading our systems, which only created more problems. I'd noticed the way he looked at her.

Carl Carolla had a thing for Erin too. I could tell because of his talk around her. He'd roll out some cockamamie story about which creep he had to deal with that day, what some wise-ass said. He said, "Joker like that, what you do, you rack up more offenses. Keep the dumb-ass violator from his appointed rounds, and hit him hard in the pocket." Carolla could be a suspect, maybe like if Erin told him to get lost after a clumsy pass.

Another cop, Rich Kleinsfeldt, resented her. Claimed women cops are a danger to everybody. Some dingbat can grab hold of their hair and then lift their sidearm, he said. Women's hair, according to dress code, has to be above the uniform collar points. Even so, it could be used for a handle, especially if it was in a braid. Another species, they are, says R.K. I'll agree that women offenders are the worst, you go to arrest them. They'll bite, yank, spit, what have you. "She's skeeter skinny anyway," Rich said. "You want that for your back?"

* * *

Something funny about the crime scene. Is that what Kleinsfeldt said? I knew one technician at the crime lab in Lancaster I could check with, but it would look odd, my poking around when the case wasn't mine. I let that idea drop.

Before what happened to Erin, I'd be on my runs, doing my job, and find myself thinking about Erin and Ooten. Ooten and Erin. The ring to it. Her power to lure him. I could understand it, yet not. I was just so disappointed in him. Hurt, you might say, though I cannot exactly say why. Ooten has awards of valor himself, the fact known by reputation and not by paper plastered on his office walls. From his example I did not display mine.

While Erin was at the front desk one morning and no public was in, I was getting pencils—pencils, by the way, not pencil. My seventeenth summer I worked at a dollar store. The boss was training me for assistant manager, said I could take college classes at night, couldn't I, so I'd be free to do a full eight hours? In his instructions, he told me to keep an eye out for what the other employees might be up to. "If they aren't stealing a little, they're stealing a lot," he said. Those words came to mind as I grabbed my second and third pencil for home. I did it right in front of Buttons, whose arm was in the cabinet too, taking a stapler. He already had one on his desk. What did he need two for? I almost think I did it to show him I wasn't such an uptight asshole after all. But I did razz him about it. He razzed me back about my three pencils.

On my way back to my desk I heard Erin say on the phone she was letting her hair grow out. Who was she talking to? Her lover? I couldn't help but glance out the window to see if Ooten's car was in the lot. It wasn't. Every action or nonaction of Ooten's I couldn't help but attach to her.

My review was scheduled for the last day of the month. You always get a little anxious at that time. No one zips through with zero criticism. The review was the same week Erin was to complete her probationary period at the same time, a thing she had to go through even though she was a trans-fer-in and not a cadet. We're a paramilitary organization, the state police, why we're called Troopers. "Soldiers of the law," we are, and we suck it up when we get assignments we don't want or when we get treated like new-bies. Erin said she was content here for the time being, mentioned how good everyone was to her, how terrific Commander Ooten was.

Did she linger on his name? How would the others feel if they got wind of her seeing him on the side? There are more minorities on the force than women. Women, in other words, still stand out. Her misbehavior would come to tarnish all other females entering the force and could severely damage Commander Ooten.

And so it was that I asked if she'd like to have coffee sometime, after shift. In my own way, maybe I was trying to be a decoy. Protect her and the com-mander both. I was a little surprised that she took me up on the invitation. Not that I look like something a dog won't eat. It's just that if she had Paul Ooten, why me? Maybe she saw me as an opportunity for a decoy too.

I suggested a seat near the window at a diner down the street, where we could watch the lazy snowflakes fall, the size of quarters that day. Erin's eyes showed her delight in it. She informed me that snowflakes fall at about the rate of a mile an hour, unless icy droplets form on them to increase their weight. How'd she know that, I asked. "Before I joined the Bureau of Liquor Enforcement, I thought of teaching biology. I'm a science junkie. Then I got out of BLE because the captain, a micromanager anyway, insisted on messing with a restaurant owner who allowed a singer to come in two nights a week."

"Say again?"

"The owner was licensed to sell liquor, could even allow people to dance in the aisles to jukebox or to live music if he wanted. His mistake? He paid a band that had a vocalist. That heinous deed made him in violation of Liquor Law Section Four-Nine-Three-Point-Ten, 'Entertainment on a licensed premise without an Amusement Permit.'"

"You're kidding," I said. "Still, if it's on the books . . ."

"It's a stupid law."

"We're not paid to write the laws."

"Ah, but there was something else. The restaurant owner was an old high-school enemy of the captain. So it was personal. It's not the only reason I left, just the last one. And, unfortunately, my judgment may have faltered when I wrote a letter to the editor about police harassment of small businesses. I disguised my identity, of course. But they were suspicious because of the way I'd been fuming about it. I got congratulations from the guys and glares from the brass."

"Ouch."

"Well, you learn to pick your battles. A lesson."

"I thought you were happy about the change."

"I am. But now I have to start over again."

She didn't get much of a chance to do that. Some evil character hit the delete key on her life.

Forget about the old days when people said tough guys don't eat quiche. Tough guys don't ever say the word depressed. I'll say it here so that maybe my actions could be understood, if ever they can.

After Erin died, on duty I'd sit off Interstate 80 and watch violators speed by. And one day, while off the rolls, I spotted a shoplifter out back of Sears in Stroudsburg look three ways and then languidly wheel a barbecue away and load it in the back of his SUV. Yesterday I saw that Gress guy, the computer jock, fudge his time card, look at me, drop it in the bin and walk away like saying, Challenge me, Muskrat, what you got in your den? And how did I know he stole time? The look. If he hadn't been smug, I wouldn't have gone to the bin and picked up the card. But he was right: I didn't challenge him. Something else was on my mind.

A few days after the coffee with Erin, I asked her out again, for a Saturday afternoon movie. We went to see *Jarhead*. Arrived in different cars. Paid our own tickets in. "You understand this is not a real date," she said. "You understand this is not real popcorn," I said. "It's packing foam." Afterward, we stood on the sidewalk outside the mall, discussing the movie. She saw stuff in it I didn't. In the chilly sunlight, talking about things outside of cop-dom, she was flat-out beautiful.

In the walk to our cars I finally couldn't keep the question away. "Want to make it official sometime? A genuine date?"

"Probably not a good idea."

"Yeah," I said. "Peace."

"Peace."

We went our separate ways.

I consider myself a balanced man, don't go off half-cocked. What my nature allows, my training reinforces. So I do not tell the rest of this lightly. It's not that hard to understand the primitives who believe in demons entering a person's skin. I say this because I don't know what came over me in the case of Trooper Erin Flannery and Paul Ooten: I became a spy. I felt righteous, principled, and therefore gave myself permissions I would never give someone else. It was the mystery of her drawing power I couldn't get out of my head, that force that makes a man like Commander Ooten forsake his marriage vows and teeter on the verge of disgracing his profession.

I took to rolling through Nazareth some weekends to see if I could spot her. I knew that's where she lived, but not precisely. Nazareth isn't that big a town: six thousand people. It's about ten miles from troop headquarters and under nine from where I live in Bethlehem—Steel City, a name that fit before the Bethlehem Steel mill and its support businesses fell victim to the Japanese business onslaught.

Driving down Center Street one day, I saw Trooper Flannery coming out of a drycleaners with her bagged uniforms. I am ashamed to say I followed her to see the apartment complex in which she lived.

And later, on occasion I would go off my route to drift down her street and see if I could catch sight of the commander's car, see it in the apartment parking lot. Sneering at my own bad behavior, I called it "volunteer surveillance." I hated what I was doing yet could not keep from the patrol. We were on extra alert because of a terroristic threat. Watch for violations on small refrigerator vehicles, the bulletin said. Stop and search if indicated. Drive by Erin Flannery's residence to see if Paul Ooten's car was there. Other guys were out at bars, cracking wise and watching games. I was stuck on one note and it was sour. Tomorrow I would shed this thing.

Don't ask me how a reporter for the *Allentown Morning Call* got it, but it happens sometimes. His piece told the basics of Pennsylvania State Police Trooper Erin Anne Flannery's demise. The state police spokesman was reserving comment on manner of death. I should think the public reader would conclude, as would any cop, that homicide was on the minds of investigators. I spent a restless night. The next day State Commissioner Corporal Robert Metcalfe announced before TV cameramen that Trooper Flannery's case was under investigation as murder, and he was sorry but he could not release any details.

"Honor, service, integrity, respect, trust, courage, and duty." Our motto. I am familiar with courage as it pertains to rescue, or in the midst of violent disputes, even in the frequent chaos of felony arrests. I've not only witnessed it but, if you'll excuse me for saying so, performed within its lighted shaft. But could it be that those were times not of action but reaction, mindless as a ball springing off the floor of a gym? Moral courage, there's the mark, and a harder one to hit.

It's clear that lying violates integrity. But does silence? We're not talking the silence of the citizens of Germany in World War II. Not that kind. In Erin's case, nothing will pull her up from the endless recycle machine, not even if I told I was there at the time of her death.

It broke. Mrs. Paul Ooten, given name Mallory, was a person of interest in Homicide Incident Number M1-645-whatever. Mrs. Paul Ooten! Our troop was on fire with speculation, with rethinking impressions of her. And then, of course, there were the terrible distance, disappointment, and suspicion toward the commander himself. I must admit I was halfway pleased there was no gloating, as I might have expected.

The commander was put on administrative leave. It wasn't the first scandal or the first capital case to stain the state police. But it was here, now, among us at Troop M, a mortal wound, it seemed to me. My fellow troopers talked themselves raw. Then, steel bands slowly tightened on our hearts. We grew silent, more involved in what we were trained to do: to be soldiers of the law. We got back to business.

There was a message slip on my desk when I came in one morning two weeks later. It called me to a meeting at Bethlehem headquarters. I brought along my personal write-up detailing my performance accomplishments this year, as we are told to do at review time. I wondered who would be giving my review now that Ooten was out.

Whatever I can say about him, I'll say I have no doubt the commander would have given me a good one. The only thing he ever admonished me about was failure to properly orient a diagram sketch of an accident scene. For all my driving about, I'd put down north for a street that actually ran northeast, and he caught it.

As I approached the conference room, I saw an officer's winter coat draped on a chair. Two rank rings decorated the coat sleeve, signifying the coat belonged to a major. When I entered the room, there sat the major at the end of the table, Commander Ooten to his right. I looked from one to the other until Ooten spoke. "Good morning, Justin." Motioning, he introduced Major Bryan Manning.

"Have a seat, Trooper Eberhardt," the major said.

My heart was pounding. What kind of promotion could I be in for?

The major began by apologizing for not making it out to Troop M barracks before. "Been busy as a bartender on payday," he said. Intended to put me at ease. I'm afraid I didn't laugh. After more chat about nothing, he said, "Tell me, Trooper, what do you recall about your CPR training?"

Confused, I stumbled through a reply, first repeating "Two hands, two inches, three compressions in two seconds. Fifteen pushes, then two ventilation breaths."

"And what is the distance of travel for compressions, Trooper?"

"Two inches, as I said, sir."

"A third the depth of the chest," the major said.

"Yes sir."

"Makes a body tired, right, Trooper?" the major asked with a smile.

Ooten pitched in: "It can be brutal."

"Sure enough I busted a sweat first time I did it," Major Manning said. "Was a big guy, close to three hundred pounds. I was drippin' sweat on him."

You do the polite thing in a situation like this. Nod, chuckle. But what the hell was this, a grilling on rescue efforts you'd give a cadet? My wooly-pully was on under my uniform shirt. It felt like ninety degrees in there.

Commander Ooten sprung the next question. "You were pretty tight with Trooper Flannery, weren't you, Justin?"

"Friends. I didn't know her well. I mean, we didn't have that much time to get to know each other." I met his eyes, guessing if the probe was meant to inquire if I had slept with her. Slept with the woman Commander Ooten was cheating with. Her lunch hour went long, people said. Dentist, doctor appointments, flat tire, things like that, she would claim.

"She wasn't here but three months, sir." All along I'd considered how quickly she and Ooten hooked up.

How can I describe the look in his eyes? Seeing me, not seeing me. Assessing, reflecting. The oil of the present saturating the rust of the past.

He said, "Carl Carolla observed you tagging after Trooper Flannery, Justin, and not once but twice. Carl thought that was odd. What can you tell us about that?"

"I ... I wouldn't know. He's mistaken." I said nothing more. Silence is a tool in interviews. And even in sales. My uncle told me that. When he'd go to close a deal, he put a pencil to his lips to signal he was through talking. "He who speaks first loses," is what he said. I recognized the tool's use now with the commander and the major, the three of us soundless while the room temp climbed even as I saw through the slats of the blinds behind the commander snow riding slanted chutes of wind.

At last Major Manning said, "Are you up to date on your CPR certification, Trooper?"

"I'd have to check the date, sir. I think I might be due."

"You've rendered CPR before, right, Justin?" Manning asked.

"No sir."

Why did I lie? I did start CPR on a victim once. It was part of an action that won me a Commendation Medal, but in the write-up it was not mentioned nor should it have been. Emergency techs had arrived at the scene seconds after I'd started, so I didn't consider it as actually "performed."

The major sat back, arms outstretched on the table, and looked at Paul, who asked me, "You usually wear a ring, don't you, guy?" Friendly, casual.

"A school ring, yes," I said, and shrugged. I hadn't put it on that day. I glanced at the commander's left hand as he toyed with a collector's pen our troop gave him last Christmas. His wedding ring was still on. I pictured his wife, Mallory, how she must look today, turmoil in her face, heartache visible in her robot motions, her walk, her interactions with her children. Commander Ooten sat there interviewing me about Erin Flannery while his family was torn apart because of his unstoppable urges toward a woman who wound up dead on the floor of her home.

No doubt his wife would be quickly cleared in Erin's case. Ridiculous, when you think about it, how she got tied to it at all. Who in this world would figure that she and Erin had in common a love of the oboe, I kid you not, a love of the oboe, which found the two of them in weekly classes at community college. Mrs. Ooten had lent Erin an old instrument her father gave her as an eleven-year-old, the name "Mallory Parsons" engraved on a gold plate on the case. The very fact that Mallory Ooten was innocently in the home of her husband's lover gave me a pang, my sympathy for her as tender as my own scoured nerves.

What I did not tell my superiors is that the night of Erin's injury she had consumed too much plum wine, and I had been the one to buy it. "I've been a little stressed out," she said. "Things."

"It can get that way."

"You know what? You're way easier to be around than I would've guessed."

"Thanks, I guess."

"It's just that on the job you're so serious."

"Is that bad or good?"

"It is what it is. Could go either way." Her hair looked like shined copper.

This was a couple of weeks after *Jarhead*. Ooten was out of town at a confab in Pittsburgh. Maybe that's why Erin weakened when I asked her out. I felt low about my reasons and almost sorry she accepted. Here she was already involved in deceit with Ooten, and now she was deceiving him with me. Of course, it wouldn't go so far as to be labeled true betrayal, I wouldn't let it go that far. But even if it did, at least the two of us were single.

We met at a Japanese restaurant, a new place I said I wanted to try near the Bethlehem Brew Works. Erin insisted on separate cars again, saying she had things to do that would put her in the vicinity anyway. We sat at one of the table-sized, stainless steel grills where the food is prepared before our eyes Teppanyaki style. The flames flew high on the volcano of onions the chef built. We marveled at his antics with thrown eggs and knives, and, with others, applauded each performance.

In between I looked for a way to caution Erin about her activities with Commander Ooten. I wanted to ask her what in the world did she think she was doing. Ask in a nice way but one that left no doubt that her new friend, myself, was there to help set her straight.

While waiting for the check, I said, "I'm going to tell you something."

She tilted her head, a smile on her lips. "Okay."

"Don't take this wrong."

"Oh boy," she said. She peered into her wine glass, refilled once already, and lifted my saké cup to drain the last few sips. Then she went for the pitcher. "Guess I'll have to do without," she said, shaking it as if more would loosen and come free. "How bad is it, what you're going to tell me?"

"You can handle it."

"Ah, thank God."

"You're a mystery to me, is all."

"Come again?"

"I can't quite figure you out."

She winked at me and reached for her puffy pink jacket from the back of the chair, saying, "Have you figured out I'm a little wasted? If I had any more I couldn't drive. You'd have to arrest me." The way she said it, like a flirtation.

We stood in the parking lot by her car, talking, and then she said, "Ugh. You know, I'm really feeling sick. I don't think I can make it home without urping." She hunched in, and I stood by her and put my arm around her. This could be the most unusual of come-ons, perhaps the same as she used on the commander to get him to take her home.

"It must be the food. It couldn't be the wine and saké. A certain person kept me from that," she said, looking at me sideways, a pixie tease in her smile.

Icy mud sprayed us as a car sped by faster than the driver should have in the lot. The snow was about three inches deep, the woods woven with chalky fog ahead of us.

"Come on," I said. "I'll take you home. In the morning I'll pick you up at your apartment and we can go get your car."

When she quickly met my eyes, I realized she hadn't mentioned whether she lived in an apartment, a house, or a boxcar.

She lived just a few miles away, near a Moravian cemetery. "I go there sometimes and just wander down the lanes. All the headstones lie flat to show that everyone is equal in the sight of God. Rich next to poor, whites next to blacks next to Mohican Indians."

"I didn't know that," I said. "I'm from Montana. We stuff 'em and put 'em in museums." She gave a soft laugh. Her eyes were closed and her head was back on the seat as I'd instructed. It's where my own should have been. I could feel the hot drink still in my veins, the sweet burn that beckons so many, the frayed ends strangely comforting.

"All but the women," Erin said. "The women are buried in their own section. Separate. Inside the church, too."

Her lips shone pink in the boomeranged light. I wanted to kiss her there, then. Instead, I turned the key in the ignition and pulled out onto the road, driving well within the speed limit, sight often flicking to the mirrors. I disdained the fact that Trooper Flannery would let herself get blotto even off duty, but the truth was I also knew in saner times I would not get behind the wheel either. She did it again, that woman. Getting men to tread over boundaries.

She seemed to feel better, once inside. "I guess it was the wine after all," she said. "I didn't eat lunch today. Hey, want some ice water? Or coffee? I'll be glad to make some." I said yes to the coffee.

That's when she got up from the couch we were sitting on. Perhaps I was sitting a little too close for comfort. I shifted to be farther away when she returned, but then I stood up and went into the kitchen with her. She faltered as she took a step, galumphing forward off the rug and slapping soles onto the tile. Laughing, she said, "Holy shit. I really am drunk . . . or something. You know what? I'm sorry, but I think I should just go on up to bed."

Sure, sure, I told her, meaning it.

"Just help me get upstairs and I'll be fine. Thank you, Justin. Thank you, really."

Was it this way with Ooten? But then she also seemed really embarrassed. Who was she? How could one woman do this to two men?

With my help she managed to mount four of the stairs. "Just flip the lock on the way out, will you, Justin? I can make it the rest of the way."

She smiled and thanked me again. I started to go down but then reached the next step up before she did, hardly aware of my action. I brought her around and pulled her to me and sank into her lips. "No," she said . . . and let me kiss her again.

What I wanted to do . . . what I intended to do . . . was scoop her up like Rhett Butler did Scarlett O'Hara in *Gone with the Wind,* but it didn't turn out that way, oh no, it didn't. She jerked back and then . . . as I try to recall this, I am not sure just what happened. All I know is I tried to grab her to keep her from falling. Instead, as she sank she twisted, and my fist connected to the left jaw. In her dive down, her head shot against the square platform of the end stair-rod, and then she flipped and her head went *smack!* on the tile, a gray tile with tan swirls in it until joined with the brightest of red.

Even as early as then I wondered if I'd let her fall. If I'd caused her to fall. My reactions are supposed to be quick. How could I let her slip by?

She was on the floor with her eyes rolled partway up. I began CPR.

You might suppose it crossed my mind to eat the hornet. Oh, I practiced caressing my weapon the way I'd seen it done in movies. And I drew other dramatic scenarios in my mind. My illicit favorite: death by scumbag. I would insert myself into a bad street scene and, while making like a hero, arrange for my own end.

I even imagined a sequence where my body would be found among the homeless at the Bethlehem mill. Once, on a perimeter canvass after a series of home break-ins, I went in at a downed section of fencing near the rear of Blast Furnace Row. Inside the steel skeleton crows flutter. Cat eyes gleam in the alcoves. Scruffy-looking souls, both men and women, cook their meals over fifty-five-gallon drums, glance at you with little interest, as though even in uniform you're just another wanderer there. That is where I belonged. Now I lay me down to sleep . . . forever. But to involve them in my final act would be to pile wrong upon wrong.

Again I was summoned to headquarters. It was a whole month after the first interview with Major Manning and the commander. This time it was two sergeants from the homicide unit.

I won't drag it out. What they laid on me I knew was coming; knew it yet pretended it wasn't imminent, that each day I awakened would be like any other before the incident.

At the autopsy for Erin Flannery it was discovered that her sternum and two ribs were cracked from the compressions I had rendered. When I first began, I did not want to remove her bra. To do so would seem a trespass of its own variety. Because I didn't remove it, the first several thrusts downward scored the flesh over her sternum. In due time I also heard a crackling, like the sound of a cereal bag being pinched tight, but I thought it was interference from the bra. With clumsy fingers, I unhinged the plastic hook in front and just kept on pumping, calling her name before I put my mouth to hers to force in another breath.

It must have gone on for thirty minutes, or so it seemed. And then, when I had no positive response, no reaction at all, curse me, I looked around trying to think of anything I'd touched, and then I fled.

The medical examiner, upon noting those injuries to the chest, instructed her assistant to swab around the mouth and to perform another separate swab on the lips of the deceased. Even this action, through DNA testing, would not have implicated me, save for the fact I volunteered a sample in one of the extra criminal investigation classes I took after joining the force. The sample was sent to the state laboratory as though it were any other, not a student's. It would be held as an unidentified profile. These are kept in the database in the hope that someday they will "hit" in another case that had other trace evidence with which to bust a suspect. Like Mrs. Ooten's fingerprint on the oboe case, my identity would not be known from that saliva sample—except that eventually my superiors pressed for a new sample to be taken. And of course, I complied.

There was the ring the commander asked about—the twist in the garrote, you might say. Nothing at the scene of Erin's death would have pointed my way. I left no fingerprints. I had not touched a glass, nor the banister. I did open the door with Erin's key, but I had on gloves, as I did when I left. Even while rendering CPR, I avoided the blood on the floor. But the ring...

The sergeant who studied the evidence seized on a peculiar mark on Erin's jaw, a curved flame shape with a slight space below, and beneath that a kind of pear shape, a teardrop with a touch of high waist. Two of each shape. Sergeant Geerd Scranton showed me a photo of it. "What does that look like to you, son?"

"I don't know, crooked carrots? With a blotch below?"

"I took up an interest in Indians when I was a boy."

"Did you," I said. Where was this going?

"My name," he said, "means 'spear brave' in Dutch. Piscataway Indians used spears. They'd hunt fish and bear with them."

"Are you onto something, Sergeant?" I asked, feigning only an intellectual interest in the case.

"It's part of a bear print. The nails, the pads. See? Perfect in the photo." He turned the photo my way.

"You could be right."

"I'm told you wear a ring with a bear print on it, Justin. Trooper Buttons says you always have it on."

"Hah. I do. Or almost always. I guess I left it on the sink this morning." I smiled. "I spent some time in Montana with my dad and uncle. God, what beautiful country. Have you ever...? The grizzly is the state mascot. Lots of people wear it on jewelry." I said.

He nodded, waited a few beats, or maybe it was minutes, or maybe it was an hour, before he said, "Why don't you just tell me about what happened, Justin? It must be very uncomfortable for you. Sergeant Kunkle, myself, Major Manning—we know there must have been some pretty powerful extenuating circumstances or you would have done the right thing. Isn't that so, son? Look, we know that sometimes we get pushed to extremes.

Maybe you tried to romance her? Maybe you had a little too much to drink?"

I sat looking at him, stunned he would suggest such things, but not arguing because arguing would only deepen what he already believed.

Again he went on like that, and I shook my head as if I just couldn't believe what test they were putting me through now. I did say I was clueless as to what response they wanted.

And then he used the tool of silence. Crows could have been squalling in the steel mill shadows. The wails of warning cats went chasing their own echoes around. The hollow laughter of the homeless kept piercing my ears.

There is a certain terror in the veins of those who would do right always. I am the junior to the senior, our standards so high there is no true escape.

Perhaps my father knew that, and maybe that's part of why he left us, his daily companions a fifth of whiskey, a bottle of bennies, and tricked-up tubing duct-taped to the exhaust pipe of his cruiser, snaked into his window on the passenger side as it sat hub-deep in mud on the side of a cornfield, a stand of trees blocking the scene from the main road, no reason known, no final written note to tell us why.

As a child, nights, I'd be in bed listening to my parents argue, my mother's voice loud and clear, my father only sometimes shouting back. After his death I tried recalling what all they argued about. I couldn't then, but today I remember a woman's name. An odd name, to me even then: Clarabelle. I remember my mother calling her "whore" and my not knowing what the word meant but that it had an awful sound, the way a roar issues deep from within a throat. Perhaps I should have known, but I was a quiet child and did not hang with any special friends.

It wasn't until I was twenty and spent a final summer with my uncle outside of Butte that I learned the real story of my father's death. Until that time, and even after, I kept hearing of what a good man he was. How positive. How good, how perfect. A model of a man. My image of him was forever ruined by what my uncle revealed and, later, by other things I came to know. I longed to be better than Enoch "Eddie" Eberhardt, and determined to shape my longing into action to become, if it is possible in this world, the truly moral man.

Commander Ooten became my model. I would learn to be like him. Anything or anyone that got in the way to diminish the image I had must only be possessed of a fierce and terrible magic. In my obsession to know what the power was that did trip him up, I laid out a woman who in no way deserved an early end, whose only fault was to be a friend to a family and to a lonely madman.

To this day I do not know if I deliberately put my fist to her jaw. But does it even matter? I either committed or omitted, failed to do what I should have, and encouraged what I should not.

It may be two years now that I've lived on the banks of the Pocono River, there until weather drives me and my fellow campers to find a collapsed barn, a forgotten shed, a building in wait for a bulldozer. Days, we hook fish and toss whatever's left to forever-hungry cats skulking in the bushes. We keep watch on our meager holdings and quickly drive out any offenders. Draw straws to see who will go buy the wine. Days are good. Blackbirds chainsaw the nights. I tell those of you who would listen that even the strongest of girders rust. We are all just wanderers here.

I/M-PRINT
A TESS CASSIDY SHORT STORY

BY JEREMIAH HEALY

TESS CASSIDY, CARRYING HER CRIME SCENE UNIT DUFFLE BAG over a shoulder, heard the uniform at the house's front door say to Detective Lieutenant Kyle Hayes, "Bad one, Loot."

Hayes just nodded, then, almost as an afterthought, glanced back at Tess. "How's your stomach, Cassidy?"

Stung by the implied dig at her professional ability, she said, "Never had a problem so far."

Hayes moved past the patrol officer. "Always a first time."

As Tess followed the detective, she noticed the uniform was a little green at the gills, and, suppressing a shiver, she remembered what the other techs in the CSU called a "debut": covering your initial homicide and autopsy.

"Well," said Hayes to the uniform inside the den, "I don't think we have to wait for the ME on cause of death."

Tess looked at the body sprawled over an oriental throw rug, then looked away, drawing a deep breath.

The house—a McMansion—had a huge living room they'd had to cross before reaching the den, which was more a library. Floor-to-ceiling bookshelves, and not the artsy, leather-bound volumes she'd seen in other rich people's places. No, lots of novels and travel guides, jackets worn, even torn from being handled, and, Tess figured, read more than once. She wasn't that involved in books herself, thanks to dyslexia. In fact, Tess nearly flunked seventh grade before her big sister, Joan, made the principal see what their parents had ignored. But Tess always, secretly, admired anyone who loved reading.

As, apparently, the dead man on the rug had. Hayes said to the uniform, "We got a name?"

"Decedent's Zederberg, Martin, middle initial 'D' as in 'David.'"

"Who found the body?"

"His wife. Nanette. Kollings is with her in the kitchen."

Tess knew Kollings, an empathetic patrol officer and a widow herself. "Other family?"

"Just a son, Steven, with a 'v.' We reached him, and he's on his way."

Hayes nodded. "How about a weapon?"

"Negative so far, sir."

"Cassidy, what would you say?"

Tess didn't mind being called by her last name. Appreciated it, in fact, as a badge of "blue" respect. But she also knew that "Kyle" used it to buffer his own emotions, because he called her sister—the lieutenant's preferred investigation partner—"Joan." The older Cassidy was out on maternity leave three weeks prior to having her baby, which Hayes wished was his baby, too. Despite his romantic hopes, Joan had chosen the law over law enforcement for a husband, marrying an attorney named Arthur.

And now Joan was at the hospital, about to deliver, while Tess was wading into a grisly crime scene commanded by a scorned, pissed-off detective.

"Cassidy," said Hayes, "Am I talking to myself here?"

"Sorry, Lieutenant." Tess forced herself to look at the body. "From the way his skull's caved in, I'd guess an axe. Or, with that big RV in the driveway, a camp hatchet?"

"Might be hope for you yet, Cassidy. That's my take, too." Hayes squatted next to the slight man's torso. "No defensive wounds on the hands or forearms, so I'm guessing this one in the back of the head was Blow Number One. Then, after the vic fell and landed sideways, Numbers Two through—what, Six, maybe?—on the floor." Hayes rose. "Barefoot, too, and bloody soles but no tracks in the living room, so probably he was already here in the den when attacked, rather than being chased into it."

Tess thought out loud. "Or running for it."

"What?"

She looked around the library. "If Mr. Zederberg knew somebody was going to kill him, maybe he wanted his books to be the last things he saw."

Detective Lieutenant Kyle Hayes just stared at Tess. "Cassidy, you are one odd duck."

Consider the source, sister Joan would have told her, so Tess took that as a compliment.

Dusting for latent prints at the threshold of the kitchen, Tess Cassidy could hear Hayes interviewing Nanette Zederberg, but not actually see them. It was like listening to a play being read aloud on the radio.

HAYES
Did your husband have any enemies?
ZEDERBERG
No. No, Marty was in medical supplies. He was always helping people, not hurting them.
HAYES
Anybody else you can think of who might want to hurt him?
ZEDERBERG
Just the man I told Officer Kollings about.
HAYES
The man?
KOLLINGS
Mrs. Zederberg was driving down the street, saw a quote, "hulking man," unquote, walking toward her—meaning northward—about two doors up from the house here.
HAYES
Mrs. Zederberg, can you describe him for us?
ZEDERBERG

Not really. I mean, as she just said, he was ... well, "hulking," the size of a professional wrestler? But also kind of mean.

HAYES

Mean?

ZEDERBERG

The way he walked. And moved his head. Like he was really angry about something.

HAYES

Did you get a good look at his face?

ZEDERBERG

No. I ... I really only glanced at him. He stared at me, I know, but I was ... well, frankly, scared of the way he seemed, so I just kept driving. Then I found the front door open here, and Marty—Oh, God, Marty in ...

KOLLINGS

Here you go, Ma'am. These tissues will help.

Good cop, Kollings.

Tess was almost finished dusting when she heard from behind her, "Cassidy, you know where the Loot is?"

The green-gilled uniform they'd met at the front door. "In the kitchen, with the widow."

"The son is here. Where should I put him?"

"Ask Hayes, but maybe call him out blind first. He might want to interview the guy without his mother knowing. Or in earshot."

"Stepmother, actually," said Steven Zederberg.

Now Tess was working the entrance to the library, and she could see Hayes with the younger man in the living room, sitting across from each other on matching armchairs. The son took after his father, slight frame and black, curly hair, with a Jewish skullcap bobby-pinned to the back of his head.

Looked a whole lot better than blade wounds. Thinking back to the corpse, though, Tess didn't remember any cap on or around the victim.

Hayes said, "You realize I have to ask some awkward questions?"

"Lieutenant, my father's just been brutally murdered, and you've told me I can't see Nanette until after you've interviewed me. So, please, ask away and be done with it so I can go to her."

Tess thought, kid's got some guts.

Hayes said, "We haven't found a weapon so far. Do you know if your parents keep an axe or a hatchet on the premises?"

"If you mean the house, no. But I'm sure Dad has one—had one in the camper."

"The recreational vehicle outside?"

"Yes. My father traveled a lot in his business, but mainly via airplane to convention cities and big hospitals. He always yearned to see the rest of the country, and so when he got a good offer for the medical supply company, Dad sold it."

"Can you tell me how much he got for it?"

A pause. "Is that really necessary for your investigation?"

"Yes."

Another pause. "All right. My father asked me to work with his lawyer on the deal."

"Why?"

"I'd just gotten my accounting degree, and Dad thought it would be good experience for me. And it was. Overall, we netted about three million."

"'We?'"

Tess looked up to see Zederberg clench his teeth. "My father did, that is." A shake of the head. "They were going to put the house on the market, too, though I told them he'd take a wicked hit—God, I'm sorry."

The son began rubbing his eyes with his fists, like a little kid. Tess's heart went out to him, but her job meant returning to the dusting.

Hayes said, "I know this is difficult for you."

"Yes," Tess hearing what she thought could be palms slapping thighs, "yes, you probably do, Lieutenant, because this is your job. But it's our lives."

Tess thought: The son's got guts and humanity.

Then Steven Zederberg made a noise that sounded almost like a laugh. "The bizarre thing is, Dad was always afraid he was going to die by fire."

"Fire?"

"Yes. The hospital he was born in burned to the ground like a week later. Then my father's first warehouse was struck by lightning when he was at his desk on the second floor of it. And, just before Dad decided to sell his company, he got caught in a hotel fire in Rochester, New York." The son hung his head. "Never thought he'd be killed like . . . this."

Hayes cleared his throat. "When you said your father and stepmother were going to 'take a wicked hit . . .'?"

"Uh, taxwise." Zederberg raised his face to the lieutenant. "While they'd lived here way beyond the minimum period for capital-gains forgiveness, the house has also appreciated to the point. . . . "

Tess couldn't follow the rest of what Steven Zederberg said, but it sounded interesting, so she resolved to ask her brother-in-law, Arthur the Attorney, about the issue.

If she ever get done with this crime scene, that is, so she could go visit Joan at the hospital.

"You look way too cute to be a cop."

Puh-leeeze, thought Tess. Where do guys find such garbage lines? Could there be a "dumb-ass.com" somewhere on the Web?

She was at the step-up entrance to the RV, about to go in to look for the camp hatchet Steven Zederberg had mentioned. The male, forties and balding, stared back at her over the bordering fence, focussing less on her face and more on her butt.

Tess said, "And you'd be?"

"Pete."

"That's your last name?"

"No." A husky laugh. "First. Pete Odabashian."

Zero hope of remembering that one. "Can you spell it for me?"

He did.

Tess said, "And you live next door?"

"Why I'm standing where I am."

"What can you tell me about the Zederbergs?"

"Well, they were quiet, that's for sure. No wild parties, probably because she's way younger than he was."

"By how much?"

"Actually we happened to talk about that once."

Tess heard his "happened" the loudest.

Odabashian said, "We were all like ten years apart."

"The 'we' being?"

"Well, Marty was the oldest, at fifty-six. I'm next at forty-seven, then Nan at thirty-six, and Stevie at twenty-five."

Using "Nan," not her full first name. "Anything else about your neighbors?"

Odabashian shrugged. "Not very religious, though I think the kid's decided to be, since he wears a yarmulke all the time."

Tess remembered that was the religious word for the skullcap. "How'd the family get along?"

"Fine, far as I could tell. I'm guessing Marty and Nan had to help Stevie out, starting a new business with student loans, an office, his own apartment, and so on. Then Marty decided to pull the ripcord on owning and running the company, and they bought this camper here. He was always puttering around in it, even forgot to close the door sometimes."

"Lock it, you mean?"

"No, not even click the door shut. I'm surprised he didn't get a squirrel or skunk building a nest in there."

"How about Mrs. Zederberg?"

Odabashian squinted. "In what way?"

A careful reply. Tess inclined her head toward the RV.

"Roughing it?"

"Ah, right. I got the impression Marty was a little higher on the great out-doors than Nan was."

"Mrs. Zederberg told you that?"

"Not in so many words. But I remember they took the camper out for a trial run, toward really touring the country in it. When Nan came back, all I heard was her not feeling safe driving it, banging her head or elbow into things. Even though the camper's enormous to look at, when Marty invited me to take a Cook's tour, it's kind of like a submarine inside, and I kept banging into cabinet corners and doorways myself. Plus there's the poisoned ivy and bug bites Nan got on their maiden voyage."

"Was that the only point the Zederbergs disagreed on?"

"Why don't we have a drink together, and I'll tell you everything you want to hear?"

God. "Like whether Mrs. Zederberg had any . . . male friends?"

"Aside from me, you mean?"

Consistency is not always a virtue, especially when it hints at a motive for killing the woman's husband. But all Tess said was, "Yes."

"How about that drink first?"

"Actually, I'd rather start by holding hands."

Odabashian seemed stunned. "You would?"

"Yes. If you were inside this camper, I need to take elimination prints from your fingers."

"That's not exactly what I had in mind."

"Tough luck. You can hop over here now, or you can cool your heels for a night or two in jail until a judge gets around to making you cooperate."

Pete Odabashian gave Tess a sour look. "Somehow, you're not so cute anymore."

Coming through the CSU door at headquarters, Detective Lieutenant Kyle Hayes said to Tess, "The vic's wallet was gone, but the stash of cash he kept in that library—and the wife kept in the kitchen—are both still there."

Suggesting a killer/robber not familiar with the household's habits. Then Tess looked up from logging in the evidence baggies used at the crime scene. Hayes was carrying two folders of different colors, neither of them ones the department used.

Tess said, "What are those?"

"Personnel files. From the vic's former business and the wife's job at the museum. She's a docent."

"What's that?"

"Cassidy, you have to get out more. A 'docent' is like a tour guide."

Tess kept her temper. "Thanks."

Hayes laid the folders on the counter next to her. "The family'd like to have the decedent in the ground by nightfall."

"What's the rush?"

"Religious thing. The ME knows about it, and he's putting Zederberg at the top of his list. Though, if it was up to the wife, we'd be looking at burning, not planting."

"Cremation?"

"Only the son's gotten pretty devout over the years, and he said it was also a religious thing to bury, and the funeral director's agreeing—naturally, since he'll get more money on the deal."

Tess was trying to think all that through when Hayes said, "I'm gonna get some coffee. Be back in ten to see how you're doing."

No "Can I get you something, too?" Tess said, "I'll be here."

As soon as Hayes closed the door behind him, Tess moved over to the folders. She was a little surprised that the owner of a company had a personnel file on himself. Opening "Zederberg, Martin," Tess read about his selling of medical supplies, some correspondence on him in turn selling his company, and some more letters about retirement options.

Then she turned to "Zederberg, Nanette." Given date of birth, she was a good twenty years younger than her husband, as Odabashian had told Tess. And not much employment history: nurse's aide, restaurant hostess, "docent" at the museum.

Luckily, Tess was back at her logging by the seven-minute mark, because Hayes burst through the door early. And empty-handed.

"Where's your coffee?"

"Cassidy, we've got a weapon."

"The weapon?"

"Well, that's something we're just gonna have to find out, aren't we?"

Silently, Tess said good-bye to witnessing the birth of her first niece or nephew.

The uniform assigned by Dispatch to investigate a bloody hatchet had enough sense to leave it on the ground.

Hayes said to her, "Any identification on the caller?"

"I can check with Dispatch, Lieutenant, but they didn't tell me squat on that."

Tess lowered her duffle bag to a patch of grass maybe ten feet removed from the weapon. She had a gut feeling the tipper stayed anonymous, though she also knew that 911 had caller ID, so they at least could trace the number.

Probably to an equally anonymous pay phone.

"Cassidy, you want to process this thing?"

Looking forward to it all day. "Yessir."

Tess bent down, trying to picture how the hatchet got there. "We're about three miles from the Zederbergs' house, right?"

"Ballpark. And in the direction the widow saw her 'hulking man' walking."

There were two huge prints, probably thumbs, in blood on the handle, but any others seemed too smudged to matter. "I don't remember Mrs. Zederberg saying anything about him carrying a bloody hatchet."

"You didn't interview the woman. She was upset, likely to miss stuff. Especially since she just 'glanced' at the guy."

"Only other people could have seen him, even focus on a big man acting odd. Why would he bring the murder weapon this far?"

"The guy could have it in a bag. Or he could just be a crazy."

"But why not wipe the thing off? Or hide it, even bury it?"

Hayes and the uniform both laughed.

Tess said, "What?"

"Cassidy," the lieutenant still chuckling, "you are a mite slow. 'Bury the hatchet?'"

"Oh."

At her computer, Tess cursed. After taking preservative close-up photos of the hatchet's handle, she'd lifted both latents perfectly from the surface. However, neither of them was in the state or federal databases.

And there were no prints in the house that didn't belong to one of the three Zederbergs, and none in the RV beyond theirs and those of the neighbor, Pete Odabashian.

Tess ran all four people through the computer. Zip also, which meant nobody had a criminal record, served in the military, or applied for any of a dozen kinds of licenses or permits.

The good news was that Tess had done all she could on the case, so now there was nothing official keeping her from going to the hospital.

"It's a boy," the new papa said, beaming in the gleaming corridor, a piece of cardboard in his hand.

Tess smiled at her brother-in-law. "That's terrific. How's Joan doing?"

"Great, just great. Still a little groggy, but only because they had to do a Caesarian section."

Meaning general anesthetic, so that made sense.

Arthur held up the cardboard. "And isn't this just the cutest thing?"

Tess glanced at "the cutest thing," then began to stare at it, and finally read the label. "What does 'I/M-Print' mean?"

He told her.

Tess nodded once. Twice. Three times. "Arthur, what happens when a married couple goes to sell their house?"

"What happens?"

"Taxwise," said Tess Cassidy, "and keep it simple."

She had to give Detective Lieutenant Kyle Hayes credit. He was willing to do what Tess asked.

They were both in the Zederbergs' living room with Nanette, son Steven, and neighbor Pete Odabashian.

The widow checked her watch and spoke with an edge to her tone. "Okay, my husband's funeral starts half an hour from now. What's this about?"

Hayes said, "Cassidy?"

Tess had already drawn and released a deep breath. "I want to take prints of all your . . . big toes."

"Our what?" Odabashian said.

"We found impressions on the handle of a hatchet, and the blood on its blade matches the decedent's DNA."

The son said, "So?"

"The prints are either the thumbs of a 'hulking man,' like the one your stepmother reported to Officer Kollings, or the big toes of somebody else."

Mrs. Zederberg said, "I don't understand."

Tess looked at her. "I got the idea when I visited my sister in the maternity ward a few hours ago. The hospital takes an 'I/M-Print,' meaning 'Infant/Mother-Print.' Or 'prints.' The mother's thumb and the infant's foot. So there's no question about somebody going home with the wrong baby."

Steven Zederberg said, "I repeat myself, but so?"

"The prints on the murder weapon weren't in any of our databases. So if the 'hulking man' wasn't the source of those prints, maybe one of you is."

Odabashian said, "Should I be calling a lawyer?"

Hayes—God bless him—chimed in, "Just let Cassidy here take prints of your big toes, okay?"

Nanette Zederberg sighed, but began to take off her shoes.

"This is absurd," from her stepson, who nevertheless began to do the same.

Odabashian said, "Not until I talk to an attorney."

Now Hayes put some steel into his voice. "You can cooperate, too, or sit in a cell until a judge tells you to comply."

Tess thought, Just what I already told Odabashian about his fingerprints. "I'll only be a minute, and this way you'll avoid any legal fees."

Odabashian gave her another sour look, but he bent to untie his shoelaces.

When all three were barefoot, Tess "rolled" their big toes. However, when she compared their prints to her latents from the hatchet, there was no match.

"So," said David Zederberg, wiping the ink off his toes with a cloth from Tess's duffle, "all this was a waste of time."

"I'm afraid so," Hayes shaking his head.

Tess decided on one last try, using what her brother-in-law had told her at the hospital. "Mr. Zederberg, as an accountant, what happens when a married couple sells their house?"

"I explained all that to the lieutenant."

"Can you explain it again?"

A sigh, much like his stepmother's. "So long as they lived in a principal residence long enough, the net equity from the transaction is protected from taxes up to a certain point. And Dad said he didn't care about the surplus profit. He'd rather pay the capital gains hit on it so he could start his new life as," a tilt of the head toward the driveway, "an RV nomad."

Tess said, "And if one of the spouses dies before the sale?"

"Then the survivor gets a 'stepped-up basis,' all the way to the fair-market value of the deceased spouse's half of the property as of the date of death, thereby saving sometimes hundreds of thousands in capital. . . . " The son looked from Tess to Hayes and back again. "Wait a minute. What are you saying?"

The lieutenant nodded, and Tess continued. "Given your new accounting business and student loans, office and apartment expenses, that house money you'd inherit without all the capital gains tax could come in very handy. Not to mention the proceeds from your father's sale of his medical supply company."

"Oh," from Odabashian, "this is really good stuff."

Steven Zederberg's face twisted. "Nanette?"

His stepmother blinked, and Tess could see a tear slide down the side of the woman's nose. "And if I had been here to die with Marty, you'd have gotten this 'stepped-up basis' from both of us, wouldn't you?"

"Nanette, how can you possibly believe—"

"Only," said Tess, "We don't think it happened that way."

Odabashian crossed his arms, nearly hugging himself. "Just better and better."

Tess looked toward the widow as she ticked off the facts on her fingers. "First, you're twenty years younger than your husband, and you didn't like the prospect of spending your prime and his money as a nomad in the camper. Second, your stepson, not you, volunteered the capital gains information to Lieutenant Hayes."

"Steven's an accountant. Of course he'd bring it up."

"Third, you were pretty quick just now to dump the 'hulking man' theory in favor of your stepson as the killer."

"This is—"

"Fourth, you were alone with your husband in this house before he died, and you found the body all by yourself. Fifth, you were a nurse's aide, so you'd know about the I/M-Print procedure. Sixth, the hospital your husband was born in burned down, so there'd be no record of his I/M-Print, meaning we'd never be able to identify the print. A nice little piece of misdirection."

Tess watched Nanette Zederberg's complexion drain of color. "Seventh, you wanted the decedent cremated, despite him being terrified of fire all his life, and his son's desire to see his father buried."

Hayes said, "When we found your husband's body, the soles of his feet were bloody. Nothing more is going to happen at the funeral home before Cassidy here can take prints of his big toes."

Tess watched the son's features crumble in doubled grief as Nanette Zederberg began to curse and cry at the same time.

A TRACE OF A TRACE

BY BRENDAN DUBOIS

I WAS TRYING TO GET THE DAMN FLUE OPEN ON MY condo fireplace when the doorbell rang. I stepped back from the fireplace, wiped my black-stained hands with a soiled rag, and went to the front door. I spared a glance out the picture window, which offered a nice view of the Atlantic Ocean and a very empty beach. It being the middle of January, the empty beach made sense, but a visitor to my second-story condo didn't.

I opened the door and a woman in her late thirties stood there, a hesitant smile on her face. Her brown hair was trimmed short, just above her collar, and she had brown eyes and a faint scar on her chin. She wore a long black winter coat with tan slacks, and over her shoulder was a leather case. She looked at me expectantly and I said, "Detective Diane Woods. Would you like to come in?"

"Please, if I'm not interrupting anything."

"Just trying to figure out how to open the flue of this damn fireplace, that's all, without breaking the lever or my hand."

She followed me into the living room, past the cardboard boxes that had yet to be unpacked. In the living room she took a couch and I took the solitary chair and I waited.

She looked around. "Still getting unpacked."

"Yes."

She shook her head, smiled. "Still find it hard to believe you came all the way east, after spending so much time in the desert. Must be a shock to the system, especially New Hampshire in January."

I tilted my head just a bit as I replied. "We have snow up in the mountains. And the desert can be very cold at night, cold enough to kill people. About the only change is the view of the ocean. And that doesn't take too long to get used to."

"I'm sure."

There were a few seconds of silence, and I said, "Detective?"

"Yes?"

"You're here because you want me to assist you. Correct?"

She looked slightly embarrassed. "It's very irregular, I know. And you're retired and you're from a different law enforcement jurisdiction. It's just that . . . well, when I met you a few weeks ago, when I found out that you had moved to our town, we had a nice conversation and you didn't seem opposed to lending a hand if the opportunity ever presented itself, and—"

"Detective," I said.

She stopped talking. Another pause. "Okay, then."

"Look. You had me when you opened the door. Any longer, I might say no. So now I'll say yes, I'll look at your case, and we'll go from there. Is that acceptable?"

The detective stood up. "Very acceptable. Can I show you the crime scene?"

I looked around at the crowded room. "Detective, it's either that or stay here and try to open the flue, or unpack some more boxes, or hang a print or two on these walls, or go through my insect collection to see what got damaged during the move. Looking at a crime scene suddenly sounds very attractive. Is it far?"

"Not far at all."

"Good. Let me get my coat."

Ten minutes later, I was in the front seat of her unmarked police cruiser, a dark blue Ford LTD with a whip antenna and lots of radio gear. There was no radar gun mounted on the dashboard. Detectives don't care who speeds and who doesn't. They are after much more important things.

We were parked on a large fishing dock that jutted into an expanse of water called Tyler Harbor. To the left was a channel that led out to the Atlantic Ocean. A small drawbridge spanned the channel, leading into New Hampshire's southernmost community on its ridiculously short shoreline, called Falconer. Before us, at the end of the dock, was a two-story wooden structure with a sign hanging over double doors. The sign was white, with painted blue lettering that spelled out Tyler Harbor Fishing Cooperative. There were four small hoists set in a row to the right of the building. The lot was plowed and surrounded by mounds of snow. Fishing craft of various sizes bobbed at their moorings as the wind whipped up little spurts of whitecaps.

"Where's the crime scene?" I asked.

"You're looking at it."

"Where?"

"Right in front of you. The fishing co-op building."

I looked again. The building seemed deserted. The doors were unattended. The parking lot behind us was empty. I sighed.

"Take me home, then," I said.

"Excuse me?"

"Take me home. We're going to be wasting each other's time. This place isn't sealed. It isn't secure. This entire crime scene has been compromised, hasn't been protected, and anything I'll do here will be a waste of time and won't be useful to you."

Her face seemed to flush. "You can determine that it's a waste of time or not. But no matter what you think, the site's secure, it's been professionally examined, over and over again, and we're now at a dead end. We've had the best from our department, from the state police major crimes unit, and the county coroner's office. We've gotten squat."

"Which is why you've asked me," I said.

"Yes."

I stared out the windshield of the cruiser, examined the exterior of the building, and said, "Do you have the case file with you?"

"Yes," she said, reaching into the leather bag. "Do you want to read it?"

"No," I said. "Not yet. Give me the particulars, will you? Before we go into the building."

"Sure."

From the leather case she took out a manila folder. She started talking without opening it. I was impressed. She obviously knew this case cold, and obviously wanted to show off.

"Our suspect is one Samuel Kosten. Age twenty-nine, resident of Tyler Beach. Lobster fisherman. Part of the Tyler Harbor Fishing Cooperative. High school dropout."

"Any previous record?"

"Some speeding tickets. One operating under the influence. Two assaults from bar fights, years ago. Nothing else."

"Victim?"

"Victim is Cassandra Malone. Also known as Cassie. Had been dating Samuel for nearly a year. A rocky relationship, according to friends and family. Usual fights and threats. Lately she told some close friends that she was determined to dump Samuel once and for all, but she was afraid of his temper."

"Aren't they all," I said. "What else?"

"A local. Employed by Public Service of New Hampshire at the Falconer Nuclear Power Plant, over there on the left."

I followed her lead. The power plant was easy to spot. Concrete containment dome, cube concrete buildings, large high-tension power lines issuing out from one of the main buildings. It looked to be a couple of miles away, across the harbor and low salt marsh and fields.

"Time of death?"

"We believe it was about two weeks ago," she said.

"Long time ago, detective."

"Sure is."

"How and where did it happen?"

"Where it happened . . . we're positive it happened in there, in the co-op building. We have a witness who places both Samuel and Cassie in the building. Same witness says Samuel left on his own, a couple of hours after they arrived and went in. Since that night, Cassie has been missing. Never reported to work, never returned phone calls from her mom and friends, and her apartment is neat and tidy. Clothes left behind, luggage left behind, no activity from credit cards, bank accounts untouched."

"I see." I looked around the parking lot. It looked cold. It had to be very cold indeed. "Do you know how it happened?"

"No. We have no body, and no usable trace evidence. Not a damn thing. He took her into that building, and only he came out."

I gently said, "That's impossible. There's always trace evidence of some kind at a crime scene. Always."

She sighed. "I know. I've always thought that, too. But this . . . this is unique. Look, let's get inside and I'll show you. That'll be easier than trying to describe it."

"Sounds fine."

I stepped out and the wind seemed to shoot right through me. It was cold, but it was a cold that was nothing like the cold out west. Out where I once lived and worked, it was a dry, achy cold, something that seemed to want to suck the moisture right out of your skin and bones. Here, it was a damp, cutting cold, coming right off the ocean, like it wanted to moisten you first, to make it easier to freeze you.

I made sure my coat was buttoned and followed Woods to the fishing co-op building. As we got closer I felt a bit better, and a bit guilty, at having earlier chastised the detective on the sanctity of the crime scene. There was a bright orange sticker covering the part of the door and adjacent wall, with her name and signature, so that was a good start. But still. Two weeks after the supposed murder. The first forty-eight hours in a homicide investigation are always key, before witnesses forget or change their stories, before evidence is removed or destroyed, before alibis are rehearsed and rehearsed so that they sound as true as gold. Two weeks. . . .

A very long time.

Detective Woods sliced through the orange sticker with a key but before she opened up the door, I said, "Hold on."

"Okay."

I turned and looked out across the lot. A bleak view indeed, with only the cruiser lending any sort of color. It was gray and white and black. A gate led to Atlantic Avenue. I'm sure that in the middle of summer, traffic was heavy on that particular stretch of road, but not today, not in January. I waited and waited and not a single car drove by.

"You said you had a witness."

"That's right."

"A witness who was here, two weeks ago, at night, and saw Samuel enter this building with Cassie and depart some hours later, alone."

"Yes."

I turned to her. "Detective, what kind of witness do you have? It's frigid out here. At night it must be even worse. You're telling me that you had a witness out here, at night in January, who saw your suspect and victim enter this building?"

"That's right."

"A defense attorney would say that's pretty convenient. Who's your witness?"

She unlocked the door. "Another problem, I'm afraid. Our witness is the resident harbor drunk. Never mind convenience. Any defense attorney will be having a day at the circus over his reliability."

"I'm sure."

"If you don't mind, I'll tell you more about our witness later."

"That'll be fine."

She opened the door and we stepped into the Tyler Harbor Fishing Cooperative. Before us was a small function room with tile floor, folding chairs and some tables, and a raised stage at one end, flanked by an American flag and the dull dark blue flag of the State of New Hampshire. It looked like the kind of place where bingo contests were held, or Saturday night ham and bean suppers, or maybe just a place to smoke and drink and trade fishing stories.

"Tell me about the cooperative," I said.

"Set up a couple of years ago with seed money from the state. Used to be, each fisherman out here was on his own when it came to his catch. He or she would come in with a day or two of work, and there'd be brokers here from Boston, undercutting each and every one of them, trying to get the best price. Here, the co-op helps set its own price, and there's even a facility here for initial processing that allows the catch to get from here to Boston restaurants in just a couple of hours."

"Business okay?"

"Fishermen never have a good fishing day, but they're doing all right. Ready to see our problem?"

"Sure."

"Right this way."

To the left was a set of heavy metal doors, with rubber trim around the bottom and tops that made it hard to push in. But Detective Woods put her shoulder to it and we went into a much larger, cooler room, and I instantly saw what the problem was.

"Well, this is certainly something," I said.

"It certainly is," she said wistfully.

The room was two stories tall, with a concrete floor with drains set in about every eight feet or so, illuminated by banks upon banks of fluorescent lights from the metal framework of the ceiling. Along the walls were waist-high stainless steel tables and adjoining sinks, and in the center was a work area that looked like it belonged in a restaurant, with a collection of knives, cleavers, and sharpening tools set on stands. There were two large refrigerators and some sort of machinery set up in the center, next to four stainless steel sinks. Diane walked over to the center, where the machinery was located. I followed, our footsteps sounding loud in the enclosed space. Near the sinks were overhead hose systems, like those of dishwashing stations in restaurants.

"This is where fishermen and their helpers can gut and clean some of the larger fish, so it can get to market quicker. Refrigerators make the ice and are used for temporary storage."

I looked around. "I guess you didn't find her head or hands anywhere, did you."

She crossed her arms. "No. And we didn't find anything else. Not a damn thing."

"Theory?" I asked.

"Best guess we have is that he took her in here, subdued her by a blow to the head or something similar. Then it gets interesting. According to the theory."

"Best theories are always the most interesting ones."

She took a breath, walked over to the collection of stainless steel tables and sinks. "We believe he took her over here after he subdued her. Draped her head over the edge of the sink. Slit her throat. Then, well, note the collection of knives and cleavers. If you take a look over here—"

Which I did, gazing into the sink, which had quite a wide drain.

"—you'll note the drain."

She flipped a switch on the side of a console. There was a whirring, grinding noise that I recognized, and when I nodded, Diane shut the switch off. The large room was quiet again.

"Industrial-strength garbage disposal," I said.

"The same. With water running, with cool nerves and steady hands, we think he dismembered the body and shoved it into the disposal."

"Where does it dispose to?"

"The harbor, right beneath us. There's a water flushing system that works with the grinder, flushes everything out."

I looked down the open drain. "Nothing?"

She shook her head. "Not a damn thing. Luminol shows some trace blood evidence, but not enough for DNA analysis. Not a drop, not a smear, nothing. We've gone through the entire building. Nothing. We even searched the overhead framework and lighting, in case an artery was sliced at the right time and we got arterial spray. Not a thing. Give any semi-competent defense attorney a crack at what we have found, some trace of blood in a place where men work day in and day out with knives and cleavers.

Lots of room there for reasonable doubt."

"I suppose you've taken apart the disposal system."

"Piece by piece. Each one examined. No bone splinters, no tissue, no dental fragments and again, we exposed every piece of metal to Luminol. Faintest traces of blood. Again, a good lawyer would claim that it was fish blood. Or something that dripped from somebody's hand or fingers as they worked on gutting a fish last week."

I backed away and took in the scene. "He was very thorough."

"For a fisherman who didn't finish high school, he was quite smart. And here, I haven't shown you the best."

Diane went around to the other side of the center island of sinks and machinery, and picked up a hand-held cleaning device of some sort, with a triggering handle and long, wand-like apparatus. She pointed the wand away from her and squeezed the handle. A burst of steam came out, droplets falling to the clean concrete.

"We're sure that after he cut up and disposed of the body, everything within reach of this piece of equipment was steam-cleaned. There's also some bleach in a rear storage area. Combine the two and we have a very troubling crime scene."

"The disposal outflow," I said. "Was it checked?"

She replaced the steam-cleaning unit back into its cradle. "Yes. Twice. By divers from the state police. With the tides and the muck down there and the time that passed since she was reported missing, not a damn thing. We even borrowed a ground-suction device that divers use, to clean up an area for exploration. Sucked the mud and muck out, passed it through a grate on land. Looking for teeth, bone fragments. Like before. Nothing."

I looked around the room again, noting where everything was located, how it was set.

"All right. Who's the witness, and what did he tell you?"

"Witness is one Joshua Thompson. Age fifty-one."

"Who is he?"

She folded her arms. "An old-timer. His family has been in Tyler for generations, fishermen all. But he doesn't fish anymore. He just drinks and smokes and hangs out at the docks, day in and day out, rain, snow, sleet, doesn't matter."

"Why was he here, the night she disappeared?"

"Just happenstance, that's all. He was here and when word got out that she was missing and that her boyfriend was a fishermen with the cooperative, Joshua came forward to let us know what he saw. Which was Samuel driving up in his pickup truck with a young woman, whom he later positively identified as Cassie. The two went in. A few hours later, only Samuel came out. End of story."

"Was he drunk at the time?"

"No doubt about it."

"What's his background?"

"Like I said, a fisherman. Went out one stormy day with his brothers on a stern trawler. Stayed out too long. Rogue wave capsized the boat, his two brothers drowned, and he was the only one left. I think he hangs around the docks to punish himself, maybe, and gets drunk to have the time pass quicker."

"At least he's found a way," I said.

"What kind of way?"

"A way of coping," I said. "Not many people do, when faced with a trauma like that. Anything else you want to show me here?"

She shook her head. "No, there's nothing else."

"All right. Let's go, then."

I started walking to the main door that led to the small meeting room. "Where?" the detective asked.

"I want to see Cassie Malone's residence, if that's all right."

She said, "Already been searched. There's nothing there."

I turned and gave her my best smile. "On the contrary, everything is there. Everything."

Outside, it was still damn cold.

* * *

Cassie Malone had lived in a condo complex on the other side of Tyler, near the prep school town of Exonia, and the moment I walked into her residence, it hit me. I was in the home of a dead person. Nothing new—I had been in the homes of many a dead person—but there was always that little shock to the system when you walk in and realize that everything here had been chosen and picked and decorated by a man or woman no longer alive. There's a darkness and coolness to a home or apartment or condo unit that is no longer owned by a living person.

The residence was standard, and I suppose it made no sense to come here—Diane and the major crimes unit no doubt had tossed the place thoroughly and professionally—but I still liked to get a feel for the person, so that she was more than just a faceless vic. I saw from her place that she liked science fiction and fantasy novels, subscribed to *Cosmo* and *Self* magazines, and that her refrigerator was fairly well stocked, with fruits, vegetables, and the usual condiments, and some containers from a previous Chinese meal.

And according to Diane, nothing was out of place. No blood spatters or smears. No journal or computer diary indicating her fear that Samuel was going to kill her someday. Just a lived-in and reasonably tidy place.

Nothing here, really, but a sense of who she had once been. Which is why I had asked to come here.

Before we left, I saw something dangling from a coat rack near the door. It was an identification badge, showing a smiling young lady with blonde hair and bright blue eyes. CASSANDRA MALONE, the identification showed, and it was her ID from the Falconer nuclear power plant. I held the badge in my hand for a moment and turned to Diane.

"What did Cassie do at the nuclear power plant?"

"Health physics technician, worked in the health physics department."

"I see."

"What do you know about that kind of job?"

I put the badge back on the rack. "I know some things. The shorthand term for her job is HP tech. Responsible for maintaining radiation records, dosimetry, radiation work permits, anything and everything involving the nuclear power side of the plant."

"You mean there's more than one side to a nuclear power plant?"

"Sure," I said. "There's part of the plant where the reactor system and all the supporting systems are located. Called the radiologically controlled area. That's the nuclear side of the plant. Everything outside of the RCA— the steam turbine, the generator, the power lines, the office buildings— that's the non-nuclear side."

Diane smiled, opened the door. "Is there anything you don't know?"

"Of course," I said, surprised she would say such a thing. "The true sign of intelligence is knowing what you don't know, and I don't know a lot."

"Could have fooled me," she said, and as we left the dead woman's condo, I wasn't sure if she was being sarcastic or humorous, and decided not to ask.

We were in the unmarked cruiser again, heading west back to Tyler Beach and no doubt to my condominium, since she hadn't offered to bring me back to the crime scene. Or alleged crime scene. Diane stayed quiet as she drove, and I thought and pondered and after a bit said, "Ever hear of John Dickson Carr?"

"Nope."

"Oh."

She glanced over at me. "Well?"

"Well, what?"

"Aren't you going to tell me who he is?"

"He was an American-born mystery author, lived for a while in England. Wrote during the so-called 'golden age' of detective stories, in the 1930s through the 1950s. He was famous for his locked-room mysteries."

"Sorry," she said, "you lost me there. A locked-room what?"

"Locked-room mystery. The type of mystery story when a body is found in a locked room, murdered, with no murder weapon in view, and with the room having been locked from the inside. Hence, the term, locked-room mystery. Supposedly an impossible crime that's unsolvable. What we have here is a derivative of the locked-room mystery. We have a murder with no body, with very little evidence, and a sly fisherman who thinks he's gotten away with it."

"So far," Diane said glumly, "the little bastard has gotten away with it."

I looked out over at the marshland, at the square and functional buildings of the Falconer nuclear power plant, and thought for a moment longer. I thought of Cassie, going in every day, working with people she liked and trusted, dealing with radiation and everything else associated with it that remained so much a mystery to so many people. And to end up dead, within eyeshot of your place of employment....

"This fisherman. Samuel. How many times have you questioned him?"

"Twice."

"Has he gotten a lawyer yet?"

"Nope."

I turned to her, with a surprised look on my face, I'm sure. "Really?"

"Really," she said. "I think the son-of-a-bitch is so confident that he doesn't have to have a lawyer with him. After all, he keeps on saying he's innocent, over and over again. As he told me the first time, an innocent man wouldn't need a lawyer. Just a guilty one."

"Interesting philosophy," I said. "This Cassie Malone. How long had she worked at the nuclear power plant?"

"Four years," she said. "Was on her way to being promoted, to a supervisory position."

I looked back to the marshland, but we had gone too far along the roadway. The power plant was now out of sight.

"All right," I said. "Look, are you taking me home?"

Diane said, "Well, it's too early for lunch."

"Any chance I can talk to your witness?"

"Joshua? Sure, I don't see why not. Do you think he'll help?"

"I don't know. I just want to be thorough."

Diane eyed me strangely. "I guess you do."

We met up with Joshua Thompson at the Honeydip Donut & Coffee shop, one of the few places still open at Tyler Beach in the middle of winter. He sat in the rear, with a mug of coffee and six honey-dipped doughnuts before him. As we talked, he slowly ate the doughnuts and sipped his coffee. He was in his late fifties, with a thick black beard streaked with gray, and his clothes were old and carefully mended. After the exchange of names and such, he raised one eyebrow and said, "I like your last name."

"Thanks," I said. "So do I."

He nodded, ate a piece of doughnut. "Same last name as a famous astronaut. Sure you know that."

"Yes, I do. But not many people remember who he was."

"Sure. People don't remember much. But I remember him, and how he died. Awful. Dead things happening . . . a man will remember that forever."

"Of course."

He leaned over the table a bit, lowered his voice. "I remembered the night my brothers died. A cold night in April. I was sleeping and the two of them were working. We were dragging about two miles out from the Isles of Shoals. Damn nets must have caught on a wreck or something. Flipped our boat over. Still don't know how I got out. But I did, and floated and called for them and called for them, all up 'til Manny Harris picked me up, a nice fella from Portsmouth, lobsterman. But they never did find my brothers. They're still out there, and that bothers me a lot."

"I'm sure it does."

He took a noisy slurp from his coffee cup and said, "I like you. You don't ask much. But you want to ask me somethin', don't you."

"Yes, I do."

"Then go ahead."

I motioned to Diane and said, "I know you were on the docks the night that Samuel Kosten showed up, with Cassie Malone. Can you tell me about it, what you saw?"

"Well." Another bite of a doughnut, and then he chewed and swallowed and said, "It was *I Love Lucy* night. I remember that. And there was no wind, which is good. I was by the far dumpsters, just taking a breather. That late at night, I just like to look at the harbor. Just look at all those boats bobbin' out there, all peaceful, all in their own little universe, all quiet and like. And then this truck came by. I was surprised, it being so late."

"Did you recognize the truck from sometime before?" I asked.

He wiped some crumbs from his beard. "Nope. But there was a bumper sticker on this truck, something about fishermen having bigger poles or something. When it parked a guy came out, and then this girl with nice blonde hair like Marcia Duller, I dated back in high school, she had hair like that. And then they went inside, and I went back to standing by the dumpsters, just looking at the boats, until he came out."

I said, "Did you hear anything from inside the building? Anything?"

A shake of the head. "No. My hearin' ain't that great."

"All right. What happened later?"

"Well. Not too sure of the time then, but then the fella, he came out, by himself. Saw his face real good by the overhead light by the door. Looked pretty damn happy with himself."

"Did he leave right away?"

"Yep. Got in his truck with the naughty bumper sticker and drove right off. A little while later, the sun came up, and I left to get some breakfast. Then, later, I heard from a cop I know that Diane and such were looking into something strange happenin' at the fish co-op, and that's when I came forward. Like a good citizen should, right?"

"Absolutely," I said. "You were certainly being a good citizen."

He smiled. "Thanks."

We chatted for a few minutes more and then we went outside into the cold, to let Joshua finish his doughnuts in peace. As we reached the unmarked police cruiser, I turned to Diane.

"Identification?"

"Sure. Joshua ID'd Samuel's driver license photo. But you see how he is. Any defense attorney will be able to cut him to pieces. I mean, look at what he said back there. He saw the whole thing the night that *I Love Lucy* is on television."

I opened the door. "Do you believe that the murder occurred on a Monday night?"

She looked surprised. "Yes. Yes, we do. How did you know that?"

"Because during its six-year run on CBS in the 1950s, *I Love Lucy* was broadcast on Monday nights."

Inside the cruiser Diane started up the engine and I said, "Let's go to your office. If you have time."

"Related to this case, right?"

"Of course."

"Then I don't mind at all."

A week later, I was back at the Tyler police station, which is in a concrete structure that wouldn't look out of place at the Falconer nuclear power plant. The interview room was adjacent to the booking area, and I was sitting there by myself when Detective Woods opened the door leading to her office and came in. Behind her was Samuel Kosten, wearing dirty blue jeans, tan workboots, and a dishwater-gray hooded sweatshirt. A Red Sox cap topped his head and he had a three-day growth of beard, and a smiling, know-it-all attitude. I wondered what the younger and attractive Cassie Malone had seen in such a specimen.

He pulled out a chair and sat down without being asked or invited, and Detective Woods sat next to me. The conference room table was black and small and scarred with cigarette butt burns and coffee cup rings. There was a shackle set up in the center for prisoners being interrogated, but Samuel wasn't a prisoner.

Not yet.

Diane made the introductions and said, "My guest here is a crime scene investigation consultant on the matter of your girlfriend's disappearance. We appreciate you coming in and taking the time to talk to us."

He shrugged. "No prob. Besides, the weather sucks anyway. Can't go out fishing even if I wanted to."

Before me was a file folder, which I opened up, and I slowly and methodically put on my reading glasses.

"You realize, of course, that the police are continuing their investigation into the disappearance of Cassie Malone," I said.

"Yeah. Though I don't know if she's gone or not, you know what I mean?"

Diane said quietly, "Are you telling us that you've heard from her?"

"Oh, hell no, not that."

"Then why are you convinced that she's not dead?"

He shrugged. "Like I told you before, and before that, and before that. Cassie was getting burned out at her job at the nuke plant. They had an outage coming up. That's when they shut down the plant and do a lot of maintenance work. Then you get to work six-tens, as they call it. Six days in a row, ten hours a day. Sometimes more if there's a problem that develops. She told me a few weeks ago she couldn't stand the thought of working another outage. She said something about just running away, just running away and not contacting anyone, so she didn't have to work the outage."

I said, "Is that what you think happened?"

"Sure. Why not?"

"And you don't think she would have contacted her mother? Or other family members? Or her place of employment?"

He laughed, and I decided I didn't like the look of his teeth. He said, "Thing about Cassie is, Cassie does what Cassie wants to. And if she wants to run off without telling anybody, including me, I wouldn't put it past her."

"I see."

I made it a point of flipping through the papers and watched to see his expression, but his expression didn't change. He seemed to be the kind of guy who liked putting one over on officialdom, whether it be a harbormaster or coast guardsmen or the local police.

I stopped flipping through the papers and said, "Could you tell us again the last time you saw Cassie?"

"Lunch, couple of weeks ago. At Jimmy's Fine Catch, over in Falconer."

"And you haven't heard from her since then?"

"Nope."

"And never saw her again?"

"Nope."

I looked to Diane and gave her the slightest of nods, to prepare her for what was coming, and she gave me just the slightest nod in return. So much was riding on that quick little gesture, from her career to bringing me in on a case like this, to possible embarrassment for the Tyler Police Department, and up to and including seeing whether or not this charming slug across from me ever got justice.

I flipped another sheet of paper. It looked like he was trying to read it upside down. Good for him. I said, "What would you say, Mister Kosten, if a witness came forth to allege that two Mondays ago, he saw you and Miss Malone enter the Tyler Harbor Fishing Cooperative building, and saw you depart without her?"

His face flushed. "I'd say he was lying, that's what."

"So. Two Mondays ago, you were never in that building."

"No!"

"And you were never in that building with Miss Malone."

"No!"

Here we go. "And you've never been in that building with Miss Malone at any time?"

His face was even more flushed. "Never! Jesus, how many times do I have to tell you? Cassie put up with me but didn't like fish that much. She's never been in that building. Not ever."

He looked to me and then looked at Diane and there was just the faintest hint in his eyes that perhaps he had gone too far. Maybe. But I thought I could tell what was going on there, that he was reviewing what he had done, how he had cut up the body and ground up the pieces and cleaned and cleaned and cleaned, and maybe, if there was something, that they'd be making an arrest, not talking, not then, they're just bluffing, that's all, keep cool, they have nothing. . . .

Now he smiled. "No, not ever."

I looked at him and said, "How long did you know Cassie?"

"Eight, nine months."

"A number of witnesses said that you had a rocky relationship. Many arguments."

"So what? Who doesn't have a fight with his girlfriend?"

I said, "Did you ever strike her?"

"Huh?"

"Did you ever hit her? Or punch her?"

"Never! And anybody who says that happened is lying. And you can count on that."

I went back to the files for a moment, and then said, "You ever see her at work?"

"Huh?"

I said, "You said you never brought her to the co-op building. Did she ever bring you to the power plant?

He shook his head. "Nah, never. Once she wanted to do it but it was too much of a hassle. Had to do a background check to get in there, even for a quick visit. Give up your birthday and your social security number. Who needs crap like that?"

"Do you know what she did for work?"

"Yeah. Something in the health physics department."

"Doing what?"

"I don't know," he said. "Some sort of technician or something—hell, what is this? A final exam or something?"

I made a point of closing the folder. "No, it's not. It's an explanation of what's about to happen next. You see, Mister Kosten, Cassie worked at the power plant in and around certain radioactive materials. She was constantly exposed on a daily basis to these radioactive materials. At no time was she ever in any danger or physical harm. In fact, the radiation that she was exposed to is strictly monitored and measured."

His face was expressionless. I went on. "But radiation is a funny animal. When you place a radioactive material next to something else, that second material also becomes radioactive. Not as much as the source material but still, it's a measurable amount. And it never goes away. Do you understand that? It never goes away. It's always there. It can't be cleaned. It can't be scrubbed. It can't wash off. It's always there. Forever."

Samuel shifted in his seat. I said, "And the funny thing is this, due to the different areas of the power plant where Cassie worked, the different types of radiation that she was exposed to, her exposure is unique. Like a finger-print. It's all her own."

I opened up the second folder. "As you can see here, this is Cassie's personnel file. And enclosed here are her radiation exposure records. Something like a DNA sample. If we can match the radiation that she received with something that she was in proximity with, we can then determine that she was there. Detective?"

Diane got up and left the room, and then came back in with a young man in a dark gray business suit. He had a large black case with him, like the old sample cases from traveling salesmen of years gone by, and he placed the case on the tabletop, and then opened it up. From inside the case he pulled out a small yellow metal box with a digital readout and dial, and a small black probe that was attached to the box by a black vinyl cord.

"Permit me to introduce State Police Detective Joseph Stevens," I said. "In addition to his regular duties, Detective Stevens has also received training from the Homeland Security Department, and is a radiation health control officer. As you can see, he has brought a sensing device with him today. Detective Stevens, if you would."

Holding the probe out before him, he swept it near Detective Woods, paying particular attention to her hands. There was the faintest click-click coming from the machine as he slowly did his work. Then he went over and did my hands, and there was the same result. Click-click-click.

When he was done with the two of us, he paused. I looked to him and nodded, and he went over to Samuel Kosten, whose face seemed to be suddenly perspiring.

When the probe reached the fisherman's hands, the faint click-click started chattering, chattering loud and fast, until it was almost a roar.

Detective Stevens made a point of reviewing the digital read outs and dials, and looking at Cassie Malone's personnel record.

"It's a match," he said.

Samuel drew his hands away, like they had suddenly been burnt. "Of course there'd be a match! Hell, I was with her! I touched her! That doesn't prove anything!"

I said, "Perhaps. But I believe Detective Stevens has one more place he wants to examine with his sensing device. Go ahead, detective."

The state police detective went back to the large black carry case and reached in and pulled out something wrapped in light blue plastic. He let it fall to the conference table with an audible thud that made Samuel jump a bit. It was about a foot long, six inches wide. Stevens unwrapped it, revealing a screw-type piece of metal.

Samuel was studiously looking at his hands. I said softly, "If I'm correct, this is a piece of the disposal unit system at the Tyler Harbor Fishing Cooperative. It was removed earlier this morning and brought here by Detective Stevens. Let's see what happens when he examines it, shall we?"

The probe went down to the exposed piece of metal, and the sensing device roared into action. Click-click-click it went, and it was amazing, just seeing Samuel Kosten's face change color from fleshy red to ghastly white. The state police detective looked to me and then Diane, and then switched off his sensing device.

"Another match," he said.

"Very good," I said. "Mister Kosten."

"Yes." His voice was barely audible.

"You've said here and in other interviews with Detective Woods that your girlfriend, Cassie Malone, was never at the Tyler Harbor Fishing Cooperative. Yet we now have evidence that not only was she in the building, but that her body was processed through the disposal system. Combine that with the witness who put you and Cassie Malone at the fishing cooperative building just over two weeks ago, I believe there are some questions that need to be answered."

Samuel murmured something.

"I'm sorry. None of us heard what you just said, Mister Kosten. Would you care to repeat it?"

He looked up at us, face still pale, eyes wide open. "I said, I think I want a lawyer. That's what I want. A lawyer."

I turned to Diane. "Detective Woods, I believe you have something to say to that."

"Yes, I do," she said crisply. "Mister Kosten, waiting in my office is an assistant attorney general from the New Hampshire attorney general's office. She is prepared to make a deal. The deal is that when she comes in here, you give a full and complete confession to the murder of Cassie Malone, and the dismemberment and disposal of her body. In exchange for that deal, the death penalty will not be considered during your sentencing. You have thirty seconds to accept this deal. After the thirty seconds are up, the window closes, and you may get an attorney, for however much you can afford, or one that the state will provide for you, and take your chance in front of a jury, where the death penalty most assuredly will be considered in your sentencing. And if you think you can sway a jury with some nonsense story about self-defense or an accident, think of what will happen when the prosecutor goes into details of how you disposed of your girlfriend's body. Mister Kosten, the clock is now ticking."

He didn't use all of his thirty seconds.

In a voice just above a whisper, he said, "I'll take the deal."

Later Diane took me to dinner in what she said was the best restaurant in Tyler, and which I didn't think would make the top twenty list in my previous hometown, and after a second glass of wine, she said, "I can't thank you enough."

"Then don't," I said. "I'm just glad that Mister Kosten will now be a guest of your state prison system for the rest of his life."

"Oh, that he will, though I'm sure that his defense attorney will scream like a stuck pig when he sees the videotape and reads the transcript of how the interview was conducted."

I took a sip from my own wineglass. "The courts have said, again and again, that it's permissible for police to lie while interrogating a suspect. You and I and that thoughtful state police detective may have approached the line, but we never crossed it."

She sighed and looked at the wine bottle. A nice Bordeaux, it tasted fine after the day I had just gone through. She said, "We're lucky that poor Cassie never explained the ins and outs of radiation to Samuel. If she had, he would have known that entire demonstration with the Geiger counter was just so much bullshit. That nothing she was ever exposed to would turn up in an examination like that, and that her exposure would just measure one thing. One thing only. Amount of exposure. Nothing like a DNA analysis. If Cassie ever told him anything, he would have walked out of there laughing."

I said, "Perhaps Cassie did tell him about it. And he promptly forgot. He seems to be that type of person."

"True. We were very, very lucky."

"How's that?"

"What you said earlier. He came that close to committing the perfect crime, without leaving any evidence behind. You said that there's always trace evidence left behind at a crime scene. Always. Well, not this time."

"But there was," I gently reminded her.

"The blood traces? Not usable and you know it. Nope, Samuel got out of there the night he killed her, clean as a whistle."

I said, "I wasn't thinking of the blood traces. No, he left something there, before he left. Something that is going to put him away for life."

"And what's that?"

I picked up the wine bottle, poured us each a fresh glass. "He left a trace of a trace. His guilt. Something that will never go away."

She laughed. "Okay. I stand corrected."

I put the bottle down, picked up my glass for a toast.

"To justice," I said, clinking my glass to hers.

She smiled, returned the gesture. "To guilt."

FIVE SORROWFUL MYSTERIES

BY JULIE HYZY

CLAIRE CORBETT LOOKED UP AS DANNY WHEELED IN the first corpse of the day. "What've we got?" she asked.

Haltingly, he read the report. "Female, age forty-four, found dead in the basement of Tus . . . cany Bay Nursing Home—"

"Tuscany Bay?"

Danny's head bobbed up. "Did I say it wrong?"

"No, no, you did fine. But didn't we just have another body from there?"

Danny's brow furrowed. Dutiful, if a bit slow, he'd been her assistant for the past twelve years. She often wondered if he could make more money flipping burgers at McDonald's than flipping bodies at the morgue. At least at McDonald's there might be a chance for promotion.

"The day before yesterday," Claire prompted.

Recollection dawned on Danny's face. "Oh, yeah. The old guy. He was from that place, too. But he, like, lived there. This lady was one of the nurses."

"Weird," Claire said, her voice showing the strain as they shifted the heavy-set female onto the autopsy table. "Maybe we should have taken a closer look at Mr. whatever-his-name-was, huh?"

Danny might not have been particularly perceptive, but he was always eager to please. Especially in trivial matters. Before Claire could get him to reposition the body, Danny had hurried to the files and dug out documents from two days before. "His name was Mr. Pah . . . try . . . zo."

Claire looked over his shoulder. "Petrizzo." She pointed. "No need for an autopsy. Eighty-seven years old, being treated for congestive heart failure, emphysema, and early stage Alzheimer's."

Danny looked confused. "Why did they bring him here? Don't the nursing homes just use hearses to go to the funeral place?"

Claire waited until Danny had settled the corpse's head onto the small wooden stand that kept it steady. "They brought Mr. Petrizzo here because he died on public property. He hadn't taken his wallet, so no ID. They brought him here until we figured out who he was."

"I still don't get why we didn't do an autopsy."

"He was reported missing fast enough that we were able to make a positive ID and get his medical history," Claire said. "No evidence of foul play. Looks like he just died. And from what I heard, he picked a beautiful place in the park, with a view of the gulf."

"That's nice," Danny said, smiling.

"So what about our girl here?"

Danny consulted the notes again.

"Com . . . complained of pain to the abdomen and head. Her super . . . supervisor said she vomited and said she was going to rest for a while. She declined medical assistance and said she thought she had the flu."

"The flu?"

Danny looked up. "Not the flu?"

Claire sighed. Whenever anyone got sick, they called it the flu. The symptoms this woman complained of were less influenza and more gastro enteritis. But neither should have killed her. "I doubt it," she said. "Was she under doctor's care for anything?"

"High co . . . co . . ."

"Cholesterol?"

Danny nodded.

"Hypertension too?"

Another nod.

"We may be looking at a heart attack or stroke. Let's see what our victim can tell us from the inside." She lowered her plastic eye protection and picked up a scalpel.

Danny lowered his eye protection as well and situated himself near the corpse's head. Claire clicked on the tape recorder and spoke into it, providing some of the body's specifics. She added, "Lividity on right side, consistent with reports of victim being found in a reclining position."

Claire pressed hard with the scalpel, carving a large Y into the waxy chest. She then stretched it open. Layers of fat made the task more arduous, but as she sawed away ribs, she noticed an enormous volume of blood, much more than she'd expected. With the body tilted on a stainless steel bed, much like a large cookie sheet, fluids ran downhill into the waste sink. Still, there was so much, Claire ran the hose into the body cavity to help clear it out.

Speaking into the microphone again, she noted the profusion of blood and speculated about the root cause. "Massive intraperitoneal hemorrhage. No evidence of trauma. Possible liver cirrhosis." She shook her head even as she said the words. Although the liver was oversized, the volume of blood was still too much to be explained away that easily. As she spoke she searched for evidence of liver cancer, a ruptured spleen, any type of aneurysm, or pancreatitis. "Nothing present to explain a hemorrhage this extensive."

Scalpel in hand, Danny cut a long curve from behind the corpse's left ear, around the back of the head, to behind the right ear. He worked the skin up over the crown of the skull until he turned the scalp inside out over the face.

Claire continued to remove organs from the cavity, weighing them and slicing specimens for further tests. "I'm ordering a tox screening on all these," she said.

Danny was preparing to start on the skull with the bone saw. Squinting at the doctor, he straightened up. "How come?"

"A hunch," she said. "Look at this." She held up the heart.

Danny came around to see. Even though he might not understand, Claire liked to instruct as she worked. She counted on Danny having been around autopsies enough to catch on. He did. "Huh. I thought you said this was s'posed to be a heart attack."

"Not likely," she said. "At first I thought maybe. What with the nausea and pain she complained about. But those symptoms are non specific; they could be almost anything." Claire kept talking, both for the benefit of the recorder and to sort out her thoughts. "The sudden onset of trouble, the hemorrhaging, and the fact that she's dead with no explanation make me think twice about this one."

Danny grabbed one of the specimens. "I'll get these out to the tox lab today."

"And we'll get answers back two weeks from now."

He stopped at the disappointment in her tone. "Isn't that the normal time?"

"Yeah, but if this lady ate something that did this—" she pointed into the body cavity, which was still deeply puddled with blood "—I'd like to know before somebody else gets hungry."

Two weeks later, very early in the morning, Mark Corbett's fingers crept beneath Claire's sleepshirt with such stealth she almost believed she was still dreaming. When his hand ran along the curve of her hip, she felt herself come awake. She pushed her face deeper into the pillow and tried to ignore the trail of goosebumps left by Mark's skimming fingers. "I'm sleeping," she said unconvincingly.

"Uh-huh." He cupped her breast, snugging closer. She let him.

"What time is it?" she asked.

He whispered into her hair. "Time for me to ravish your body."

"I was dreaming we were in Paris."

"So pretend we're making love at the top of the Eiffel Tower."

Claire peeled open one eye. "It's four in the morning."

"Mm-hmm," Mark said. He brushed the hair off Claire's neck and pressed his lips into the tiny nook that always made her melt.

"Oh," she said, and closed her eyes.

As he murmured next to her ear, Claire heard something else. Her eyes popped open. "Hang on," she said.

Mark kept nuzzling.

"Mark." She reached back and pushed at his hip. "Listen. Is that you?"

He boosted himself, tilting his head toward the bedroom door.

Digital notes of Beethoven's "Für Elise" drifted up the stairs. "Shit!" Mark said. He bounded off the bed.

Claire watched him go. Buck naked. "You must've been pretty sure of yourself, mister," she said as he ran out the door. Turning, she leaned over his side of the bed and clicked on the lamp. Yep, there were his sleep clothes, dropped into a hasty pile.

When Mark returned he was still on the phone. Nodding. Scratching his bare chest. "Got it. See you there," he said before hanging up.

"Some day I ought to turn you down," Claire said, smiling. "Just so you can feel what the rest of the husbands in America go through."

Mark grabbed clean underwear from the drawer. "I gotta go," he said, heading for the bathroom.

"Now?"

"Dead guy found in the parking lot of Tuscany Bay Nursing Home."

"Tuscany Bay?" Claire sat up. "That's odd."

Mark pivoted, came around to the other side of the bed and rescued his discarded clothing.

"What happened?" Claire asked. "Homicide?"

"I assume so. Don't know yet."

Sarasota, Florida, is beautiful almost any time of the day, but Mark enjoyed the cool freedom granted by the pale morning light best of all. By the time he got to Tuscany Bay's parking lot, the sun still hadn't broken over the horizon and the world was bathed in cool shades of gray.

"Gonna be warm today," one of the evidence technicians said. "Good thing they found this guy before the sun came up." He waved a hand in front of his face. "Coulda been a lot worse."

The body lay face up on the ground next to a dark blue Dodge Neon. Spotlights had been set up in a perimeter around the area, and a few onlookers had gathered to watch. One of the uniforms, Bailey, stood nearby. "What do we have?" Mark asked him.

"Male, age fifty-six. Worked here as a nurses' aide." Bailey cocked his head toward the expansive elderly care facility just south of the lot. "Name is Damon Tarabulus. Complained of not feeling well, so he left early." Bailey consulted his notes. "Was supposed to get off at eleven. Left at nine instead. Nobody noticed his car here till about an hour ago, when one of the maintenance guys saw him slumped over the wheel."

"Evidence of foul play?"

"Wallet and keys are still here. No sign of struggle." Bailey shook his head. "Parameds pulled him out but he was cold. Preliminary guess, he came out here and closed his eyes for a minute before starting the car. Too bad. He never opened them up again."

Mark stepped over to the body and made a slow circuit. Dark hair, Caucasian, six feet tall, maybe more. Damon Tarabulus wore a blue patterned smock, solid blue cotton pants, white gym shoes, and a final grimace that spoke of great pain. Not a specimen of perfect health, this Tarabulus carried about sixty extra pounds and had the wrinkled skin of a smoker.

ETs were photographing the car's interior, the body, and the surrounding area. One of the techs interrupted Mark's musings. "How much you want us to do?" she asked.

Mark knew the kit she carried contained tools to pick up everything from fingerprints to fibers. "Keep it simple. There's probably nothing here," he said. "But they want us to have a look-see because of that other death here a few days ago. Just to be safe, we'll impound the car. Look at it later if we have to." He turned to Bailey. "Anybody notify the victim's family?"

"Estranged wife," he said. "We're locating her now."

Mark put money on this being a heart attack or stroke, despite the victim's relatively young age. There was nothing to suggest otherwise—no gun shot, no head trauma—nothing looked out of place. Well, other than the fact that the guy was dead.

By the time the sun came up, Damon Tarabulus's body was wrapped, loaded, and ready for transport to Sarasota Memorial Hospital for autopsy. Mark resisted the urge to tuck a note for Claire under one of the body bag's tight straps.

"Follow the victim to the morgue," Mark told Bailey. "I guess I better talk to some of the people who knew him."

For it being so early in the morning, Tuscany Bay was bright and bustling. A forty-something nurse named Brenda ushered Mark in through the back door. "Come on in, Detective," she said. The gray corridor was lit by narrow fluorescent overhead fixtures. "I just can't believe it," she continued in a hushed voice. "I mean, Damon seemed so robust." She turned. "He wasn't mugged or anything, was he? The paramedics said they thought it might be his heart."

Mark started to answer, but she interrupted.

"I mean, why are you coming in to talk to us? Why a detective? What is it you're not telling us?"

"Just procedure," he began, but she'd pushed open double doors. A group of elderly people stared up at him. Some leaned on walkers, others sat in wheelchairs and on sofas. Despite the room's brightness and its cheery butter-yellow color, Mark smelled the potent combination of mustiness, disinfectant, and stale body odor.

"Word spreads like the plague around here," Brenda whispered close to his ear. "They've been up since Damon's body was discovered. Most of them watched out the window."

The group shifted closer. Too close.

"Before you go," Mark said, eager for any opportunity to retreat, "was Damon well liked?"

Brenda wrinkled her nose. "I didn't care for him. No one did."

He jotted that down. "What about the nurse who died here a few weeks ago?"

"Lisa? She and I worked different shifts so I never got to know her. But if

JULIE HYZY | 129

you come in later you can talk with some of her friends. In the meantime, these are the people who know everything that goes on here. Ask them." She winked, and left.

The elderly patients parted to allow Mark into their midst. Hands clawed at him, pressuring him toward the room's center. He had a flash-forward vision and wondered if he and Claire would live out their final years in a place like this. Despite the tasteful décor and the expensive furnishings, he had an inexplicable urge to run fast and far before the grasping arms of old age could squeeze the life out of him.

Across the room, a large woman with dyed black hair worked knitting needles, an orange scarf puddled at her feet. Mark figured it was already two yards too long. Near the window two women gazed out at the Florida greenery, wistful expressions on both their faces.

One of the taller men shuffled up to Mark and introduced himself. "I'm Ace," he said. "My nickname. Used to own an Ace Hardware." He pointed to the wing chair. "Sit here."

Ace called over to one of the window women. Small-boned and hunched, she had thick gray hair, and watery eyes. Both hands gripped the handles of a walker, and a red rosary dangled from the right. While she made her way over, Mark sat, finding himself at eye level with all the residents. He flipped a page of his notebook and clicked his pen a couple times just to avoid their vacant stares.

"Why are you here?" a woman asked. Her fingers tapped a Parkinsons-like rhythm against her lips. "Was Damon murdered? Do you know who did it?"

"I don't think . . ." Mark began.

"And what about Lisa Hume?" another woman asked.

A voice from behind Mark: "Yeah, what killed her?"

The woman with Parkinsons placed a shaky hand on his arm. "Nobody ever tells us anything. What happened to her? Is somebody going to kill us too?"

Mark raised his voice just a little. "That's what I'm here to ask you about." They silenced and waited for him to continue. Just like little kids, he thought.

Ace hurried to help the woman with the walker into an adjacent wing chair. "This is Rita Petrizzo," he said to Mark. "Her husband is one of the people who you recently found."

Mark's mind raced. He didn't recall a third death. Not from here. But he wanted to be polite. Leaning forward, he took the elderly woman's tiny hand in his. "I'm very sorry," he said.

"My husband good man." Mrs. Petrizzo's old-country voice cracked. "But he not so good up here. . . ." she tapped at her temple. Wide tears shimmered in her rheumy eyes. "My Angelo. Why nobody bring him back here? Why he die alone? He no want to die alone. He supposed to stay with me."

Oh jeez. Mark did remember that one. Since it hadn't been a homicide the matter hadn't ever come under official scrutiny. Once it had been determined that the old guy had been under a doctor's care and had passed away apparently peacefully on an idyllic afternoon, Mark had erased the incident from his mind. "I don't have an answer for you," he said.

Mrs. Petrizzo turned away in disgust, clutching her rosary. Fingering one of the red beads, she sat in the chair mouthing silent prayers, twisting over her shoulder long enough to glare. "I pray you die, you sum-a-bitch," she said, then spat on the floor.

For fifteen minutes Mark fielded more questions than he asked. Although some of the residents were lucid—Ace and the knitting lady, for instance—most asked him wild and unanswerable questions, talking about kids who never visited and loved ones who'd died.

As he rose to leave, he saw Mrs. Petrizzo start after him, her rosary clacking against the walker's metal framework as she inched forward in fits and starts. As much as he would have preferred to bolt, he turned and made his way back to her.

"Mrs. Petrizzo, let me say again how sorry—"

"Shut up you mouth," she said. "You no see what 'dey do to us. Dey kill my Angelo." She waved a hand upward. "Dey try kill us all."

"Who?" Even as the word popped from his mouth, he regretted it.

The hand holding the rosary came up, quivering. She crooked her index finger and gestured him to come closer. She kept her hand aloft and he could see how much the effort cost by the blue-white grip her other hand maintained on the walker. "You find dem," she whispered hoarsely, shaking the rosary near his nose. The prayer beads were so close they looked like red eyes, with angry black pupils staring straight into his face. "God punish dem."

"I'm sure—"

She pointed her finger hard. The rosary shook. "You find who take my Angelo out to die." Mrs. Petrizzo narrowed her eyes, then tapped Mark on the cheek, almost affectionately. "You find dem, and den I pray for you soul."

When Brenda rescued Mark a few minutes later, he asked her about Mrs. Petrizzo's outburst.

"They get a little loopy sometimes," Brenda said. "And she's been lost since her husband died." She gave a half hearted shrug as she led him back into the administrative section. "Did you get any good information in there?"

He flipped his notebook closed. "Hardly," he said. "But I do know they hated Damon."

"Good riddance to bad rubbish."

"Tell me why you didn't like him."

"He was mean. Ridiculed the patients when he thought no one was looking, made them ask for every little thing, and he drank. A lot."

"And he wasn't fired ... because?"

"He was on review for coming in drunk. But management's hands are tied. The staff complained about his work habits, but heaven forbid he get fired." She rolled her eyes. "Our management team is pathetic. They're so afraid of lawsuits of any kind. And let me tell you, Damon would've figured out a way to sue them." She leaned in and lowered her voice. "He took them to the cleaners once for an on-the-job injury. Management was afraid to touch him."

"But they're not afraid of residents' lawsuits because of how they are treated?"

"Right," she said. "The residents were afraid to speak out against him. They knew Damon would retaliate if they did. And who listens to these old folks anyway? Beside us nurses, I mean." Brenda seemed completely oblivious to the irony of her earlier "loopy" comment with regard to Mrs. Petrizzo. "We do what we can to keep things nice around here. But with a wimpy management and no formal complaints, what else can we do?"

"That's just wrong."

"Yeah," she said as though he'd just pointed out that the floors were green.

An hour later, Mark had talked with the staff on duty, and had made arrangements to come back to meet with the night shift. As he left the facility, he shook his head. From the looks of the body at the scene, this was a natural, albeit unexpected death. But the fact that so many people disliked the guy made Mark just a little extra curious.

Flipping open his cell phone, Mark hit speed dial number one. She answered after two rings.

"You at work yet?" he asked.

"Just got in," Claire said. "And I see we got your guy from Tuscany Bay."

"Good. Keep him on ice till I get there. I want in on this one."

"You got it."

Three hours later, Claire peeled off her latex gloves and shook her head. "Danny," she called to her assistant. "Have we gotten those tox reports back from a couple of weeks ago?"

"Reports?" He jumped up from the corner where he'd been waiting for his next task. "Yeah. I think they came today," he said with enthusiasm before leaving the autopsy room.

"What are you looking for?" Mark asked.

Claire pointed inside Damon Tarabulus's body cavity. "Two weeks ago I found the same sort of hemorrhaging in the body of a nurse from Tuscany Bay."

"You think there's some virus going around there?"

"I think they both ingested a poison," she said as Danny returned with the tox screening.

"Poison? Like what?"

Claire flipped through the reports. "Negative, negative, negative . . . " She blew out a breath of frustration and looked up. Danny's and Mark's faces were expectant, eager. "I screened for all the normal stuff," she said. "Unless I know what to look for, I don't know what additional tests to order." Biting her lip, she turned to Mark. "I need to take another look at what both victims ate."

"Must be something only they shared," he said. "None of the residents have gotten sick, so it probably isn't in the cafeteria food."

"Except for Mr. Petrizzo," she said. "We just assumed he died of natural causes, because of his age." She pursed her lips, thinking. "We've done autopsies because relatively young staff members died, but if the older folks are dying too, and those aren't considered suspicious, we wouldn't necessarily know, would we?"

Mark's face told her he was following her train of thought. "Let me check with Tuscany, see if they're seeing more deaths than usual."

When Mark visited Tuscany Bay this time, he came through the front door. A windowed sunroom occupied the space to the right, and he smiled at the two women sitting there. One of them was the heavy-set, dark-haired woman, but this time the knitted item in her lap was bright blue. The woman next to her napped in a wheelchair, until the knitting lady shoved her with an elbow. "Look, it's the detective. Hallo, detective!" she shouted.

The wheelchair woman jerked. She looked around, then dragged the back of a speckled hand across her mouth as she nodded hello. A moment later, she'd drifted back to sleep.

Brenda met him at the juncture to the office hallway. She held papers in her hand and a somber expression on her face. "I've got that information you asked for," she said. "Let's head over to the staff lounge, and we'll go over it."

On their way to the facility's far reaches, they walked through resident corridors. Quite a few doors were open. "These don't look like hospital rooms," Mark said as he craned his neck to see better. "They're huge."

"This is an assisted-living facility, not just a nursing home."

Mark shook his head.

"Come here." She walked back a few yards to what would be a corner unit and knocked at the open door of room 1100.

"Bright," Mark said, toeing the fire-engine red carpet inside the threshold.

"Residents have total control of their apartments." She glanced down at the garish rug and stuck out her tongue. "I'm glad we have professional designers for the common areas of the place." She knocked again. "Mrs. Petrizzo?"

Not Mrs. Petrizzo again. "I don't want to bother anyone," Mark said.

"May we come in?" Brenda asked, her voice high and polite. Then to Mark, "It'll be fine. They love company. And this apartment is one of the nicest we have. The view of the garden is breathtaking."

At that moment, Mrs. Petrizzo rounded the corner in herky-jerky walker movements, the ever-present rosary clutched in her right hand. When she made it to the doorway, her face scrunched, then recognition dawned. "You find who take Angelo away?" she asked.

"He's here to investigate." Brenda answered, very slowly and a little louder than necessary. "He needs to get more information."

Petrizzo turned her back.

Mark grimaced. This could turn into the visit from hell.

Brenda walked straight in, following the old woman. "These are self-contained apartments," she said, oblivious to his discomfort.

"You visit her often?" He nodded his head toward Mrs. Petrizzo.

"Actually this is my first time in here since she and her husband switched to this unit," Brenda said. "I tend to avoid the cranky ones." She winked, then spoke loudly once again as they all made it into the main room. "It's incredibly expensive to live here—I couldn't afford it—but we've got a waiting list a mile long."

Mrs. Petrizzo turned. "My Angelo say 'Nothing but the best!' He good man."

Brenda continued the tour, "And another thing we offer here—"

"Shut up you mouth," Mrs. Petrizzo shouted. "You no tell me who took away my Angelo."

"I told you before, Mrs. Petrizzo," Brenda said soothingly, "we think your husband walked away on his own. Nobody would have taken him off the grounds."

Mrs. Petrizzo harrumphed. "Why you come here?" she asked them.

Brenda answered again, a little less patiently. "Detective Corbett here is investigating the recent deaths."

The old lady seemed to consider that. She shuffled off to the kitchen while Brenda continued the tour. Behaving more like a realtor than a nurse, Brenda made her way through the rooms, first pointing out the kitchen with its top-of-the-line appliances, then the living room, the bedroom, and finally the bathroom: safe, secure, and all handicapped accessible.

When they returned to the kitchen, Mrs. Petrizzo beckoned them forward. "I make coffee," she said. "Sit."

Mark would have much preferred to get out of the woman's apartment and back to his office, but he wanted to get the resident information from Brenda before he left. To his great dismay, she smiled at the old woman and said, "I've passed my limit for today, thanks. But I'm sure the detective here would like some."

He tried to protest. "No—"

"Sit, sit," Mrs. Petrizzo said, gesturing with her spoon toward a chair . "I no have company long time. Sit."

It just seemed wrong to let an old woman wait on them while they sat and talked, but she seemed pleased to have visitors. Biting the insides of his cheeks in frustration, Mark took the chair opposite Brenda's. "So what did you find?" he asked.

"I don't know what all this means," Brenda said, as she spread the papers across the tabletop. She took pains to lower her voice. Mrs. Petrizzo was humming and not paying them any attention. "Statistically speaking, we have seen a bump in resident deaths, but nothing crazy."

"How many?"

Brenda whispered. "In a facility this size, we can expect one to two losses per month. The past six months we've averaged over two per month."

Mrs. Petrizzo leaned over the table, placing a basket of cookies on the table before them. A moment later, she added a bowl of candy. "Help yourself."

Mark and Brenda paused their conversation momentarily until Mrs. Petrizzo shuffled back to the counter.

He ran his finger down the names of the deceased. "Is there anything these people might have had in common?"

"Nothing I can think of," she said. "Umm . . . let's see. About five months ago we did have one weird coincidence. Mr. Gomez passed away, and a day later, his wife followed him." She raised her voice and turned to Mrs. Petrizzo. "Do you remember Mr. and Mrs. Gomez?" she asked over her shoulder.

The old woman grunted an affirmative reply.

Brenda said, "They say Mrs. Gomez died of a broken heart. Isn't that sweet?"

Mark swallowed. He had a sudden urge to rush home and grab Claire and take her on that trip to Paris she'd always been dreaming of. Today. Right now. Before chubby middle-aged nurses could say things like how sweet it was that they'd died together. He cleared his throat. "Can I get copies of these?" he asked, standing.

"These are copies," Brenda said. "You can take them with you."

Mrs. Petrizzo placed a mug of coffee on the table before Mark just as he gathered his papers to leave. "I'm sorry," he said. "Thank you for your time. But I really need to get back."

She pointed a gnarled finger at him. "Wait. You come with me."

Mark followed her to a brass étagère whose style went out in the last century. She lifted a rosary away from its draped position over a corner of an eight-by-ten portrait, and pulled the picture up.

"This my Angelo."

He took the frame from her hands. "He must have been a—" The words died on his lips. The corpulent face staring up at him was familiar. But the name was all wrong. Angelo, yes. But not Petrizzo. This was Angelo Gilardi, the mobster from Chicago. Everybody on the force knew this face. When the well-known criminal relocated to Sarasota, Mark's department had been put on alert. Gilardi, however, who'd been in his seventies at the time, never made a move. It was as if, after all those years of butchering people up north, he'd decided to live a quiet, law-abiding life in this fair-weather haven. Eventually the department lost interest, and subsequently lost sight of the guy. He'd been here, living under a different name, and nobody had ever known.

Mrs. Petrizzo's moist eyes blinked up at him.

"Thank you," Mark said placing the picture back on the shelf. "This helps a lot."

"Angelo no want to die alone," she said in a soft voice. Mark thought she might start crying but her voice grew hard and she pointed to the kitchen. "Bitch in there no tell me nothing. She know who take Angelo away. Take him away to die alone." She shook her head and tears gathered in her eyes again. "Strangers find him. Strangers." As Mark started to move away, she gripped his arm with a bony hand. "You understand?"

"I do," he said.

When Mark's cell phone rang two days later, he was sitting on the sofa in front of the TV, sound asleep. Claire's head was on his lap, and his fingers were tangled in her hair. "Für Elise" jarred them both awake, but at least this time he'd kept the handset within reach.

"Shit," he said, disbelievingly when he got the news. "I'll be right there."

Claire sat up. "What happened?"

"Tuscany Bay again. But this time it's somebody I know." He boosted himself up and checked his watch. "I may not make it back tonight. But I'll be there first thing tomorrow. Don't start without me."

"You look terrible," Claire said when Mark made it into the medical examiner's office the next morning.

"Thanks, honey. I love you too."

"What's going on at that nursing home, anyway?"

"Hell if I know. And because the victim was rushed to the hospital this time, we've got less physical evidence than we would if she'd been found dead. I've got the crime lab taking a look—" He stopped himself, remembering that he'd asked the lab to keep Damon Tarabulus's car impounded. "Hang on a second." Still talking as he dialed, he asked, "You think these people were poisoned, right?"

"It's the only thing that makes sense right now, why?"

"If they all came across the same substance, there might be some spillage or residual on their clothing or—"

When the crime lab answered, Mark asked for additional tests to be run on each victim's clothing and on Damon Tarabulus's car's upholstery. "You never know," he mouthed to Claire.

The tech on the phone said he'd do his best, but cautioned they might not have kept enough from the first victim, the nurse in the basement. "We didn't have any reason to suspect a problem, so I don't know how much we saved," he said. "But I'll check."

"Thanks," Mark said, and hung up.

Claire came around her desk and rested a hand on his shoulder. "I waited till you got here. You sure you're up for this?"

"Not really." He rubbed his hands over his face, then stood. "Let's get it over with."

In the cool autopsy room, Claire adjusted the neckline of her sterile gown to give her enough leeway to comfortably lean into the corpse. She settled her shoulders and spoke into the microphone as she worked.

Arms folded as he watched, Mark shook his head. What was going on at that crazy place?

"Take a look," Claire said after she'd removed the ribs. "This is what I've been talking about."

"That's a lot of blood."

"Whatever killed those other two killed this woman too. What was her name?"

Mark pulled his lips tight before answering. "Brenda." He'd been to enough autopsies to treat them with casual indifference, but he'd never watched when he'd known the victim before. Using the tips of his gloved fingers, he pulled his T-shirt high up to his mask-covered nose, and took a big breath.

"You okay?" Claire asked.

The overwhelmingly pungent smell, like summer garbage left out in the sun too long, was getting to him. "Yeah," he lied. He looked at Brenda's face. Thought about her comment about people dying together. About how sweet that was.

Deep in the body cavity, Claire's hands stopped moving. "You sure you're okay?"

"Yeah." He shifted his weight. "You finding anything unusual?"

"Well," she said, stringing the word out thoughtfully, "the one thing I've noticed is that all three victims have more undigested matter than I would expect to find."

"They ate a big meal before they died?"

Claire shook her head. "No. They haven't digested properly. I noticed it with the first one, Lisa Hume. I thought it odd that she hadn't digested more fully. All the reports suggested she tried to sleep for several hours before she died."

"What does that mean?"

"At first I didn't think it meant anything. You know as well as I do that witness accounts of time aren't always accurate. But then Damon Tarabulus's autopsy gave me a similar finding, and now Brenda's here does too." She talked a little faster. "I'm starting to suspect that whatever killed them also slowed their digestive processes. In fact," she said, bending over the corpse again, "I'm going to send this out for more comprehensive tests."

To Mark, the stomach contents looked like little more than unappetizing mush. "How can they find anything in there?" he asked.

"It helps if we know what to look for," she said, poking through the material in the stainless steel pan Danny held. "But I can tell you a few things just by looking. For instance, this is almost completely undigested." She held up what looked like a shell fragment. When Claire swiped at it with her gloved finger, Mark noticed it was red, about the size of a jellybean.

He pointed. "That's . . ."

"That's what?"

"I've seen something like that before." Mark wracked his brain trying to place the little bean in context.

Claire flipped up her eye shield and studied the shell, then searched the remaining matter in the bowl. "Here's another piece," she said. "And another one. It looks like a seed. A big seed. Danny," she called. "Go see if we've got any books on poisonous plants."

Ten minutes later, Claire looked up from the book Danny had hustled to find. "Got you, you little bugger!" she said, triumphantly. "*Abrus precatorius.* That's what we're looking at. Listen . . . " she read the plant's description aloud to Mark and Danny. "Also known as the Jequirty bean. It's a non-native, invasive plant here in Florida. If the shell is compromised, then ingesting a single pea can be fatal. And the poison, abrin, slows the metabolism as it kills."

"Nasty stuff." Mark said.

"This is probably the most dangerous plant we know of in this country. There's almost no chance of surviving once a bean has been ingested. But poisonings are so rare we don't normally test for abrin. No wonder we didn't find it in the tox screenings."

"So you think this is from a plant that grows on Tuscany's grounds?"

She stared off into space for a long moment. "Yeah, but I can't imagine all of these people picking beans off a plant and eating them. Can you?"

A memory tap-danced just out of reach and hard as Mark tried, he couldn't access where he'd seen the little red bean before. "Let me take a look at the book," he said.

Claire was still reading as she twisted the text to face him. "Interesting. Another name for the bean is the Rosary Pea because people use them—"

"Holy shit," Mark said.

When Mark visited Tuscany Bay again, he headed straight for apartment 1100 and knocked on the open door. "Mrs. Petrizzo?" he called. "It's Detective Corbett."

He waited and a minute later, she made her way slowly toward him. She called out, "You find who take my Angelo away?"

"No."

Stopping in her tracks, she fixed him with an angry glare. "Wha' good are you?" Turning away, she labored to turn her walker back the way she'd come.

"I have a few questions for you, Mrs. Petrizzo."

She ignored him, making her careful way into the living room.

"Why didn't you tell me your husband was Angelo Gilardi?"

She answered over her shoulder. "Wha' difference it make? Somebody take him away. You find who take him."

"Who do you think took him?" Mark asked.

Her skinny shoulders shrugged.

"Do you think it was Lisa Hume?"

Mrs. Petrizzo spat. "Bitch," she said. "She give my Angelo bad medicine."

"And Damon Tarabulus," Mark said, following her toward the out-of-date étagère again. "You didn't like the way he treated you or your friends."

Another shrug.

"What I don't understand is what you had against Brenda," Mark said.

"Why you ask me?"

"I think you killed Lisa Hume, Damon Tarabulus, Brenda Pikorski, and

Roberto and Felicia Gomez." He spread his hands. "There may be more."

The old woman threw her head back and laughed. "How do a little lady like me kill so many people, hah?"

"Where is your rosary, Mrs. Petrizzo?"

Her shrewd glare dissolved, replaced by a sympathetic expression he'd never seen on this woman before. "I no kill nobody," she said softly. "You work too hard and you see things," she said. Suddenly, she winced.

"Are you all right?"

She nodded, but her eyes clenched shut. "My heart no so good no more." Her skinny arm flailed out and she pointed to the nearby kitchen. "Help me sit."

Mark guided her to one of the wooden seats. "Can I get you anything?"

She shook her head. "You stay with me," she said. "I be okay."

"I'll go get someone," he said.

"No, no." She wiped at her brow. "I need sit." Glancing up, she pointed to a tumbler of water. "Please."

He obliged.

She then waved toward a plastic container on the countertop. "Sit with me. Make some coffee."

Mark picked up the cranberry red bowl. "This?"

She nodded. "You make coffee, sit with me a while. Help old lady feel better."

"I don't think so, Mrs. Petrizzo."

"You no like my coffee?" The solid-steel was back in those watery eyes.

He hefted the container. "You're a wily thing, aren't you?" He took Mrs. Petrizzo by the elbow and brought her to her feet. "Let's go."

She fought, scratching at him, but her chicken arms were no match for Mark's strength. "You no touch me. You leave me alone!" As they moved into the living room, her leg gave out and Mark tried to catch her before she fell. But just as he helped her right herself, she wrenched from his grip and clawed at the brass étagère. Her bony hand snatched at Angelo's portrait, grabbing the rosary from its perch. Her fist tightened around the rosary beans. Before he could react, she shoved it into her mouth and started to chomp.

"No!" Mark shouted for help and wrestled to pry open her jaw.

When the wily old lady grinned it was a pitiful sight—the string of beads hung from her lips, and bean meats oozed out the sides of her mouth. "I no go jail, you sum-a-bitch," she said around clenched teeth. "I die first." She smiled up at the ceiling. "I coming, Angelo!"

Less than thirty-six hours later, after enduring a futile stomach-pumping, Mrs. Petrizzo's body was wheeled into the autopsy room where Claire waited with her scalpel. "Why would anyone choose such a painful way to go?" she asked as she made the first incision.

Mark sat nearby, watching Claire and Danny work. "She was surrounded by pain her whole life. First as her husband doled it out and then when she inflicted it. Maybe it's all she knew."

"By the way," Claire said, as she poked through Mrs. Petrizzo's skinny corpse, "all the other tox screenings came back positive for abrin." Danny had already begun sawing the skull open and Claire looked over at him. "I'd love to understand this lady. What kind of screwed-up brain did she have?"

Mark stood, coming around to watch. The procedure didn't bother him as much this time. "Best we can guess is that she learned the business of revenge from years of living with her husband."

Claire didn't look up. "And she used rosary beads to kill people. What a lunatic."

"We got her to talk a little before she died. Once the poison started taking effect she was ready to confess. She claimed she wanted to cleanse her soul so she could get into heaven."

Danny snorted a laugh. Claire shook her head.

Mark continued. "She and Angelo targeted the Gomezes to get their apartment. That was their first abrin killing. And it went perfectly. Smooth. Undetected. But then Angelo died, and Mrs. Petrizzo went a little nuts in the head." Mark blew out a breath. "The thing is, she was hell-bent on revenge for her husband's death."

"Even though he probably did die of natural causes when he wandered off," Claire said, as she directed the running hose into the body. "No surprises here. I see the same hemorrhaging I did with the other victims. I'm just sorry I didn't find those red seeds in Lisa, or Damon. We might've been able to save Brenda."

"Oh, I didn't tell you." Mark said. "She managed to get Brenda to eat the seeds. Petrizzo told her they were candy. But the other victims drank their poison. We found abrin in the coffee. Looks like the old lady maintained a separate grinder for her special guests. She invited them in, made a pot of her brew, and a day or so later, they're dead. Ties in with the fact that all the victims had carpet fibers from her apartment on their clothing."

"Good work, detective." Claire smiled. "But what made you look at her coffee?"

"She offered me some."

Claire looked up. "Oh, no."

"Don't worry." Now it was his turn to grin. "I knew better."

"But how? Who would ever suspect a sweet little old lady? Especially one carrying a rosary around all the time."

"I did."

She blew out a heavy breath. "Thank God."

"Speaking of which, or should I say 'whom,'" Mark said, "according to Mrs. Petrizzo, God supposedly sanctioned this little killing spree." He nodded toward the body on the table. "She kept ranting about how he guided her rosary and about sorrowful mysteries. You're Catholic. Any idea what she meant?"

"Rosary mysteries. Wow. I haven't heard that in years." Claire's gaze swept to the ceiling. "There are five mysteries per rosary, one for each decade. She was talking about meditations."

Mark shot her a quizzical look. "Meditations?"

"If I recall correctly, certain days of the week are devoted to certain meditations—you're supposed to reflect on each of the mysteries in between praying the decades. There are all sorts of different mysteries—Glorious, Joyful, Sorrowful. This lady was responsible for five deaths, right?"

"Yeah."

She scratched at her chin with the back of her gloved hand. "Weird how that worked out. Five murders. Five sorrowful mysteries. It's almost as if she planned them to match her holy meditations."

Mark stared at the corpse's wide open chest, watching as Claire removed the heart and placed it into a container to be weighed. He thought about the old woman's cold-blooded devotion to her deadly rosary.

"Could be," he said, "only this lady wasn't sorry at all."

MITT'S MURDER

BY JOHN LUTZ

THE JOGGING TRAIL IN SPEEDERS PARK WAS ONE OF THE area's favorites among early morning exercisers. Softly asphalted paths wound through mature elm and maple trees, around a pristine blue lake whose banks were lined with white quarry stones. Speeders Park was nothing if not scenic.

It wasn't officially named "Speeders Park." It was called that, rather than the name of some long-dead city father, on its entrance sign, because the street that bordered its western edge was Sallab Road. Sallab was a beautiful straight and level stretch traveled by drivers just off the nearby interstate. Used to highway speeds, people with a tendency to go fast couldn't resist the wide and level road. The local police had given out reams of speeding tickets on that stretch of road for so many years it had become a notorious speed trap. It didn't seem to slow anyone down, but it did provide a steady source of revenue for the county.

Former major league catcher Mitt Adams stayed in reasonably good physical condition by jogging every morning on the park's mile-long running and bicycle path, the one passing closest to Sallab Road. Mitt had been retired from baseball for ten years. He'd been stocky and immovable behind home plate and many a runner trying to score had come out sore and bruised, whether safe or out. Now pushing fifty, Mitt was still stocky and strong, though a bit paunchier. And he was still not a man to be run over, on or off a baseball diamond.

Mitt was in a different kind of diamond business now. He was public relations director and representative of Diamond Square, a company that wholesaled jewelry and industrial diamonds. Being a celebrity front man for the firm, he always wore a large diamond set in an eighteen-karat gold ring on his left hand. His World Series ring he wore on his right. He liked to watch the morning sunlight glint off both rings as he pumped his stocky arms while he jogged.

He wasn't the only one who noticed this mesmerizing play of light.

Mitt had jogged most of his regular five miles and the former athlete was huffing hard when he rounded the slight grade beyond a stand of maples and began the stretch of path that paralleled Sallab Road. The killer watched from another copse of maple trees, less than a quarter of a mile ahead and toward the bend away from the road. When Mitt entered the trees, for a few seconds he'd be invisible from the road or from farther down the winding trail.

Here came Mitt, puffing like a miniature steam engine, legs and arms working like pistons, eyes squinted against the sun, perspiration pouring down his broad face from beneath a sweat band with his old team logo on it. The killer smiled. Mitt, team player to the last.

Sweat at the corners of Mitt's eyes stung and obscured his vision. Seeing became even more difficult when he passed from bright sunlight into the shadows beneath the trees. His eyes didn't have time to adjust as a dark form suddenly appeared before him.

Puzzled, Mitt huffed and puffed to a halt. The killer brandished a knife, and ordered Mitt to accompany him off the trail and into the trees. Mitt could hardly refuse.

As soon as they were in the shadows, Mitt barely saw an arm slash upward toward his midsection. Something long and sharp sliced like ice into Mitt, beneath his sternum, up, up into his heart. The pain was like an explosion, but brief.

Did I tag him? Mitt wondered inanely. Did I tag the bastard? He took three more steps, the third one when he was already dead, and crumpled to the ground a few feet off the path.

The killer glanced around, confident that he hadn't been seen, then bent low and removed the diamond ring from the third finger of Mitt's gnarled left hand. Mitt had lost weight lately with his regular jogging and was in great shape for a dead man, so the ring slid off easily. The killer ignored the World Series ring.

He wiped clean the long folding knife he'd thought he might have to use to remove the diamond ring, placed it and the ring in his pocket, then jogged off into the bright sunlight beyond the trees.

Mitt had died almost immediately. The killer was glad there hadn't been much blood. Things had gone swimmingly, if you weren't Mitt.

In his office at police headquarters, Captain Wayne Loman sat back and looked across his desk at the two people he'd summoned to get him out of deep doo-doo. When a local celebrity like Mitt Adams was murdered, the pols and public expected—no, demanded—action followed by results. Loman knew the best way to accomplish both those things was sitting right there in front of him in the persons of Miles Dougherty and Catt Balone. Dougherty had long been top dog of CSI in a major city in Florida, home of wacko crime, and Balone had been his assistant. Florida also being the home of wacko politics, both had been forced from their jobs for political reasons. Now they were in private practice here in the Midwest with their own investigative agency, Dougherty and Balone. Loman wasn't too proud to ask for help.

Catt, a tall, curvaceous woman with attractive if predatory features, stared at Loman with her cool green eyes. Miles Dougherty was her physical opposite, short, dumpy, balding, amiable looking. He had a pleasing smile that seemed always present. He was about forty-five to Catt's thirty-five. Loman knew that when he was about twenty-five, Miles Dougherty had been a decorated Navy Seal.

"So whadya got?" Catt asked him, lounging in one of the two chairs angled toward the cluttered desk.

"Murder," Loman said.

"Mitt Adams?" Miles asked, having kept up on the news.

Loman nodded.

JOHN LUTZ | **149**

"So whadya got?" Catt asked again. Same expression, feline observing mouse, speculating.

"As he did most mornings, starting about six-thirty, Mitt was jogging in Speeders Park. He was found by another jogger who noticed him lying off the path in the shadows and called nine-one-one on her cell phone. Mitt was stabbed to death by a knife with a long, thin blade, very sharp. His keys and a roll of bills were in a packet attached by a Velcro strap around his right ankle. The diamond ring he always wore was missing, but not his World Series ring."

"A thief can fence a diamond ring without too much danger," Miles said. "That World Series ring would arouse suspicion. Not too many fences would touch it."

"A real fan might," Catt said. She smiled, looking dangerously feline. "A Cubs fan."

"What's the ME say?" Miles asked. He kind of liked this, entering a case when the investigation was well under way. The first forty-eight hours had passed and the police had gotten nowhere. His smile was inward. Time for the real experts to show how it's done.

Catt was staring at him. She knew what he was thinking. She always did. Sometimes she gave him the creeps.

" . . . dead when he hit the ground," Loman was saying.

"At least he didn't suffer," Catt said. Miles wondered if she was serious. Being stabbed in the heart was never a walk in the park. Or a jog. "For long, anyway," she added.

"What'd your CSI people come up with?" Miles asked.

"Mitt was lying curled on his right side on the ground, right arm and leg bent beneath him. Minimal bleeding from the knife wounds, and from facial injuries sustained when he fell, indicated he was dead before he hit the ground. The weapon hasn't been found. There were no discernable footprints in the area, which was on hard, grassy earth beneath some trees. There was some blood, though, and it appeared the killer stepped in it with the edge of one shoe. Probably didn't even know he did it."

"What kind of sole?" Catt asked.

"Smooth. No way to tell if it was composite or leather, with such a small sample. And there was no particulate matter in the blood other than what was indigenous to the scene." Loman sighed. "I tell you, we've got nothing other than that the weapon was a long, thin-bladed knife."

"And sharp," Catt reminded him.

Miles wished she'd stop being sarcastic. But he knew she wouldn't. This was the woman who'd raised her extended middle finger at a bossy police lieutenant at a murder scene while snapping on her white Latex glove.

"Might the person who discovered the body have stepped in the blood?" Miles asked.

"That would be a woman named Adelaide Clark, an emergency room nurse who jogs the trail in the park every morning before going in to work at Mercy Hospital. She says she never got closer than ten feet away from the body. She was pretty sure Mitt was dead. According to her statement, she backed away, trying not to disturb even the area around the body, before making her nine-one-one call. Records show the call came in at seven-twenty."

Catt sat up straighter. "If she's a nurse and was only pretty sure he was dead—"

"I know," Loman said. "I'm just summarizing her statement. She admitted she was rattled."

"Why? She'd seen dead bodies before, in her job."

"It wasn't what she was looking at," Miles said, "it was whom."

Catt nodded her acknowledgement and approval, maybe of his grammar. She much admired good grammar, even if she didn't bother using it herself. "Starstruck, huh?"

"Mitt almost made it into the Hall of Fame," Loman said.

"Caught two no-hitters," Miles said.

"Two-forty lifetime batting average," Catt said. "Hit seventeen home runs one decade."

Miles grinned. Nothing and no one awed Catt.

"Killer leave anything at the scene?" he asked Loman. "Other than that very partial footprint?"

"Not a hair, not a thread, fingerprint, useful footprint, or any suggestion of any kind of body fluid," Loman said. "Mitt jogged that same path regular like clockwork. The intersection at the northwest corner of the park's a busy one, and there are cameras set up to catch speeders so we can get their license plate numbers and ticket them later. One of them's aimed north, down Sallab Road along the edge of the park. The tape's marked with time and date. The interesting thing about the camcorder is it coincidentally takes in the park's only vehicular traffic entrance and exit. If the killer used his car to get in and out, we've got it on tape."

"Too far away to read the plate numbers?" Miles asked.

"'Fraid so. We aren't that lucky."

"Let us work on the tape," Catt said. "Maybe we can enhance it."

"Will do." Loman began swiveling back and forth in his desk chair. "The camera also caught a traffic cop handing out a ticket near the park entrance. Date and time stamped on the image. Seven-sixteen a.m."

"In the time frame," Catt said.

"Cop said he saw nothing suspicious along that edge of the park, and the speeding ticket went to an eighteen-year-old kid doing twelve miles an hour over the limit."

"Crime scene still cordoned off with tape?" Miles asked.

"It is. I saw that the scene was kept undisturbed."

"Knowing you were gonna call us," Catt said.

"Well," Loman said. "Suspecting."

"Speaking of suspects," Miles said. "Are there any?"

"Not per se," Loman said.

"Very good," Catt said, beaming.

"Then I presume no motive," Miles said.

"One possible," Loman said.

"Who we talking about?" Miles asked.

"The husband or lover of the woman Mitt was seeing behind his wife's back."

"How do we know there was such a woman?" Miles asked.

"Mitt's wife told him," Catt said, before Loman could answer.

Loman shook his head in mock admiration. "Women's intuition. I marvel."

"Give us some names," Catt said. "Friends, business associates, neighbors, fellow joggers. Everybody but the killer. That would take all the fun out of it."

After a look at the crime scene that was every bit as unrevealing as Loman had described, Miles and Catt went into interview phase with Mitt's extramarital interest.

"I've already told all this to the police," said Nora Cross.

Catt said, "You don't know how many times we've heard that."

They were in Nora's third-floor condo. It was small but in a smart neighborhood, not far from Speeders Park. The furnishings were traditional and tasteful, lots of dark wood and mocha-colored leather, plush beige carpeting, wooden window treatments of the sort that used to be called venetian blinds. Catt and Miles sat on a sofa opposite Nora, who was posed prettily in a leather wing chair. The sofa faced the wide window. Catt decided she liked the bars of sunlight lancing in through the blind slats, even the illuminated swarming dust motes.

Nora, who should have dusted more often, was a starved looking blonde woman about thirty with haunted gray eyes. She looked like a smaller, younger Lauren Bacall. Thirty made her considerably younger than Mitt. She worked for a diamond retailer that had an account with Mitt's company. She explained how a year or so ago, for her and Mitt, business had become pleasure.

"It sneaked up and surprised both of us," she said, not sounding at all credible.

"Were you aware Mitt's wife knew about you two?" Miles asked.

"Yes. Mitt was, too. It was the kind of thing none of us talked about. No one among the three of us wanted to upset the balance. Life wasn't working quite right for any of us, but it was working." Her eyes misted up and a tear tracked down her cheek, but she didn't wipe it away, didn't even blink. Ignoring the tear might make it cease to exist. This was a woman who didn't cry easily.

"Any idea who might have killed Mitt?" Catt asked bluntly.

"It wasn't his wife. Linda wouldn't hurt anyone. Well, maybe me, but who could blame her?"

"You have a very charitable attitude toward your lover's wife," Miles said.

Nora shrugged. "Love happens."

So do trophy wives, Catt thought.

"Did Mitt seem upset about anything lately?" she asked. "Did he give any indication he might have known his life was in danger?"

Nora hesitated. "I didn't tell the police this, because I don't like stating anything other than what I know is fact. Mitt didn't confide in me, but I got the impression something was very wrong at work."

"What gave you that impression?"

Nora gave a slight but eloquent shrug. "Mitt might have been a big league catcher, but I knew the signs."

"Was he worried about losing his job?" Miles asked.

"Nothing like that. More like he didn't know what to do about whatever he thought was wrong."

"You said 'thought was wrong,'" Catt pointed out.

"Yes, I got the feeling Mitt wasn't sure anything was wrong. That's why I hesitated giving the police the name Mitt mentioned."

Miles would have sworn he felt his ears prick up.

Catt arched an eyebrow. "Name?"

"Kerrington," Nora said. "I heard Mitt mutter it one day when he was deep in thought. I think the man's first name is Roger. I can't be positive of that. Mitt and I had been drinking. We weren't drunk, but liquor tended to loosen Mitt's tongue."

Catt wrote the name down in her leather-bound notepad. "What did he tell you about Kerrington?"

"Not much, really. But I gathered he was the fellow employee causing

Mitt's concern, and it might have had something to do with stealing from the company."

Motive, Catt and Miles thought simultaneously. Kerrington might have killed Mitt to keep him from telling anyone about misdirected money or diamonds.

Nora stretched her lithe body and leaned back in her chair. The solitary tear that had tracked down her cheek was no longer visible. "That's really all I can tell you, unless you insist on the sordid details of our affair. You'll be disappointed to learn that sex was pretty normal."

"We're not into sordid yet," Miles said, smiling. He thanked Nora and stood up.

Catt slipped her notepad into her purse and stood up also. "I'm curious," she said.

"I noticed," Nora said with a faint smile.

"Why did you tell this to us and not to the police?"

Nora shrugged again. She really was good at it. You could almost see what might have been bothering her running down off her shoulders. "You know how water dripping on stone will finally wear it away?"

Catt nodded.

"You were the last drip," Nora said.

Miles was about to pull the car away from in front of Nora's condo when his cell phone vibrated. He did more listening than talking before breaking the connection and sliding the phone back in his pocket. "Loman's got a witness who said he passed Mitt on the jogging trail at seven-twelve the morning of Mitt's death."

"And the nine-one-one call came in at seven-twenty," Catt said. "That pretty much brackets the time of death. Mitt must not have been dead long when his body was discovered."

"Progress," Miles said. Though he wasn't exactly sure how they were any closer to the killer.

"If we can believe the witness," Catt said, more realistically.

Miles pulled away from the curb and drove toward the address of Roger Kerrington.

"We gonna call and see if Kerrington's home?" Catt asked.

"It's Sunday," Miles said. "He should be there."

"Or in church," Catt said. "Maybe confessing."

Roger Kerrington was home. His wife insisted on being present when he talked with Miles and Catt. The couple was childless and lived in a neat, well-furnished suburban house in keeping with Kerrington's salary at Diamond Square. If he was stealing, he wasn't using the proceeds to live large. Or maybe he was smart enough to salt it away until he had enough to live the luxurious life he imagined. Contrary to popular belief, some thieves did know when to quit.

Kerrington was a short, squat man about forty, well-muscled, with a square jaw and square-rimmed glasses. Squared away, Catt thought. He was wearing khaki walking shorts, a brown knit pullover with a collar, and white jogging shoes. Catt wondered if their soles would show traces of Mitt's blood.

It didn't take long to get to the meat of the interview.

"You say Mitt was killed around seven-fifteen?" Kerrington asked.

"Near as we can tell," Miles said.

Kerrington rubbed his square jaw, looking like a man pretending to think. "I was feeling ill that morning. Some kind of bug. I went in to work late."

"He didn't get out of bed until after eight o'clock," his wife said. Her name was Belinda and she was a smaller version of Kerrington only without the square glasses. "I know because I was in bed with him."

"Asleep?" Catt asked.

"Reading a good mystery. My husband's snoring was keeping me awake." She smiled woman to woman at Catt. "You know how it is."

"No," Catt said. "I wouldn't put up with snoring."

Throughout the interview, Miles and Catt didn't mention Nora's belief that Mitt thought Kerrington was doing something detrimental to

Diamond Square, Inc. Probably something illegal that provided a motive for murder.

When they left the suburban ranch house, Catt said, "He's got a solid alibi, even if Belinda's lying."

"Was she lying?" Miles asked. He knew Catt had an uncanny ability to read body language.

"Like a rug," Catt said.

After leaving the Kerringtons, they talked to the witness who'd seen Mitt jogging at seven-twelve the morning of his death. His name was Jack Ozman, and he was an insurance agent who ran in the park every morning. He had not a single hair on his head and sparse blond eyebrows. His smile was as expansive as his waistline, and he pumped Catt's hand, then Miles's, as if trying to draw water from wells. Catt thought somebody should tell him that after being shaken like that, the prospective customer's hand might be too sore to hold a pen and sign on the dotted line.

"How did you know the exact time you saw Mitt?" Miles asked Ozman.

"I'd just checked my watch to make sure my run was on schedule, and when I looked up, there he was. We nodded at each other as we passed, like we do—did most mornings."

"Do you know any other people who jog or walk regularly in the park about that time?"

"Lots of them," Ozman said. "We're all mostly from the neighborhood around the park. I've tried to sell most of them insurance."

Catt made a low grumbling sound, not a purr.

"Then you know names?" Miles asked.

"Like any good salesman, I know their names."

Miles and Catt exchanged glances.

"Eureka," Catt said.

"Kerrington?" Miles said.

Ozman beamed. "Sure, Roger Kerrington. I see him most mornings. He's underinsured and doesn't know it. But I didn't see him the morning Mitt was killed."

"You're sure about that?" Catt asked.

Ozman looked insulted. "Hey, it's the kind of thing a salesman remembers. Names and faces."

When they'd left Ozman, Catt said, "The salesman will be able to sell to a jury. The guy'll make a great witness."

"For Kerrington," Miles said. "Maybe Belinda Kerrington was telling the truth and her husband actually wasn't in the park that morning."

"She was lying," Catt said with her usual certainty.

They drove silently for a while. They knew what they needed, but they also knew there wasn't enough evidence to obtain a search warrant for the Kerrington residence.

"What we could use are a few reliable witnesses who saw Kerrington in the park the morning of Mitt's murder," Catt said.

"It should be possible," Miles said. "Assuming he was there."

Catt wasn't so sure, having little faith in the reliability, or believability, of eyewitnesses.

At the next stop sign, she said, "I'd sure like to get my hands on Kerrington's shoes."

Miles said, "Forget the shoes for now. Kerrington doesn't live within easy walking distance of the park. Let's find out what kind of car he drives."

"If there's blood on the shoes," Catt said with a grin, "there's a good chance for blood in the car."

"Mitt's blood."

"It'd be great if we could get enough on Kerrington to hold him overnight," Catt said.

"Why's that?"

"See if he snores."

Miles and Catt were just finishing a late lunch at a steakhouse not far from Speeders Park when Loman phoned Miles's cell phone from police headquarters. Loman seemed upset.

"Somebody in the department's leaking to the media," he said. "We're gonna get some terrible press 'cause of that traffic cop writing a ticket nearby almost at the precise time Mitt was murdered."

"That seems to be the case," Miles said. "But so what? The cop wasn't a mind reader with X-ray vision."

"You know how it is, Miles. The news media'll be bitching because of how we allocate our people, calling us incompetent, making life hell around here top to bottom to sideways."

"Meaning?"

"There's suddenly twice as much pressure on us to solve this murder. Pressure on me, pressure on thee."

"Downhill," Miles said.

"Pardon?"

"Nothing. We'll keep you informed, Wayne." Miles broke the connection.

"What was that all about?" Catt asked.

"Pressure," Miles said.

"Pass the artificial sweetener," Catt said.

Catt was right about the unreliability of witnesses. Six people in the park said they were reasonably sure they'd seen Roger Kerrington on the joggers' path the morning Mitt was killed. The trouble was that seventeen joggers or walkers would testify they hadn't seen him that morning. And of course, no one had seen anything relating to Mitt being killed except for the woman who'd noticed the body.

Miles and Catt did run a Department of Motor Vehicles check on Kerrington. A black Ford Explorer SUV was registered to him.

Late that afternoon, a messenger arrived at Miles and Catt's office with a package. Miles smiled at Catt as he signed for it.

"Blown up sequential photos from that traffic camcorder," he explained, tearing open the package. "We can at least get a glimpse of every car coming or going at Speeders Park, from an hour before the murder to an hour after Mitt's body was discovered."

"That could be a lot of vehicles," Catt said.

It turned out to be forty-seven. The relatively low number was due to the early hour of the photos, which were time-lapse stills, marked with the precise time and date, taken from the camcorder tape. Trouble was, thirty of the vehicles were SUVs. Fourteen of them could be eliminated because they were too light a color to be Kerrington's black vehicle. The others were indistinctly shaded in the grainy black-and-white images. They might have been red, blue, green, or black. And because of distance and poor imagery, any number of them might have been Ford Explorers.

"Narrowed down to sixteen," Miles said, sitting back exhausted from examining the stills with a magnifying glass. "Not enough to implicate Kerrington and prove his wife is lying about him being home in bed."

"It doesn't prove his SUV wasn't in the park's lot that morning," Catt pointed out.

"For all your skepticism," Miles said, "you talk like an optimist." He pulled his Rolodex across the desk and thumbed through the index cards for a number. He started to peck with a finger on his desk phone, but halfway through the number he hung up the receiver and used his cell phone.

"Who are you calling?" Catt asked.

"Worldwide Security," Miles said.

Catt was surprised. Worldwide was one of the largest private security firms in the world, providing every kind of protection for VIPs and their families, from corporate CEOs to potentates of major nations. "You know somebody there?"

"The president, Willis Burr. We grew up in the same neighborhood, dated the same girls, and made some of the same mistakes."

"You think Worldwide can enhance those images so we can read a plate number?"

"I doubt that," Miles said, "but they might have some photos of their own. Worldwide has its own satellite. Three of them, in fact. And there's a good chance one of them was in range of this city when the murder took place."

Catt wasn't surprised when Miles didn't get through to Burr. He didn't get through even to an assistant. He left a message and hung up, noticing the expression on Catt's face.

"Not to worry," he said.

"Skepticism and worry," Catt said. "Not the same thing."

When Catt went into the office the next morning, her skepticism disappeared at the sight of Miles's extra-wide amiable grin. "Your guy came through," she said.

He nodded. "A messenger will deliver a DVD within the hour. There'll be a slight angle, but a Worldwide satellite passed overhead just east of the area at the time of Mitt's murder."

"Your old pal Willis Burr knows what friends are for."

"Don't think I don't owe him for this," Miles said.

"Wouldn't dream of it. I know what friends are for, too."

When they viewed the satellite DVD an hour later, they were disappointed to find that, while the vehicles entering and leaving Speeders Park were in sharper focus than on the traffic cam photos, their license plates still couldn't be read. However, it was possible to identify the make and comparative sizes of some of the SUVs and eliminate eight more. That meant six of them might be Kerrington's Ford Explorer.

But there was something else on the DVD, something that made it possible to determine the precise time of the murder. The satellite imagery was marked by a date-and-time bug in the lower right corner, ongoing in hundredths of seconds. The video stream enabled them to see Mitt's murder. Well, almost. The zoomed-in aerial view of the park showed a tiny figure on the jogging trail standing motionless minutes before another, bulkier figure arrived, apparently at jog pace. Mitt. The bulkier figure slowed, moved close to the other figure. Then both disappeared into the darker area of the woods. Half a minute later, one of the figures emerged and began moving at a moderately fast pace along the jogging path, away from the scene. There was no doubt that Miles and Catt had just witnessed the murder of Mitt Adams.

"After killing Mitt, the murderer jogged away along the trail," Catt said. "Somebody must have seen him."

"We do have witnesses who'll say Kerrington was jogging in the park that morning," Miles pointed out.

"And a ton more witnesses who say they never saw him there."

Miles and Catt viewed the video stream again, but from a wider angle. There were other joggers and walkers on the winding path, but none near the point of the murder at the time it happened. And from satellite distance, amazing as the enlarged imagery was, it was impossible to know one small dark moving figure from another. As far as anyone could judge from the DVD, the figure emerging from the woods might be Mitt. Only it wasn't Mitt, because he was dead on the ground.

"The fact is," Catt said, "we've still only got a lot of circumstantial evidence, and Kerrington's got a solid enough alibi to walk if there's a trial. We still don't have enough to obtain a search warrant for his house. And if we did have a warrant, we might not find anything incriminating unless there are blood stains on Kerrington's shoes, or maybe the carpet of his car or house." She stared out the window at a breeze barely moving the trees. "All that circumstance might be enough to get an indictment, but what we really need is something to sell a jury. Otherwise, the defense and prosecution will simply be playing dueling witnesses and paid experts, and you might have noticed our side's outnumbered."

"We have enough for a conviction," Miles said, leaning back in his desk chair almost far enough to tip.

"You've figured a way to get Mrs. Kerrington to tell the truth?" Catt asked.

"No," Miles said, "but I might know how we can nullify the defense's witnesses and place Kerrington in the park at the time of the murder."

SIX MONTHS LATER

Halfway through the trial, it didn't look good for the prosecution. Bo Hastings, the DA who led the prosecution team, was distraught. He was a small man with a barrel chest and a facial resemblance to Napoleon. The resemblance was made stronger by the black helmet of hair he wore Napoleon style. Catt knew it was a wig and figured she probably shared that knowledge with everyone else.

"The fact that we found no blood on the shoes or in Kerrington's SUV or house has just about killed us," Hastings told Miles, Catt, and Loman, in his office in the Hall of Justice.

Catt sat up straighter, arching her back. "There's still a—"

"I know," Hastings said, "mountain of evidence. Take away the wife's testimony that Kerrington didn't leave her sight around the time of Mitt's murder, and that mountain would bury Kerrington. But the evidence is circumstantial. The traffic camera's got an SUV like his entering and leaving the park around the time of the murder. The satellite photos show somebody who could be Kerrington accosting somebody who could be Mitt on the jogging path, going with him into the woods, then emerging and driving away in an SUV that might be the same SUV we saw entering and leaving the park at a time that suits our case, while we ignore all the other SUVs."

"Have we tried to get satellite shots of an SUV leaving and returning to Kerrington's house that morning?" Catt asked.

"That was going to be our ace in the hole," Hastings said. "But timing and cloud cover worked for Kerrington. No such shots were taken that we could zoom in on." Hastings made a tent with his fingers and looked as depressed as if Josephine had left him. "And tomorrow the defense is going to put on an almost endless parade of witnesses who jog or walk every morning in the park and will swear they don't recall seeing Kerrington there." He sighed. "We have only three who say they saw him, and three more who think they might have. Who you gonna believe if you're a juror?"

They all knew the answer.

"Any ideas?" Loman asked.

"I'd like to see some satellite shots of the jogging trail," Miles said, "to make sure of something I noticed."

"What part of the trail?" Hastings asked.

"Any part."

Everyone in the room stared at him.

"I think," Miles said, "I can give you the something that'll sell the jury."

The next morning in court was the low point for the prosecution. One credible witness after another testified that he or she hadn't seen Kerrington in the park the morning of Mitt's death, lending more and more validity to Kerrington's alibi. In a largely circumstantial case, the barrage of defense testimony should prove fatal to the prosecution.

It didn't help that Hastings chose to ask the witnesses only the same, single question in his cross-examinations.

After a two-hour recess for lunch, it was the prosecution's time for rebuttal.

Hastings began by making a show of strutting before the jury and glancing at his watch. Miles noticed that he'd changed watches during the recess, from his gold Rolex to what looked like a bargain oversized watch with an obviously imitation leather band.

"The prosecution has put witness after witness on the stand," Hastings said, "regular joggers or walkers in Speeders Park, who testified they did not see the defendant in the park during the time frame of Mitt Adams's murder." Hastings tapped his watch's plastic face several times sharply with a fingernail. "I believe them all."

There was a notable reaction among the jurors. Not exactly a gasp, but a simultaneous slight shifting of weight. As if maybe the assumed outcome of the trial was shifting.

"The reason for their testimony is here," Hastings proclaimed. He held up his arm to show them his wristwatch, face out.

"As you know, the jogging trail in Speeders Park circles a large lake.

Anyone wanting to travel in either direction along that path makes a choice before they set out—whether to go clockwise or counterclockwise. In this country we do almost everything physical and requiring circular motion counterclockwise. Racehorses run counterclockwise. Same way with race cars or almost anything else that races. Dancers circle the floor counter-clockwise. Track and field runners run along the track counterclockwise. Baseball players circle the bases counterclockwise. And almost every morn-ing former big league catcher Mitt Adams jogged counterclockwise along the park's path. That was natural for him. First to second to third to home. Only that morning Mitt never reached home."

Hastings had the jurors leaning slightly forward now. He seemed to become possessed by a kind of fierce joy. This was his game and he was on top of it.

"Anyone else moving that same direction almost certainly wouldn't have seen Mitt unless they were in sight of each other when they began. Few of the counterclockwise people see each other during their morning exercise." Hasting stopped pacing and faced the jury with his arms crossed. "But they see virtually every jogger or walker moving clockwise on the path, because they will pass each other."

Hastings paused. He was good at pauses.

"Every one of the defense witnesses who testified they did not see the defendant in the park at the time of Mitt's murder ran or walked counter-clockwise along the trail—the same direction as the defendant. Of course they're telling the truth. Of course they never saw him."

Another dramatic pause. Even better than the first. The earth seemed to hesitate in its rotation.

"The witnesses we the prosecution will call, who will testify that they either saw or thought they saw Roger Kerrington in the park, at the time, in the vicinity, on the morning of Mitt Adams's murder, will also testify that they traveled clockwise along the trail. They didn't see Kerrington as a dis-tant figure, or see him only from the back if at all. They saw him face to face as they passed each other. One such witness who saw Roger Kerrington in the park that morning is worth a hundred who swear they were there but didn't see him, if that one witness jogged or walked clockwise." Hastings took a deep breath and tented his fingers. "I will give you six."

And he did. He even showed them satellite images of a figure in what looked like a white hat, one of the witnesses, passing a figure that might well have been Roger Kerrington on the path near where Mitt's body was found, and at the approximate time of the murder.

The jury was out less than an hour before returning a guilty verdict.

In exchange for not being charged with perjury, Belinda Kerrington revised her testimony and stated that Kerrington had left the house early the morning of the murder, claiming he had errands to run. He'd confided to her later that he'd driven to the park and jogged as usual until he found the right spot, then slipped into the woods and waited for Mitt. She showed police where stolen diamonds, including the one in Mitt's ring, and a folding knife with a long thin blade were buried in the flower bed in the backyard. She underwent, and passed, a polygraph examination. It was unlikely that Roger Kerrington would have the slightest grounds for appeal.

Hastings paid for dinner that night at Chez René, the best French restaurant in the city. Miles, Catt, and Loman were his guests. The champagne was excellent.

They toasted traffic cameras, time-marked and dated satellite photography, clocks, and justice.

THE RETIRED ARSONIST

BY EDWARD D. HOCH

LEOPOLD'S WIFE MOLLY SOMETIMES SAID THAT HE worked almost as hard since his retirement as he'd done during those long years as captain of the city's violent crimes squad. While not really true, there were often times when a call from his successor, Captain Fletcher, was enough to rouse him from the stupors of advancing age. One such call came while he was eating breakfast on a sunny September morning, contemplating a quiet day in the backyard with a good book.

"I hate to bother you," Fletcher began, "but something's come up."

"Something always comes up," Leopold said with a smile. "What is it this time?"

"I've had a call from Fire Marshal Pedley. He's at the scene of an overnight blaze and he asked if you could come down and look at it."

"Me? I'm no arson investigator. And I'm retired, remember?"

"He especially asked for you. Connie is on her way out there. She can pick you up and you won't even have to drive."

Connie Trent had been a lieutenant on the violent crimes squad ever since Leopold retired and Fletcher replaced him as captain. He'd always liked her, and when she picked him up in her car twenty minutes later somehow it was like old times. She was middle-aged now, but still retained the youthful charm and intelligence he remembered so well.

"What have we got, Connie?" he asked, sliding into the front seat next to her.

"A bad arson, Captain."

"You always forget I'm retired," he said. "Not a captain any longer."

"You'll always be one to me." She went on, "It's messy. The nozzle man, first firefighter into the building, was killed by a flashover. That makes it murder if we ever catch the guy."

"Why does Pedley want me?"

"I don't know. Something he found at the scene."

He remembered an arson case about fifteen years earlier, when he was still captain. A firefighter had been shot inside a burning building, apparently by the discharge of a box of cartridges. Leopold proved it was something else. Now he reminded Connie. "Remember that one?"

"Sure, I was there with you when you cracked the case. But there are no bullets involved here. It was just the fire that killed him."

They pulled up in front of a warehouse on the south side of town, near the docks. The streets were still clogged with fire engines, though the blaze seemed to be out. Even as they left the car one of the engines turned back toward the station, its bell clanging mournfully. A woman firefighter stood outside the building, awaiting their arrival. "Watch the hose," she warned. "I'll take you up to Marshal Pedley." Connie remained outside.

Leopold had known him years ago when he first joined the fire department. A smart young man whose father had been a fire marshal in New York City, Pedley came to the job naturally. Leopold hadn't seen him in years, but he recognized him at once. He was middle-aged now, but he still had the chiseled features and jutting jaw that Leopold remembered. He'd removed his smoke mask but still wore his helmet with the chin strap hanging loose. The fire had been reduced to charred beams hung with smoke, water dripping on them from above. A faint odor of gasoline lingered in the air.

"Sorry to get you down here, Leopold," Pedley said, shaking hands. "You'd better put on this helmet in case things start falling."

"Thanks." He fitted the heavy contraption over his head.

"I know you're retired, but I felt I had to get you in on this. One of our best men died in the fire, Sam Crandel from Engine Twenty-one. He was the first in with his hose and he caught a flashover. It was shortly after one this morning."

"Arson?"

"There's not much doubt." He steered Leopold toward a charred shelf near the door. "This was a little alarm clock rigged to set off a small fire-bomb of some sort, maybe just a firecracker. Ever see anything like it before?"

"Plenty of times. But arsonists today are usually a bit more sophisti-cated."

"How about this?" he asked, shining his powerful flashlight at a copper pipe just above their heads. Leopold made out a bit of string with a tiny piece of red plastic attached, perhaps five feet above the charred remains of a foot-high stool. Pedley reached up and detached it.

"Is it—?"

"A balloon filled with a liquid accelerant, probably gasoline. You can still detect the odor. I believe there were several. Once the original flames burst them they created fireballs that spread quickly throughout the building. It's a terrible hazard to firefighters and probably cost Sam Crandel his life."

"This is what you brought me to see."

Pedley nodded. "I wanted to know if your memory was the same as mine."

Leopold moistened his dry lips, conjuring up a half-forgotten name from deep within his memory. "Parker Oslo, the arsonist. This was his spe-cialty. But that was—what? Almost twenty years ago? He must be still in prison if he's not dead."

"Could we check? I didn't want to suggest it until I was sure, and I remembered you were the one who tracked him down."

"Connie Trent is outside. I'll ask her to check on him."

Connie had a way with computers that Leopold would never equal. Working from her laptop in the car she quickly accessed Parker Oslo's name. "Here he is. He drew a twenty-year sentence in nineteen eighty-nine.

He was released on parole a year ago. Want his address?"

"Is he still in town?"

"Yep. Got an apartment on Schaefer Street."

Leopold grunted. "How old would he be now?"

"Sixty-seven, according to his record. Old enough to be retired."

"Do arsonists ever retire?"

"I doubt it," Connie replied.

Schaefer Street had once been home to some of the city's top executives. A white colonial house that had been the address of the telephone company's president was now a funeral parlor. An adjoining house had been divided into four apartments, with an enclosed outside staircase ruining the perfect symmetry of the structure. It was there that they found Parker Oslo's apartment, at the top of the outside staircase.

Leopold's knock was answered by a young man wearing jeans and a faded rock group T-shirt. "Yeah?"

"We're looking for Parker Oslo," Connie said.

"Not here."

She showed her ID. "Where can we find him?"

"Jeez, is this about his parole?"

"Who are you?" Connie asked.

"I'm his son. Randy Oslo."

"Do you live here with him?" Leopold asked.

"I'm staying here a while, between jobs. I was only a little kid when he went to prison. It's time I got to know him."

"Is your mother in town?"

He shook his head. "California. That's where I lived for sixteen years. She divorced him after his conviction."

"When will he be home so we can talk to him?" Connie asked.

"He works part time at the supermarket down the block. You can probably find him there. He works till the business slacks off, then they send him home."

They found the market without difficulty, one of those customer-friendly places that employed retired men to help carry groceries to your car if needed. "That's Oslo," Leopold said, spotting him near the entrance.

"Are you sure?"

"I'm sure. He's missing the little finger on his left hand."

Again, he allowed Connie to conduct the questioning. She approached the man and asked, "Are you Parker Oslo?"

His years in prison had left him with a pallid complexion that Leopold had seen many times before. For his part-time job he wore a plaid shirt and jeans, with a baseball cap hiding strands of stringy white hair. He seemed older than his sixty-seven years, but Leopold knew prison could do that. "That's me," he admitted in a gruff voice. "Who wants to know?"

"Lieutenant Trent," she said, showing her ID. "Is there somewhere we could talk? We have some questions to ask."

"I heard about the fire on the news. I suppose it's that again. Can't you people ever leave me alone?"

"You're a convicted arsonist," she reminded him.

"I'm retired."

"My experience is that arsonists and pedophiles never retire."

"Firebugs, maybe, but not arsonists."

"There's a difference?"

"Sure. An arsonist does it for money, a firebug is nothing more than a pyromaniac."

"Was there money in burning an empty warehouse?"

"Maybe insurance." Oslo pushed the cap further back on his head. "What time did the fire start?"

"About one o'clock this morning."

"Then I've got an alibi; I was playing poker with some guys from ten o'clock till nearly two."

"The arsonist used a timer," Leopold said, speaking for the first time. "It could have been set well before ten o'clock."

Oslo squinted at him. "Who are you? I remember you from somewhere."

"Retired Captain Leopold. I'm the one who arrested you the last time."

"Yeah. You were younger then."

"Weren't we all?"

"The arsonist used your technique," Connie told him. "Complete with balloons. That's why we're here."

He merely smiled at that. "It's not patented. I won't sue the guy."

"It's no joking matter. A firefighter was killed. We're trying to determine if you were involved."

"I never killed anyone," he insisted. "I got that sentence because it was a third felony conviction."

"I remember a firefighter was badly burned by one of your balloon bombs."

"I didn't do it to kill people."

"Why did you do it, Oslo?" Leopold asked. "You never stayed around to watch your fires so you're not a pyromaniac."

"I did it for cash." He glanced over his shoulder. "I gotta get back to work or I'll lose my job."

Connie wanted to question him further but he was already walking back to the store. "We'll catch him later," she said. "Let's check in at headquarters."

The death of a firefighter had brought out the media in force. Leopold was almost pleased that none of the younger TV journalists recognized him as he followed Connie into the building. They found Captain Fletcher in conference with Marshal Pedley and the dead fireman's widow. Janice Crandel was a short young woman with dark hair and a pretty face now marred by tears. In happier days she was a woman who took care of herself, with perfectly manicured nails peeking out of a Band-Aid on one finger. She sat across from Fletcher but was more intent on what Pedley was telling her.

"I want you to know he died a hero, Mrs. Crandel. I knew Sam to be a brave firefighter, always one to lead his team into the flames. He'll be buried with full departmental honors."

"All the honors and death benefits you have won't bring him back," she told them, shaking her head. "He gave you twenty-four years of his life. You can't know what it was like to be married to him. He was already a fire-fighter when we met. He'd come home after his shift and tell me about it, about the terrible tragedies, the dead children, the arsonists, all of it. All the years he'd spent with the department. I wanted to share it with him. Sometimes I wished I could join the department myself, but Sam would just laugh and say I was too short."

It was Fletcher who asked Pedley, "Do you have any ideas about this?"

The fire marshal frowned. "An empty warehouse usually means insurance, unless we're dealing with a firebug. Do you know who owns that place?"

Fletcher motioned toward Connie. "See what you can find out about that." He turned back to Janice Crandel. "Thank you for coming in. I'll have an officer drive you home."

Leopold walked outside with her. The breeze had blown her tears dry and she looked up at him. "I hope you get the man who killed my husband."

"We'll get him," he promised.

"He'd been home sick with a stomach bug Monday night. I wanted him to stay home last night, but he insisted on going in. If he'd listened to me he'd be alive now."

But someone else would be dead, Leopold said silently.

After she'd gone Fletcher asked Connie what luck they'd had with the arsonist. "We found Parker Oslo quite easily. He's living right where he's supposed to be and his son is with him temporarily. He claims he was playing cards with friends when the fire started this morning, but that means very little when a timer is used."

"Do you think he'd risk going back to prison?"

Connie thought about it. "If someone paid him enough. I don't think he'd do it just for a thrill."

"Find out who owns that warehouse and question him."

"I want to go along too," Leopold requested. "If it's really Oslo behind this, I'd like to be with you when you collar the bastard."

Connie smiled at him. "Be my guest, Captain."

The warehouse was owned by a New York realtor named Mitch Kovak who divided his time between Manhattan and Leopold's city. They were in luck, finding him in his suite at the Rainbow Tower, one of downtown's newest office buildings. Kovak was a big, jovial man not much younger than Leopold, but showing no signs of retirement. He kept them waiting only a few minutes before his secretary ushered them into his office. Its windows offered a panorama of the city and Leopold couldn't help noticing that the ruined warehouse was visible along the waterfront.

"I'm Lieutenant Trent," Connie told him, "and this is Captain Leopold, retired. He's helping us because he knew the man who could be a suspect in torching your warehouse last night."

"Well!" He swiveled his chair to peer out the window. "You know, the corporation owns so many old buildings like that, I didn't even realize it was ours until my secretary told me this morning. You say you have a suspect?"

"A convicted arsonist who used the same torching technique in the past," Leopold explained. "Ever have any dealings with a man named Oslo?"

"Never heard of him."

"I assume the building was insured."

"Of course. We've got insurance on everything. I hope you're not implying I'm a suspect in this."

"No," Connie told him, "but the ex-convict we're investigating only performed arsons for hire. He wouldn't have done it unless he was getting paid."

"It wasn't by me," Kovak insisted. "You'd better get yourself a new suspect."

"What was that warehouse used for?"

"It was empty, far as I know. My secretary tells me at one time we used it for large rolls of newsprint for the local paper, but that was years ago. They were shipped downriver by barge and stored there till the paper needed them."

"Has your company received any recent threats, anything that might hint at a motive for the fire?"

"Nothing. I doubt if many people even knew we owned the building."

Outside, Connie suggested she take Leopold back home. "I'll spend the rest of the afternoon going through the arrest records for other arsonists. No need for you to be saddled with that."

"Is that a lieutenant's job?" he asked.

"It is when a police officer or firefighter is killed. Fletcher wants us to find this guy, whether it's Oslo or someone else."

That evening he recounted his day's activities to Molly over dinner. It was a treat to have something to tell her. Usually their evening conversation was filled with talk of her court cases and impending trials. "Don't overdo it," she cautioned. "You're not a kid anymore. I hate to think of you crawling around in burnt-out buildings."

"I wasn't crawling," he assured her. "Pedley and I just walked through the place."

"Are you finished with it?"

"I might take a ride over to that warehouse tomorrow. Don't worry, I won't go in there alone. I just want to look it over again."

Leopold wasn't sure what he was looking for, and when he pulled up to the warehouse the next morning all he saw was one of those emergency enclosure trucks with two workers boarding up the broken ground floor windows. He got out of his car and walked over to the older man who seemed to be in charge. "Bad fire here yesterday," he said, making conversation.

The man had on jeans and a sweater, though the temperature was still around sixty. He wore a peaked cap with a football logo on it and hammered the plywood sheets over the broken windows like someone who didn't much care for his job. "Yeah," he replied after a moment. "This place has been a nuisance lately."

"Were there other fires?"

"No, just break-ins. Probably kids wanting to smoke pot or make out."

"Was this recently?"

"What's today? Thursday? The fire was yesterday morning. I guess the first break-in was early Monday morning. They have a watchman who drives around every morning and checks on these places. He called us about a broken window, this one near the door. I boarded it up and the next morning he called again. Someone had pulled out my nails and gotten in the same way again, left a spot of blood this time. I told him if it happened again he should call the cops."

"Could you show me the window you're talking about?"

The man frowned at Leopold. "You a cop or something?"

"Leopold. I'm retired but helping in the investigation. And you're . . . ?"

"Rafferty. Come on, I'll show you the window."

Virtually every window in the building had been smashed by the fire itself or the efforts to extinguish it. Rafferty and his assistant had boarded up the ground floor ones, and he showed Leopold one right next to the metal overhead door, apparently used by trucks. The window extended almost to the ground and once the glass was broken entry would have been easy. "No alarm system?" Leopold asked, examining the plywood that had covered it.

"The building's been empty for three years. Nothing to steal."

"So this window was broken Monday morning and someone broke in again Tuesday morning?"

"That's right."

"Did you check around inside?"

"Nope. Not my job."

He returned to what was his job, and Leopold started back to his car. That was when he spotted a young man across the street who looked familiar. He ducked quickly into an alleyway between two warehouses as Leopold came after him. There was no chance he could have caught the youth in any sort of foot race, but he had the advantage of half a lifetime in the city's streets. He knew where the runner had to exit and he circled quickly around the block.

"Hello, Randy," he called out when he spotted him again. "It is Randy, isn't it?"

Randy Oslo trotted to a halt and stood staring at Leopold. "What do you want? I've done nothing."

"I just want to talk. What are you doing over here?"

"I came to see this place where the fire was. You were questioning my dad about it."

"Do you know something about it, Randy?"

"No, why should I?" he answered a bit too quickly.

"Your dad—"

"Am I responsible for the sins of my father?"

"Certainly not. I hope you're not following in his path."

"Don't worry," he said and turned away. Leopold let him go. There was nothing more he could say.

That evening Leopold went to the funeral parlor where the dead firefighter was laid out. He didn't often attend the wakes for murder victims because he was usually busy tracking down the killer. But this one was different. Fletcher and Connie were working on it, and he'd done all that he could.

"Thank you for coming," Janice Crandel said, shaking hands. "I still can't believe he's gone." Several of his fellow firefighters were there in uniform, perhaps thinking that it could have been any of them laid out among the flowers.

"I hope to be at Saturday's funeral too," he told her.

"It's all so fast. A week ago we were talking about an October vacation to Maine. Now he's—"

It was difficult trying to comfort her and Leopold was relieved when she excused herself to greet a friend. He signed the register and was heading for his car when he encountered Marshal Pedley. "Anything new on the arson?" he asked.

"Not really. I was checking the call to nine-one-one reporting the blaze.

These things usually come in by cell phone but this was from a coin telephone at a gas station. The voice seemed muffled or disguised."

"You think it was the arsonist?"

Pedley seemed uncertain. "Or someone who knew about it and didn't want the call traced. There's something else odd. Do you have a few minutes?"

"All the time in the world."

"Let's sit in my car and talk."

Leopold climbed into the SUV and the fire marshal took out his notebook. "The call came in to nine-one-one at one-o-eight a.m. Wednesday morning. Now look at this." He lifted an evidence bag from the back seat and showed Leopold the charred remains of the timing device he'd seen at the fire scene the day before.

Leopold saw what he meant. The clock had stopped as soon as the flames engulfed it, but he could still make out the alarm hand pointed at 1:10. "Interesting," was his only comment.

"What do you think it means?"

"That the clock was fast, and the fire had already started when the someone reported it at one-o-eight."

Pedley nodded. "Or else the arsonist wanted to tip us off early."

Leopold told him what he'd learned about the broken window at the arson site. "If the arsonist broke in and set his bomb to go off early Tuesday morning, why would he return before that and advance the timer?"

"Maybe he didn't," Pedley suggested. "Maybe someone who knew about it tried to keep the bomb from going off."

"Like who?"

"Like Parker Oslo's son?"

It was a possibility Leopold hadn't considered. "But it did go off, not Tuesday morning but early Wednesday morning."

Pedley was silent for a moment, considering another possibility. "Suppose Oslo's son set the bomb, trying to emulate his father. Oslo discovered it and disconnected the timer. That might be more likely."

"We still have the problem that it did go off, that the fire did start and Sam Crandel died. So what was accomplished by delaying the fire by one day?"

"I suppose the two break-ins might be only a coincidence. The window was broken by kids and the arsonist went in that way simply because the board was easier to remove." He opened the car door. "I just wanted your opinion on this, Leopold. I don't know that it's getting us anywhere."

"Wait a minute. You just said it might be more likely that the fire was started by Oslo's son. Why is that?"

"I found the device on a shelf, right where I showed you. Professional arsonists prefer setting their bombs on the floor so the flames can spread upward from the lowest point in the room."

"So that would rule out Parker Oslo?"

Pedley shrugged. "It would seem to. But if his son was copying his method he might not have known of this aspect."

"Let me think about it," Leopold said. "I may want to visit Mitch Kovak again tomorrow."

He phoned Connie in the morning to alert her of his planned visit to Kovak. "That's not interfering with your investigation, is it?"

"No, go ahead. Just make sure he understands you're not part of the official investigation."

Kovak was having a busy day but he finally agreed to see Leopold for a brief period in the afternoon. His greeting came straight to the point. "If it's about that warehouse again, I can tell you the company has decided to demolish it. The fire damage plus the age of the building doesn't make it worth rebuilding."

"But you still get the insurance money."

"Of course. Collecting insurance on fire damage isn't a crime."

"Not unless you started the fire."

Kovak eyed him grimly. "Are you here in an official capacity, Captain?"

"I'm retired, as you know. Lieutenant Trent asked you about a convicted arsonist named Parker Oslo."

"And I said I never heard of him. I still say that. Good day, Mr. Leopold. I'm afraid I must cut our conversation short."

He drove down to Connie's office at headquarters, still trying to sort it out in his mind. He thought she might be able to help after he told her what he'd learned, but she just made things more complicated. "Don't you see?" she asked, trying to be logical. "If Oslo—or his son—set that time bomb in the warehouse on Sunday night, or early Monday morning, and the other one came by to disconnect it, then how did the place catch on fire?"

"Maybe Randy Oslo planted the bomb and told his father about it. Parker realized he'd done something wrong and took him back for a bit of instruction in the fine art of arson. They went in together and left together, with the time bomb reconfigured to the father's wishes."

"Do you believe that?"

"No," he admitted. "Marshal Pedley tells me professional arsonists usually start their blazes at floor level. If Oslo was advising or teaching his son, he'd have moved the time bomb off that shelf."

"So where does that leave us?"

That was when he remembered something about the crime scene. It was a little thing, perhaps meaningless, but he asked if she had the police photographs handy. "Right here." She handed him the folder.

"That's the way I remembered it," he said. "Connie, I want you to listen to a theory I'm developing. Just listen until I'm finished, and then tell me if I'm crazy."

Connie Trent listened.

On Saturday morning they attended Sam Crandel's funeral together, along with the mayor, the fire chief, and other dignitaries. The church was warm and crowded, and more than Crandel's wife were shedding tears. Outside, an honor guard of firefighters paid their respects. It was one of the most moving experiences Leopold remembered. Later, at graveside, a piper played a final tribute to Crandel's memory.

"That's about it," Leopold told Connie.

"Yeah." She gazed across the open grave at the mourners. "Come on."

Leopold hung back, because it was Connie's show. She walked over to where a relative was escorting the black-clad widow back to the car. "Mrs. Crandel," she said.

"Yes?"

"I'm sorry to intrude at this time, but I have to request that you accompany me to headquarters for questioning about the death of your husband."

"What?" Her face froze, and suddenly her eyes darted left and right as if seeking some escape. "No!" she insisted. "No no no!"

She broke away from the relative's comforting grip, but by this time Connie had a firm hand on her. Leopold followed them to Connie's car.

She asked Leopold to sit in while she read Janice Crandel her rights and opened up the questioning. He was asked to repeat what he'd explained to Connie the previous afternoon. He sat off to one side, trying to stay inconspicuous as he spoke. After all, he was retired.

"It wasn't just one big thing," he began as Mrs. Crandel watched him intently. "It was more like three or four little things that came together." He counted them off on his fingers, tapping the index finger of his left hand. "First, there was the fact that someone—undoubtedly the arsonist—smashed a window and entered that empty warehouse on Sunday night or Monday morning. It seemed likely that the firebomb and timer were planted then, but an odd thing happened the following night. Someone broke in again, through the same boarded-up window. I considered several possibilities involving a convicted arsonist and his son, but then fact number two was added to the mix. The fire was reported to 9-1-1 by someone with a muffled voice about two minutes before the timer was set to go off. Sure, the clock being used might have been wrong, but maybe the arsonist wanted the firefighters to arrive before the fire got too much of a headstart."

Janice Crandel tried to say something then, but her broken words turned into a sob. Leopold went on, keeping his voice soft but authoritative, the way he'd done so many times in interrogation sessions over the years. "I thought about this and suddenly it seemed to link up with the two break-ins at the warehouse. I asked myself what else had happened during those two days. And then I remembered. Your husband Sam had stayed home sick, unable to work because of a stomach bug. A terrible thought crossed my mind. Had the arson been postponed because its main motive was to kill Sam Crandel? Was there any possible verification of this? Yes, there was—the phone call that was clocked in possibly two minutes before the firebomb was timed to go off. I remembered Marshal Pedley showing me a bit of rubber from a balloon tied to an overhead pipe. Gasoline-filled balloons were a favorite technique used by Parker Oslo, and the fireball they caused was a deadly threat to firefighters. Your husband, Janice, was a nozzle man, the first into many burning buildings with his hose."

"How could I have known about arsonists and fire balloons?" she asked, pleading for a way out that was not to come.

"Because Sam told you about them. You said yourself that Sam told you everything about his job, about the tragedies, the children, the arsonists. He was with the department twenty years ago when Oslo was operating. He might even have told you the man was on parole now."

"Why me? Maybe someone else wanted to kill him."

Leopold touched another finger. "Third, at the crime scene Marshal Pedley pointed out the remains of one of the burst balloons. He reached up some six feet above the floor and took it down, but I noticed a charred footstool just below it. It appeared the arsonist might have used it to position the balloons, implying it was a short person. You're short, Janice, as you admitted yourself. So we have a short arsonist who could have known about Oslo's technique and also that Sam wouldn't be at work Monday night."

"Why would I go to all that trouble if I wanted to be rid of him?"

"If he was killed in the line of duty, you'd receive the death benefits. They could be substantial."

Her voice had hardened now. She'd decided to deny everything. "Go ahead, do your damnedest! I'll have the news media on my side. I'm the brave widow of a dead firefighter, remember?"

That was when Connie spoke. "You realize we're taping this interview. You were read your rights. Now I'm going to require a DNA or blood sample from you."

Janice Crandel's face froze. "For what?"

"When the arsonist returned to the warehouse Monday night to remove the enclosure over the window and get back inside, there was a drop of blood left on the plywood. I noticed the bandage on your finger and we just want to see if your blood matches it."

As Leopold told Molly later, that was the end of the story.

PATRIOTIC GESTURES

BY KRISTINE KATHRYN RUSCH

PAMELA KINNEY HEARD THE NOISE IN HER SLEEP, giggles, followed by the crunching of leaves. Later, she smelled smoke, faint and acrid, and realized that her neighbors were burning garbage in their fireplace again. She got up long enough to close the window and silently curse them. She hated it when they did illegal burning.

She forgot about it until the next morning. She stepped out her back door into the crisp fall morning and found charred remains of some fabric in the middle of her driveway. There'd been no wind during the night, fortunately, or all the evidence would have been gone.

Instead, there was the pile of burned fabric and a scorch on the pavement. There were even footprints outlined in leaves.

She noted all of that with a professional's detachment—she'd eyeballed more than a thousand crime scenes—before the fabric itself caught her attention. Then the pain was sudden and swift, right above her heart, echoing through the breastbone and down her back.

Anyone else would have thought she was having a heart attack. But she wasn't, and she knew it. She'd had this feeling twice before, first when the officers came to her house and then when the chaplain handed her the folded flag that just a moment before had draped over her daughter's coffin.

Pamela had clung to that flag like she'd seen so many other military mothers do, and she suspected she had looked as lost as they had. Then, when she stood, that pain ran through her, dropping her back to the chair.

Her sons took her arms, and when she mentioned the pain, they dragged her to the emergency room. She had been late for her own daughter's wake, her chest sticky with adhesive from the cardiac machines and her hair smelling faintly of disinfectant.

And the feeling came back now, as she stared at the massacre before her. The flag, Jenny's flag, had been ripped from the front door and burned in her driveway.

Pamela made herself breathe. Then she rubbed that spot above her left breast, felt the pain spread throughout her body, burning her eyes and forming a lump in the back of her throat. But she held the tears back. She wouldn't give whoever had done this awful thing the satisfaction.

Finally she reached inside her purse for her cell, called Neil—she had trouble thinking of him as the sheriff after all the years she'd known him—and then she protected the scene until he arrived.

It only took him five minutes. Halleysburg was still a small town, no matter how many Portlanders sprawled into the community, willing to make the one and a half hour each-way daily commute to the city's edge. Pamela had told the dispatch to make sure that Neil parked across the street so that any wind from his vehicle wouldn't move the leaves.

And she had asked for a second scene-of-the-crime kit because she didn't want to go inside and get hers. She didn't want to risk losing the crime scene with a moment of inattention.

Neil pulled onto the street. His car was an unwieldy Olds with a souped-up engine and a reinforced frame. It could take a lot of punishment, and often did. As a result, the paint covering the car's sides was fresh and clean, while the hood, roof, and trunk looked like they were covered in dirt.

The sheriff was the same. Neil Karlyn was in his late fifties, balding, with a face that had seen too much sun. But his uniform was always new, always pristine, and never wrinkled. He'd been that way since college, a precise man with precise opinions about a difficult world.

He got out of the Olds and did not reach around back for a scene-of-the-crime kit. Annoyance threaded through her.

"Where's my kit?" she asked.

"Pam," he said gently, "it's a low-level property crime. It'll never go to trial and you know it."

"It's arson with malicious intent," she snapped. "That's a felony."

He sighed and studied her for a moment. He clearly recognized her tone. She'd used it often enough on him when they were students at the University of Oregon and when they were lovers on different sides of the political fence, constantly on the verge of splitting up.

When they finally did, it had taken years for them to settle into a friendship. But settle they did. They hardly even fought any more.

He went back to the car, opened the back door and removed the kit she'd requested. She crossed her arms, waiting as he walked toward her. He stopped at the edge of the curb, holding the kit tight against his leg.

"Even if you somehow get the DA to agree that this is a cockamamie felony, you know that processing the scene yourself taints the evidence."

"Why do you care so much?" she asked, hearing an edge in her voice that usually wasn't there. The challenge, unspoken: *It's my daughter's flag. It's like murdering her all over again.*

To his credit, Neil didn't try to soothe her with a platitude.

"It's the eighth flag this morning," he said. "It's not personal, Pam."

Her chin jutted out. "It is to me."

Neil looked down, his cheek moving. He was clenching his jaw, trying not to speak.

He didn't have to.

Somewhere in her pile of college paraphernalia was a badly framed newspaper clipping that had once been the front page of the Portland *Oregonian*. She'd framed the clipping so that a photo dominated, a photo of a much-younger Pamela with long hair and a tie-dye T-shirt, front and center in a group of students, holding an American flag by a stick, watching as it burned.

God, she could still remember how that felt, to hold a flag up so that the wind caught it. How fabric had its own acrid odor, and how frightened she'd been at the desecration, even though she'd been the one to set the flag on fire.

She had been protesting the Vietnam War. It was that photo and the resulting brouhaha it caused, both on campus and in the State of Oregon itself, that had led to the final breakup with Neil.

He couldn't believe what she had done. Sometimes she couldn't either. But she felt her country was worth fighting for. So had he. He joined up not too many months later.

To his credit, Neil didn't say anything about her own flag burning as he handed her the kit. Instead he watched as she took photographs of the scene, scooped up the charred bits of fabric, and made a sketch of the footprint she found in the leaves.

She found another print in the yard, and that one she made a cast of. Then she dusted her front door for prints, trying not to cry as she did so.

"A flag is a flag is a flag," she used to say.

Until it draped over her daughter's coffin.

Until it became all she had left.

"I called the local VFW, Mom," her son Stephen said over dinner that night. Stephen was her oldest and had been her support for thirty years, since the day his father walked out, never to return. "They're bringing another flag."

She stirred the mashed potatoes into the creamed corn on her plate. The meal had come from KFC. Her sons had brought a bucket with her favorite sides and told her not to argue with them about the fast food meal. She wasn't arguing, but she didn't have much of an appetite.

They sat in the dining room, at the table that had once held four of them. Pamela had slid the fake rose centerpiece in front of Jenny's place, so she wouldn't have to think about her daughter.

It wasn't working.

"Another flag isn't the same, dumbass," Travis said. At thirty, he was the youngest, unmarried, still finding himself, a phrase she had come to hate.

The hell of it was, Travis was right. It wasn't the same. That flag those people had burned, that flag had comforted her. She had clung to it on the worst afternoon of her life, her fingers holding it tight, even at the emergency room when the doctors wanted to pry it from her hands.

It had taken almost a week for her to let it go. Stephen had come over,

Stephen and his pretty wife Elaine and their teenage daughters, Mandy and Liv. They'd brought KFC then, too, and talked about everything but the war.

Until it came time to take the flag away from Pamela.

Stephen had talked to her like she was a five-year-old who wanted to take her blankie to kindergarten. In the end, she'd handed the flag over. He'd been the one to find the old flagpole, the one she'd taken down when she bought the house, and he'd been the one to place the pole in the hanger outside the front door.

"The VFW says they replace flags all the time," Stephen said to his brother.

"Because some idiot burned one?" Travis asked.

Pamela's cheeks flushed.

"Because people lose them. Or moths eat them. Or sometimes, they get stolen," Stephen said.

"But not burned," Travis persisted.

Pamela swallowed. Travis didn't remember the newspaper photo, but Stephen probably did. It had hung over the console stereo she had gotten when her mother died, and it had been a teacher—Neil's first grade teacher? Pamela couldn't remember—who had seen it at a party and asked if she really wanted her children to see that before they could understand what it meant.

"I don't want another one," Pamela said.

"Mom," Stephen said in his most reasonable voice.

She shook her head. "It's been a year. I need to move on."

"You don't move on from that kind of loss," Travis said, and she wondered how he knew. He didn't have children.

Then she looked at him, a large broad-shouldered man with tears in his eyes, and remembered that Jenny had been the one who walked him to school, who bathed him at night, who usually tucked him in. Jenny had done all that because Stephen at thirteen was already working to help his mom make ends meet, and Pamela was working two jobs herself, as well as attending community college to get her degree in forensic science and criminology. A pseudoscience degree, one of her almost-boyfriends had said. But it wasn't. She used science every day. She needed science like she needed air.

Like she needed to find out who had destroyed her daughter's flag.

"You don't move on," Pamela said.

Her boys watched her. Sometimes she could see the babies they had been in the lines of their mouths and the shape of their eyes. She still marveled at the way they had grown into men, large men who could carry her the way she used to carry them.

"But," she added, "you don't have to dwell on it, every moment of every day."

And yet she was dwelling. She couldn't stop. She never told her sons or anyone else, not even Neil, who had become a closer friend in the year since Jenny had died. Neil, a widower now, a man who understood death the way that Pamela did. Neil, whose grandson had enlisted after 9/11 and had somehow made it back.

She was dwelling and there was only one way to stop. She had to use science to solve this. She couldn't think about it emotionally. She had to think about it clinically.

She had her evidence and she needed even more.

The next morning, the local paper ran an article on the burnings, and listed the addresses in the police log section. So Pamela visited the other crime scenes with her kit and her camera, identifying herself as an employee of the state crime lab.

Since *CSI* debuted on television, that identification opened doors for her. She didn't have to tell the other victims that she had been a victim too.

She took pictures of scorch marks on pavement and flag holders wrenched loose from their sockets. She removed flag bits from garbage cans, and studied footprints in the leaf-covered grass to see if they looked similar to the ones on her lawn.

And late that afternoon, as she stepped back to photograph yet another twisted flag holder beside a front door, she saw the glint of a camera hiding in a cobwebby corner of the door frame. The house was a starter, maybe twelve hundred square feet total. She wouldn't have expected a camera here.

"Do you have a security system?" she asked the homeowner, a woman Travis's age who looked like she hadn't slept in weeks. Her name was Becky something. Pamela hadn't really heard her last name in the introduction.

"My husband put it up," Becky said, her voice shaking a little. "I have no idea how it works."

"When will he be back?" Pamela asked.

Becky shrugged. "When they cancel stop-loss, I guess."

Pamela felt her breath slide out of her body. "He's in Iraq?"

Becky nodded. "I put the flag up for him, you know? And I haven't told him what happened to it. I've gotta find someone to fix the holder, and I have to get another flag."

Pamela looked at the house more closely. It needed paint. The bushes in front were overgrown. There were cobwebs all over the windows, and dry rot on the sills. Obviously the couple had purchased it expecting someone to work on it. Either the money wasn't there, or the husband had planned to do the work himself.

"I can fix the holder," Pamela said. "If you have a few tools."

"My husband does," Becky said.

"I have a few things to finish, and then you can show me," Pamela said.

She dusted for prints, and then, for comparison, took Becky's and some off the husband's comb, which hadn't been touched since he left. Then Pamela went into his workroom, which also hadn't been touched, and took a hammer, some screws, and a screwdriver.

It took only ten minutes to repair the flag holder. But in that time, she'd made a friend.

"How'd you learn how to do that?" Becky asked.

"Raised three kids alone," Pamela said. "You realize there's not much you can't do if you just try."

Becky nodded.

Pamela glanced at the camera. Untended since the husband left. It was probably in the same state of disrepair as the rest of the house.

"Can I see the security system?" she asked.

"It's not really a system," Becky said. "Just the cameras, and some motion sensors that're supposed to alert us when someone's on the property. But they clearly don't work anymore."

"Let me see anyway," Pamela said.

Becky took her past the workroom, into a small closet filled with electronics. The closet was warm from the heat the panels gave off. Lights still blinked.

Pamela stared at it all, then touched the rewind button on the digital recorder. On the television monitor, she watched an image of herself fixing the flag holder.

"It looks like the camera's still working," she said. "Mind if I rewind farther?"

"Go ahead."

Backwards, she watched darkness turn to day. Saw Neil inspect the hanger. Saw Becky crying, then the tears evaporate into a stare of disbelief before she backed off the porch and away from the scene.

Back to the previous night. No porch light. Just images blurred in the darkness. Faces, not quite real, mostly turned away from the camera.

"Got a recordable DVD?" Pamela asked.

"Somewhere." Becky vanished into the house. Pamela studied the system, hoping that she wouldn't erase the information as she tried to record it.

She rewound again. Studied the faces, the half-turned heads. She saw crew cuts and piercings and hoodies. Slouchy clothes worn by half the young people in Halleysburg.

Nothing to identify them. Nothing to separate them from everyone else in their age group.

Like her, her hair long, her jeans torn, as she stood front and center at the U of O, a burning flag before her.

She made herself study the machine, and figured out how to save the images to the disk's hard drive so that they wouldn't be erased. Then she inspected the buttons near the machine's DVD slot.

"Here," Becky said, thrusting a packet at her.

DVD-Rs, unopened, dust-covered. Pamela used a fingernail to break the seal, then pulled one out and inserted it in the slot. She managed to record, but had no way to test. So she made a few more copies, feeling somewhat reassured that she could come back and try to download the images from the hard drive again.

"Will this catch them?" Becky asked while she watched the process.

"I don't know," Pamela said. "I hope so."

"It's just, they got so close, you know." Becky's voice shook. "I didn't know anyone could get that close."

It took Pamela a moment to understand what she meant. Becky meant that they had gotten close to the house. Close to her. The burning hadn't just upset her, it had frightened her, and made her feel vulnerable.

Odd. All it had done to Pamela was make her angry.

"Just lock up at night," Pamela said after a minute. "Locks deter ninety percent of all thieves."

"And the remaining ten percent?"

They get in, Pamela almost said, but thought the better of it. "They don't usually come to places like Halleysburg," she said. "Why would they? We all know each other here."

Becky nodded, seemingly reassured. Or maybe she just wanted to abandon an uncomfortable topic.

Pamela certainly did. She wanted to play with the images, see what she could find.

She wanted a solid image of the culprits, one that she could bring to Neil.

Maybe then he would stop complaining that this was a petty property crime. Maybe then he might understand how important this really was.

But it was her own words that replayed in her head later that night as she sat in front of her computer.

They don't usually come to places like Halleysburg. We all know each other here.

She had lied to make Becky feel better, but the words hadn't felt like a lie. Thieves really didn't come here. There was no need. There were richer pickings in Portland or Salem or the nearby bedroom communities.

Besides, it was hard to commit a crime here without someone seeing you. Except under cover of darkness.

Her home office was quiet. It overlooked the backyard, and she had never installed curtains on the window, preferring the view of the year-round flower garden she had planted. At the moment, her garden was full of browns and oranges, fall plants blooming despite the winter ahead. She had little lights beneath the plants, lights she usually kept off because they spiked her energy bill.

But she had them on now. She would probably have them on for some time to come.

Maybe Becky wasn't the only one who felt vulnerable.

Pamela put one of the DVDs in her computer, and opened the images. They played, much to her relief, so she copied the images to her hard drive and removed the DVD.

Her computer at home wasn't as good as her computer at work. But it would have to do.

She didn't want to do any work on this case at the state crime lab if she could help it. The lab was so understaffed and so overworked that it usually took four months to get something tested. When she last checked, more than six hundred cases were backlogged, some of them dating back more than nine months. Those cases were bigger than hers. The backlogs were semen samples from possible rapists and blood droplets from the scene of a multiple murder case.

She couldn't, in good conscience, bring something personal and private to the lab. She would work here as long as she could. Then if she couldn't finish here, she might be able to convince herself that the time she took at the lab would go toward an arson case—a serious one, not a petty property crime, as Neil had called it.

Petty property crime.

Funny that they would be on opposite sides of this issue too.

Pamela went through the images frame by frame, looking for clear faces. Her computer didn't have the face recognition software that one of the computers at the lab had, but she had installed a home version of image sharpening software. She used it to clean out the fuzz and to lighten the darkness, trying to find more than a chin or the corner of an ear.

Finally she got a small face just behind the flag, a serious white face with a frown—of disapproval? She couldn't tell—and a bit of an elongated chin. Enough to see the wisp of a beard, a boy's beard, more a wish of a beard than the real thing, and a tattooed hand coming up to catch the flag as the person almost blocking the camera yanked the pole out of the holder.

She blew up the image, softened it, fixed it, and then felt tears prick her eyes.

They don't usually come to places like Halleysburg.

No. They grew up here. And worked at the grocery store down the street to pay for their football uniforms at the underfunded high school. They collected coins in a can on Sunday afternoons for Boosters, and they smiled when they saw her and respectfully called her Mrs. Kinney and asked, with a little too much interest, how her granddaughters were doing.

"Jeremy Stallings," she whispered. "What the hell were you thinking?"

And she hoped she knew.

Neil wouldn't let her sit in while he questioned Jeremy Stallings. He was appalled she'd even asked. "That sort of thing belongs on TV and you know it."

But she also knew he probably wouldn't do much more than slap the boy on the wrist, so what would be the harm? She hadn't made that argument, though.

Instead, she waited on the bench chair outside the sheriff's office conference room, which doubled as an interview room on days like this, and watched the parade of parents and lawyers as they trooped past.

No one acknowledged her. No one so much as looked at her. Not Reg

Stallings, whose brother had sold her the house, or his wife June, who had taken over the PTA just before Travis got out of high school. No one mentioned the friendly exchanges at the high school football games or the hellos at the diner behind the movie theater. It was easier to forget all that and pretend they weren't neighbors than it was to acknowledge what was going on inside that room.

Then, finally, Jeremy came out. He was wearing his baggy pants with a Halo T-shirt hanging nearly to his knees. He wore that same frown he'd had as he took the flag off from Becky's front door.

He glanced at Pamela, then looked away, a blush working its way up the spider tattoo on his neck into his crew cut.

His parents and the lawyers led him away, as Neil reminded all of them to be in court the following morning.

Neil waited until they went through the front doors before coming over to Pamela.

She stood, her knees creaky from sitting so long. "He confess?"

Neil nodded. "And gave me the names of his buddies."

Pamela bit her lower lip. "Funny," she said, "he didn't strike me as the type to be a war protestor."

Neil rubbed his hands on his pristine shirt. "Is that what you thought?"

"Of course," Pamela said. "Every house he hit, we're all military families."

"Who happened to be flying flags, even at night." There was a bit of judgment in Neil's voice.

She knew what he was thinking. People who knew how to handle flags took them down at dusk. But she couldn't bear to touch hers. She hadn't asked Becky why hers remained up, but she would wager the reason was similar.

And it probably was for every other family Jeremy and his friends had targeted.

"That's the important factor?" she asked. "Night?"

"And beer," Neil said. "They lost a football game, went out and drank, and that fueled their anger. So they decided to act out."

"By burning flags?" Her voice rose.

"A few weeks before, they knocked down mailboxes. I'm going to hate to charge them. There won't be much left of the football team."

"That's all right," Pamela said bitterly. "Petty property crimes shouldn't take them off the roster long."

"It's going to be more than that," Neil said. "They're showing a destructive pattern. This one isn't going to be fun."

"For any of us," Pamela said.

Her hands were shaking as she left. She had wanted the crime to mean something. The flag had meant something to her. It should have meant something to them too.

God, Mom, for an old hippie, you're such a prude. Jenny's voice, so close that Pamela actually looked around, expecting to see her daughter's face.

"I'm not a prude," she whispered, and then realized she was reliving an old argument between them.

Sure you are. Judgmental and dried up. I thought you protested so that people could do what they wanted.

Pamela sat in the car, her creaky knees no longer holding her.

No, I protested so that people wouldn't have to die in another senseless war, she had said to her daughter on that May afternoon.

What year was that?

It had to be 1990, just before Jenny graduated from high school.

I'm not going to die in a stupid war, Jenny had said with such conviction that Pamela almost believed her. *We don't do wars any more. I'm going to get an education. That way, you don't have to struggle to pay for Travis. I know how hard it's been with Steve.*

Jenny, taking care of things. Jenny, who wasn't going to let her cash-strapped mother pay for her education. Jenny, being so sure of herself, so sure that the peace she'd known most of her life would continue.

To Jenny, going into the military to get a free education hadn't been a gamble at all.

Things'll change, honey, Pamela had said. *They always do.*

And by then I'll be out. I'll be educated, and moving on with my life.

Only Jenny hadn't moved on. She'd liked the military. After the First Gulf War, she'd gone to officer training, one of the first women to do it.

I'm a feminist, Mom, just like you, she'd said when she told Pamela.

Pamela had smiled, keeping her response to herself. She hadn't been that kind of feminist. She wouldn't have stayed in the military. She wasn't sure she believed in the military—not then.

And now? She wasn't sure what she believed. All she knew was that she had become a military mother, one who cried when a flag was burned.

Not just a flag.

Jenny's flag.

And that's when Pamela knew.

She wanted the crime to mean something, so she would make sure that it did.

She brought her memories to court. Not just the scrapbooks she'd kept for Jenny, like she had for all three kids, but the pictures from her own past, including the badly framed front page of the *Oregonian*.

Five burly boys had destroyed Jenny's flag. They stood in a row, their lawyers beside them, and pled to misdemeanors. Their parents sat on the blond bench seats in the 1970s courtroom. A reporter from the local paper took notes in the back. The judge listened to the pleadings.

Otherwise, the room was empty. No one cheered when the judge gave the boys six months of counseling. No one complained at the nine months of community service, and even though a few of them winced when the judge announced the huge fines that they (and not their parents) had to pay, no one said a word.

Until Pamela asked if she could speak.

The judge—primed by Neil—let her.

Only she really didn't speak. She showed them Jenny. From the baby pictures to the dress uniform. From the brave eleven-year-old walking her brother to school to the dust-covered woman who had smiled with some

Iraqi children in Baghdad.

Then Pamela showed them her *Oregonian* cover.

"I thought you were protesting," she said to the boys. "I thought you were trying to let someone know that you don't approve of what your country is doing."

Her voice was shaking.

"I thought you were being patriotic." She shook her head. "And instead you were just being stupid."

To their credit, they watched her. They listened. She couldn't tell if they understood. If they knew how her heart ached—not that sharp pain she'd felt when she found the flag, but just an ache for everything she'd lost.

Including the idealism of the girl in the picture. And the idealism of the girl she'd raised.

When she finished, she sat down. And she didn't move as the judge gaveled the session closed. She didn't look up as some of the boys tried to apologize. And she didn't watch as their parents hustled them out of court.

Finally, Neil sat beside her. He picked up the framed *Oregonian* photograph in his big, scarred hands.

"Do you regret it?" he asked.

She touched the edge of the frame.

"No," she said.

"Because it was a protest?"

She shook her head. She couldn't articulate it. The anger, the rage, the fear she had felt then. Which had been nothing like the fear she had felt every day her daughter had been overseas.

The fear she felt now when she looked at Stephen's daughters and wondered what they'd choose in this never-ending war.

"If I hadn't burned that flag," she said, "I wouldn't have had Jenny."

Because she might have married Neil. And even if they had made babies, none of those babies would have been Jenny or Stephen or Travis. There would have been other babies who would have grown into other people.

Neil wasn't insulted. They had known each other too long for insults.

Instead, he put his hand over hers. It felt warm and good and familiar. She put her head on his shoulder.

And they sat like that, until the court reconvened an hour later, for another crime, another upset family, and another broken heart.

ARTICULATION OF MURDER

BY MICHAEL A. BLACK

I WATCHED THE NEWSCAST OF THE WILDFIRES winding down the mountain as I held the model in my hand. My fingers probed the impressions of the bite marks that I was sure were Fernando Montoya's. He now had a minimal overbite, the fortunate byproduct of porcelain veneers, which I was certain hid the peg laterals that I knew would convict him. Or at least I hoped they would. The search warrant for the original plaster impression of his bite had yet to be issued.

My lab assistant, Rachel Pruit, sidled up next to me and squinted at the television.

"That where you're going, Doctor?"

Her unruly crop of red hair and freckled face made her look like a life-size Raggedy Ann doll. I'd hired her to do small jobs around the office, like pouring models and setting up articulations.

"Friction, Arizona," I said. "Second hottest place in the United States."

"Second hottest? What's the first?"

"Bullhead City. It's a couple miles south." I articulated the maxillary and mandibular models using the bite registration material.

"Want me to mount that for you?"

I shook my head. It would create too many openings on cross-examination for Montoya's attorney to impugn my investigative techniques. I'd learned that the hard way many trials ago, and this was one trial I didn't intend on losing. The victim, Sandra Tilly, had been a beautiful nineteen-year-old coed when she'd begun her walk from the college library a year ago. Now she was a statistic, a bright smiling face in a photograph on her parents' mantel. A beacon of lost hopes and dreams of a shattered family. The killer had left his bite marks on her shoulder and breasts at some point during the brutal rape and murder, and although there was a mountain of inconclusive trace evidence, his distinctive bite pattern would let the truth shine through. Even the most skillful defense attorney wouldn't be able to ease that indelible image from the jurors' minds. All I had to do was find conclusive proof that it matched up to Montoya's.

I set the yellow die stone models between the metal tongues of the articulator and began mixing some plaster. I'd have to mount the maxillary model first, and then, once it had dried, mount the mandibular.

"You sure you don't want me to do that for you, doc?"

"Very sure," I said. Just then my hygienist, Roland Vanderberg, walked in and gave me an equally perplexed look.

"Doctor Link," he said, still staring at the rubber bowl in my hand, "there's a phone call for you."

I'd just gotten the plaster mixed with the right amount of water so that I could slap it on the die stone-model and then affix it to the articulator. It wasn't a good place to stop.

"Just take a message," I said, realizing that I'd let my receptionist go home a tad too early today. "I'm in the middle of something."

Vanderberg gave me one of his customary looks of smug superiority. As hygienists went, he was capable and talented, and he was applying to U of I Medical Center, my alma mater, for dental school. He was handsome and charming to the patients, but I had taken a dislike to him. Usually, when someone enters the field of dentistry, they are imbued with an urge to help people. Or at least, in my opinion, they should be. Vanderberg seemed motivated more by venality than altruism. His first words to me, after I'd hired him, was a disparaging remark about the Buick I drove. He'd asked why I didn't drive a Porsche. When he found out I did forensic dentistry for the police, he seemed dumbfounded, asking if it was lucrative. He had a lot to learn.

"It's some guy who says he needs an emergency appointment," Vanderberg continued. "Says you were recommended to him."

I tried to control my frown as I used the spatula to scoop enough of the soupy plaster on the yellow model.

"I'm going out of town tomorrow, remember?" I said. "Dr. Major is taking all my calls for the next few days."

"Okay, doctor," he said, his tone not masking his disapproval.

I set the metal tong in place, then slathered on the plaster. It would take a few minutes to harden, and then be ready to trim down. When I was finished, I wanted to place it in a special locked cabinet that I used for my forensic investigations. Then I'd be ready to go home and pack for my early-morning trek to the airport. This was one trip I wasn't looking forward to, even though weddings are supposed to be joyous affairs.

"Excuse me, Doctor." It was Vanderberg again. "You got a second phone call."

I'd just finished trimming the excess plaster off the model. "Another patient with an emergency?"

"No, it's that cop. He says it's urgent."

I grinned, despite myself. "He always says it's urgent. Send it into my office." The call wouldn't take more than five minutes, which would give enough time for the plaster to set before doing the mandibular. Eventually, I'd need the original model, without the veneers, to demonstrate the articulation of the peg laterals over a life-size photograph of the wound site to the jury, but we had to obtain a search warrant before I could get it from his dentist. It was either that or I'd have to drill off Montoya's new veneers and get the impression, which wouldn't be as exact a match as the original plaster model. That was probably what Detective Keldon wanted to talk to me about.

I sat behind my desk and answered with my most professional sounding, "Dr. Link."

"Yeah, Jim, it's Keldon. Just calling to check if we're on for Monday's performance."

Keldon had asked me to accompany him before the judge to describe exactly what was needed for our search warrant regarding the importance of getting the original model of Montoya's bite. Once we had that, I could do a dog-and-pony show for a grand jury and he'd be indicted quicker than the blink of an eye. We figured the grand jury would allow Keldon to swoop in and arrest Montoya before he could sneak away to Mexico.

"Shouldn't be a problem," I said. "I'm catching my flight to Arizona early tomorrow, got the rehearsal Friday night, the wedding Saturday, and the return trip Sunday. I'll be back in plenty of time."

"Okay," he said. I detected something in his voice. Apprehension, maybe? "Doc, you're sure about those things, aren't you?"

The question didn't surprise me. Keldon had called me in as an accredited forensic dentist after the bite marks were discovered during the autopsy. I'd gone to the morgue and examined the body, something I don't like to do unless I have to. She'd been stripped and dumped in a pond, which destroyed or tainted any DNA residuals in the bite marks, but the distinctive patterns gave me hope. When Keldon pulled Montoya in for questioning, because he'd sought "a dating relationship with the victim" and had been rebuffed, I sat in on the interview due to the bite marks. Montoya sat across from us, a perpetual smirk on his face, as his lawyer monitored our questions and translated his responses from Spanish. We both knew Montoya spoke English, but it was obvious he was enjoying the game. He figured he'd covered all the bases. It was when he got up to leave that his smile betrayed him. An almost perfect alignment of dentition, which I knew immediately had to be attributed to porcelain veneers. Later, Keldon and I sifted through the collection of Montoya's previous arrest photos and found one where he'd been grimacing at the camera in defiance. I used a magnifier to examine the exposed array of teeth and confirmed what I already knew: he had a pair of peg laterals hidden beneath the new veneers.

"Peg whats?" Keldon had asked.

"Peg laterals," I said, pointing the picture. "Underdeveloped incisors on the maxillary."

Keldon had looked at me like I was speaking Klingon. I imagined his expression wasn't too much different on the other end of the phone today.

"I won't know for sure until I can get the original plaster impression of his bite from the dentist who did them," I said, pausing to look at the careful re-creation of maxillary and mandibular impressions the purple Impregum displayed of the bite pattern I'd taken from the wounds on Sandra Tilly's body. "But I'm as sure as I can be at the moment." I heard him sigh. "I'm afraid you'll just have to trust my gut instinct on this right now."

"It's not that, Jim. I'm just a bit concerned, is all."

"Why's that?"

"Montoya's got a new shyster representing him. Donnie Plutarch. I wouldn't put nothing past him. He's the best that all that drug money can buy."

"Once we get those X-rays and the impression, it won't matter if he knocks his client's teeth out."

I heard Keldon's low chuckle. "He'll have to stand in line if he wants to do that, with me at the head. Still, if he gets wind of our plans, he'll have a motion to suppress before we can say brush your teeth."

"I'll be coming back Sunday afternoon. I'll meet you at the courthouse early Monday morning."

"Great. Have a nice trip. See you then."

The plane banked steeply after the initial takeoff, and I watched the white clouds against the blue sky outside my window, while the other side showed a square frame of rapidly diminishing buildings and fields. The pilot straightened the big jet and we continued to climb, angling west as we sought our cruising altitude. We passed through the cloud layer and I leaned back in my seat, trying to relax. Trying to put all the thoughts of the Montoya case behind me. I'd left my family at home on this trip, my wife Donna electing to stay and help set our daughter up in her new dorm room at college. I figured it would be a good mother-daughter bonding experience, and I would only be in the way. But thoughts of Debbie away at college brought the unpleasant memory of Sandra Tilly, and how her college experience had netted death instead of a degree. His stubby lateral incisors sinking into her flesh from the tearing, mandibular closure. All the more reason to put an animal like Montoya behind bars for good.

I caught a glimpse of the woman next to me staring at my clenched fingers around the armrests.

"Nervous flyer?" she asked.

I smiled. "Just thinking about some dental work."

"Ooooh, dentists. They're the worst." She lowered her tray and set up a laptop. I grinned to myself at her pronouncement, and began to think about the dentist I was going to see.

Edward Turnbaum and I had gone through dental school together. He'd been a perpetual clown when I'd first met him, not seeming serious about anything. How he made it through the rigors of U of I Dental, I wasn't sure. But upon graduation, his practice took off like a rocket. Putting his gregariousness to work, he quickly began amassing patients at an astounding rate, until he'd reached the point of total saturation. He'd even contacted me about joining him so he could keep up. We'd met again, after ten years, at a party commemorating the anniversary of some mutual friends. Turnbaum, or Dr. Eddie as he liked to be called, came up to me like we were long-lost buddies, pumping my hand and slapping me on the shoulder. I watched from across the room at the reception as he began to work the crowd, going up to each person and introducing himself. Sometime between dinner and the drinks that followed, I saw him leaning over a supine figure on a reclining chair, probing the oral cavities of the dinner guest with his mouth mirror and a small flashlight.

"You've definitely got an abscess there," Dr. Eddie was saying. "Easily fixed with a few visits." He removed a probe from his pocket. "In fact, I think I see some incipient gingivitis here, too." He paused long enough to grab a drink from a passing waiter, swirl the probe in the amber liquid, and resume his diagnosis. "Why don't I just do a bit of preliminary work right away, say, Monday morning? Give me your number and I'll have my receptionist set up an appointment."

Amazed at his audacity, I quickly slipped to the other side of the room as the reluctant "patient" made a series of "goos" and "un-huhs" while the probing fingers held his jaw open.

It surprised me when, out of the blue, Dr. Eddie called me and asked me to be his best man at wedding number three. I knew he'd gone through two wives, the last one being a very comely assistant, whom he now described as "the ex from hell."

"I moved out West," he'd said over the phone. "Friction, Arizona. It's great out here. You'll love it."

More out of curiosity than residual friendship, I agreed to make the trip. I wanted to see how the gregarious Dr. Eddie was faring in the land west of the Pecos. Plus, I'd gone to Arizona State as an undergrad, so it would be a good excuse to revisit some old haunts.

We touched down at Phoenix about two and a half hours later, and I reset my watch, marveling that the trip had only taken about thirty minutes out of my day. The pilot had said that it was a balmy hundred and ten degrees, and I could feel the oppressive desert heat seeping up through the floor of the portable gate. Since I just had carry-on luggage, I was able to skip the baggage claim and go right to the car rental place. Eddie had volunteered to pick me up, but I'd declined, not wanting to be dependent on the perennial groom for my transportation. Besides, I hoped to find the time to see some of Arizona again. The desert can be stark and cruel, but it had its own beauty. I got to the car rental line at almost the same time as a swarthy-looking guy who looked strangely familiar. A moment later it came to me. After we'd all boarded, I'd seen a couple of people who must have been flying standby amble down the center aisle. This guy had been one of them. He'd stood out to me because of his immense, prognathic jaw. He eyed the line as he stepped in front of me, causing me to almost stumble. Our eyes locked for a moment and he looked away again, mumbling an apology, but still crowding in front of me. This was a guy in a hurry.

I, on the other hand, had nothing but time. Or so I thought.

"Hey, hey, hey, how's the second best dentist who ever graduated from U of I?"

I knew who it was before I looked.

Eddie Turnbaum was ambling my way, his right arm locked around the waist of a very pretty young girl. She could have been his daughter, but from the placement of his hand low on her ass, I knew she wasn't. He'd let his hair grow a bit longer than the last time I'd seen him, and it was combed straight in such thick, pompadour fashion that I knew immediately that it wasn't all his. He had jowls, and the over-sized T-shirt he wore, with "Party Animal" on the front, couldn't hide the pearlike shape that jiggled under it.

I switched my carryon to my left hand and extended my right, but Eddie wasn't having any of that. He released the girl, moved forward, and gave me a big hug. I've always found the modern custom of men hugging a bit disconcerting, but this was like being grabbed by a bear. I was suddenly afraid he was going to plant a sloppy kiss on my cheek next. But luckily, he didn't.

"What are you doing?" he asked. "I told you we'd pick you up."

I smiled and went into my standard spiel about not wanting to put him out.

"Awww, hell, Jim. I got plenty of cars." He flashed a dazzling grin that told me he'd whitened his teeth, and turned to hold his hand out toward the babe next to him. "And this is Alicia."

He beamed as she and I shook hands. Her grip was strong, her teeth also dazzling white, and up close she looked even younger than she had from twenty feet away.

After a seesaw debate that I thought was going to develop into a wrestling match, I finally broke away from the happy couple and went to the counter to get my car. Resigned, Eddie followed me there and leaned both of his big forearms on the flat surface. The young girl waiting on me made the mistake of smiling, and that was all the opening the Party Animal needed.

"Say, you've got a pretty nice smile there, young lady," he said, flashing his own pearly whites. "Except for that slightly off-key central."

Her face scrunched up slightly as she tried to ignore him.

"Don't listen to him," I said. "Ali McGraw had a smile just like yours, and she did fine."

"Who's Ali McGraw?' the girl asked, looking even more confused.

"Jim, please," Eddie said, laying a hammy hand on my shoulder. "All I'm saying is, I could straighten that tooth with minimal intrusion. I could fix you up with a transparent orthodontic appliance that would do the job and no one would even notice you were wearing it." He grinned again. "I mean, how would you like to have a smile like this?" He snapped his fingers and Alicia moved up next to him, pressed her nubile body against his. After canting her head to exactly the right pose, she smiled. "A little touch-up here, and some whitening, and I'll have you looking like Shania Twain. It'd go good with your dark hair."

The girl kept watching him as we concluded the rental transaction. As she gave me the keys and the directions to find the car, Eddie snapped a business card on the counter.

"Call my receptionist for an appointment," he said. "I'm over in Friction."

I felt a sense of relief as I got into my rental car and exited the parking garage, trying to memorize the way so I'd have a smooth return trip Sunday morning. When I pulled out onto the access road, I heard a horn blaring and, sure enough, there was Eddie, party animal extraordinaire, honking at me with his flashy red Lexus. With his trophy fiancée in the front seat, I could only imagine how cramped I would have been in the back with my suitcase. I followed him to Friction, which proved to be a short, twenty-minute ride. In the background I could see the mountains, their tops covered with the black soot from the recent fires. I silently wondered if it wasn't some sort of omen for the coming festivities.

Luigi, the tailor, was pinning the cuffs of the tuxedo pants when Eddie asked him how his bridge was working out. Luckily, I'd called him with my measurements, so I didn't anticipate this eleventh-hour fitting would be too radical.

"The bridge is good, Doctor," Luigi said, smiling to show off the handiwork: a row of perfect central and lateral incisors. He bent to one knee and tugged on the pants. "If I hem them here, they'll hang like this."

I glanced down as Eddie moved in closer.

"That's perfect," he said, then turned to Luigi. "Open up. Lemme see."

Luigi obediently stretched his jaws apart as Eddie took a small penlight and shone it into the tailor's oral cavity. He grunted a few times, then pulled at Luigi's right cheek. "Pull your lip back." Again, the tailor did what he was told. Eddie grunted a few more times, then nodded. "Okay, I'm noticing a bit of excessive wear on the second molar. I'm going to have to make a minor adjustment on that one."

Luigi, still pulling his cheek away from his teeth, nodded. His eyes looked solemn. Eddie pulled out a palm pilot and pressed a couple of keys. "How about tomorrow, ten-thirty?" he asked.

"Okay, Doctor. I'll bring over your best man's tux. How's that?"

"That," Eddie said with a grin, "is great."

I couldn't believe that he was scheduling a patient on his rehearsal day, but when Eddie saw my expression he only winked and grinned. We'd made plans to go out to dinner, so I went back to the hotel to freshen up and call my wife. Everything was fine, Donna assured me, and asked how I was doing.

"Marvelous. I can't wait to get out of here."

"I take it Fast Eddie hasn't changed?"

"Remember that old song, 'Middle-Aged Crazy'?"

Her laugh sounded musical and I wished I was back next to her.

I went down to the lobby about thirty minutes later, checked the front of the place for any sign of Eddie's Lexus, and then went back and sat on one of the chairs. A copy of the local paper was folded on the small coffee table so I picked one up and began reading about the recent fires. They were directly attributed to the rainy spring, which caused an excess of mountain vegetation that dried to straw-colored tinder over the hot summer. All it took was one lightning strike, or one carelessly dropped cigarette, to set off a conflagration. A loud voice interrupted my reading and I looked over the rim of the paper.

"I'm expecting a very important package to be overnighted to me," the voice said. It was harsh-sounding and held the hint of implied malice, with a slight lisping sound due to the prognathic jaw's malformation. Its owner surprised me. The same guy who'd been on the plane, and then ducked in front of me at the car rental place. "The name's Marco Fabian. I want to be notified immediately. Got it?"

The mousy little clerk gave his assurance and Mr. Fabian walked away looking like an angry pelican. I went back to reading about the wildfires.

Eddie had shown up without his bride-to-be, saying that she needed the time alone to check on her gown and get with her girlfriends. I mentally debated asking him if this upcoming nuptial was in his best interest, but decided to keep my mouth shut. He must have read my mind, though.

"I know what you're thinking," he said with a grin. "Out of the frying pan and back into the fire."

I smiled. "How sure are you this time?"

His grin faded slightly. "Sure? Hell, I knew I had to have Alicia as soon as I saw her." A wistful look settled over his face. "Why? You think she's too young for me?"

There was no sense playing Dear Abby at this point. His mind was already made up. "True love conquers all."

He smirked and looked down at his plate. "Yeah, I just hope that the third time's the charm."

Somehow, I didn't think it would be.

As I got ready for bed that night, I made mental plans to get up early on Friday and go for a run. It was good to be in Arizona again and the sights brought back a lot of old college memories, but the aroma of burnt wood that had occasionally engulfed me as I'd walked outside was troubling. The newscaster had assured everyone that the fires were now under control, but I couldn't help but think they'd only temporarily stopped, waiting for a new flashpoint.

Sleep eluded me as I lay in the strange hotel bed, and I found myself thinking about how I'd present my suspicions to the state's attorney Monday regarding the likelihood of Montoya's peg laterals matching up to the bite. It was a situation that required a clear and obvious preponderance of the evidence. Keldon had phone records showing that Montoya had repeatedly called Sandra Tilly, and her roommate had also given a statement that Sandra had confided her revulsion of him. That gave us motive, and his bite, the natural one, would tie him to the crime. I was confident I could persuade the judge, and once I had the original plaster model of his pegs, the jury. I had photos of Sandra Tilly's body that could be blown up to life size. My most effective methodology was to take a video of myself beside the life-sized photo, running the model of the suspect's teeth directly over the bite marks. I didn't use sound. It was more effective to speak directly to the jury, pausing the video if necessary, and playing it back with each opportunity. If I had had the impression while her body was still available, I would have filmed myself using the actual bite wound. But either way, it left an unforgettable impact on the minds of the jury. I remembered seeing Sandra Tilly's body when I took the photos, and resolved that nothing was going to go wrong with this one. I wanted to see Montoya take the fall.

My plans to go for that morning run on the treadmill were cut short by an incessant ringing that stirred me at seven-thirty. It was Eddie.

"Up and at 'em," his voice said. "I'm on the way over. We got work to do before we pick up your tux."

"We do?"

"Yeah." His voice lowered slightly. "I need a favor. I sorta overbooked myself this morning, scheduling Luigi, so I was thinking if you wouldn't mind helping me out, we could get done in plenty of time to get to the rehearsal."

"What are you talking about? I'm not licensed to practice in this state."

"You could help me with the lab stuff," he said, "unless you're too used to working on dead people." His horselike laugh punctuated the sentence.

So I was relegated to serve as Eddie's gofer. I sighed. "Give me thirty minutes."

True to his word, I saw Eddie leaning against the front counter drumming his nails on the solid wood top. The desk clerk was engaged in a conversation with my ubiquitous buddy, Marco Fabian himself. As I walked up, I could hear his whistling lisp berating the clerk.

"Has my package arrived yet?" he asked. "I instructed the person yesterday to notify me as soon as it arrives."

"Not at this time, sir," the clerk was saying. Fabian still looked like that angry pelican. He spouted off a few more orders to the clerk and turned to leave. That's when Eddie's venality got the better of him.

"Say," the party animal said, "I happen to be a dentist and couldn't help but notice your jaw. You have a skeletal Class III malocculsion, better known as an anterior crossbite. May I?" He reached up and tried to touch Fabian's protruding jaw. The other man's head jerked back defensively.

"Keep your hands off me!" he said. He drew his balled-up fist back.

Eddie recoiled and for a moment I thought he might even blush. "Hey, I'm a doctor of dental surgery, sir. A professional. I specialize in helping people like you." He leaned his head back, scrutinizing the prognathic jaw. "There are several procedures I could use, but they would all leave you looking like Rock Hudson."

Rock Hudson? I mentally groaned.

The dark eyes glowed with anger. I was afraid Fabian was going to deck Eddie so I stepped up, trying to use my midwestern roots to extinguish this fire.

"Say, didn't I see you on the plane from Chicago?"

Fabian turned his dark gaze on me. It looked cold enough to freeze water. Without speaking to either of us, he stormed away.

I looked at Eddie. "What exactly were you trying to do?"

He rolled his head in an aww-shucks gesture and grinned, showing his white teeth again. "Hell, I'm always cruising for a new customer, and the best way to do that, I've found, is self-promotion. That's why I'm so successful."

I glanced after Fabian's retreating form as he entered the opening elevator. "You call that success?"

"Hey, I wasn't like you, having GI bennies pay for my schooling. I had to work my way through college selling these aluminum pots and pans. That's how I learned, you've got to be able to approach people, to sell yourself."

I shot him a skeptical look.

"You should have paid more attention in your practice management class." He flashed a sly grin. "If there's one thing I learned, it's that there's a sucker born every minute. Plus, I've got two greedy exes to support."

I was willing to bet that this time next year, the number would be three.

"How about that Luigi?" Eddie was grinning as we headed over to the church. "Don't that tux fit like it was made for you?"

"As well as I'm sure his bridge does."

Eddie laughed. "I'm just like a Lexus. Relentlessly pursuing perfection. And the dollars that go with it."

Alicia, who was in the backseat, reached over and slapped his shoulder. "Don't be so cynical."

"What?" Eddie made a half-assed attempt to look wounded. "I got a right to do follow-up work on things, don't I? Jim'll tell you."

Not wanting to get in the middle of what I hoped would be their penultimate pre–wedding day disagreement, I kept my mouth shut.

"So I bill his insurance for a little occlusal adjustment. Who gets hurt?"

"You should be nicer to him, all he did for you with the tuxes," she said.

"Nicer? He's got some great-looking choppers now. Thanks to yours truly."

"And what about the insurance company?" she shot back. "Somebody still has to pay, right?"

"And that's all part of the game of life," Eddie said, his expression showing that he obviously felt he'd scored the deciding run. "You didn't see him offering to give us a free ride on the tux rentals, did ya?"

I stretched and glanced in the side mirror, catching a glimpse of a silver Lincoln following us. The "objects may be closer than they appear" mirror made it impossible to tell, but I almost thought I caught a glimpse of a long-jawed driver who looked vaguely familiar. I turned to look out the back window, but the Lincoln slowed and made a right turn.

"See something?" Eddie asked.

I shook my head. "Not really."

"Oh," he said, "I figured you spotted a nice looking chick."

Alicia reached up and slapped him again.

As wedding rehearsals went, this one was pretty typical. The minister gave us the rundown, and we practiced our entries. I was partnered with a maid of honor who looked young enough to be my daughter. I wondered if anyone would mistake Eddie for the father of the bride. Still, Alicia had turned out to be a very nice young lady, and, since it was her first wedding, she'd insisted on wearing white. I glanced at my watch and mentally calculated the hours until my return flight on Sunday.

Eddie had informed me that we were dropping Alicia off at her girlfriend's so she could have her bachelorette bash. "Then we're going to your hotel for my party," he said.

"Haven't you already had one of those?"

"Yeah." He grinned. "Twice. The third time's gotta be the charm. I've got a couple of strippers lined up that'll do the deed. They been rehearsing this act called 'The Dentist.'"

"Hey wait a minute," I said. "I don't want to get mixed up in that sort of thing."

"Aww, relax. They're strippers, not hookers." He grinned again. "Plus, it'll just show some innocuous business name."

Frowning, I shot him a glance that told him how I felt about it.

When we got to the hotel, our first stop was the bar. Eddie had two martinis and I had a virgin piña colada. I figured one of us needed to remain sober. He was busy punching in numbers on his cell phone and frowning when the call seemed to take time getting connected. Finally he got hold of someone and reconfirmed the strippers were coming. He was getting sloppy now, as he covered the mouthpiece with his hand and asked me loudly, "What's your room number again?"

I felt like belting him, but relented, against my better judgment. I said, "Four twenty-five," in as low a voice as I could.

"Got that? Four twenty-five!" He was speaking so loudly now practically everyone in the damn bar must have heard him. "Forty minutes? Good." He terminated the call, then leaned drunkenly toward me, placing a hand on my shoulder and confiding that he was ready for them.

"You don't look so ready," I said.

"Whatcha mean?" His face grew lugubrious for a second, as if I'd insulted his manhood. Then the sly look reappeared and he withdrew a mouth mirror out of his pocket. "Don't leave home without it."

I nodded, but he shook his head.

"This," he said, edging closer to me and looking around to make sure no one else saw, "is what they call a multifaceted tool." He gripped the small, circular mirror and twisted. Suddenly the end slipped off and a shiny blade protruded from the end. His voice was a whisper now. "See, when they tie me up, so they think I can't grab their boobies, I just slip this outta my back pocket, and presto! In no time flat my hands are free to roam."

I watched his self-congratulatory simper as he tried to reassemble the mouth mirror. Finally, I grabbed it and did it myself, handing it back to him and watching him try three times before finally slipping it back into his rear pants pocket.

He had one more drink while I nursed mine, glancing at my watch. Maybe he'd be so drunk that I could just slip the strippers a quick tip and get rid of them at the door. I could tuck Eddie onto the couch in the room so I could get some sleep. It was already getting late, by my standards.

We went up to the room and Eddie ordered a bottle of champagne on ice. When he mumbled to charge it to the room, I thought seriously about cutting his wedding gift in half. Donna had convinced me that it would be best, considering the groom's proclivities, to just give money inside a card. The universal gift. But I was thinking about including a copy of *How to Win Friends and Influence People.*

The knock at the door startled me. Figuring it was the strippers arriving early, I went to open it and got the shock of my life. Roland Vanderberg stood in the doorway looking somber. His next words answered my unspoken query.

"Dr. Link, we have to leave right away."

"What are you talking about? And what are you doing here?"

He licked his lips. "It's your wife and daughter, sir. There's been an accident."

Eddie came over and stood by the doorway looking as dumbfounded as I felt. He blinked several times and began fishing in his pocket for his keys.

"Where are they?" I asked, reaching for my cell phone.

"I've got the hospital number on my cell," Roland said. "Let's go down to the lobby."

He stepped back, allowing the door to slowly close. I rushed over, grabbing it, but it swung inward from a hard push. Roland came inside with it, followed by Mr. Pelican himself, Marco Fabian. He held a long pistol that I realized had a sound suppressor on it.

"Don't move," he said.

I looked at the black hole of the barrel and raised my hands.

Fabian motioned for Eddie to raise his also, but the alcohol was obviously overriding his better judgment. He smirked and said, "Why? What are you gonna do? Shoot me?"

Fabian moved forward with a quick step and backhanded Eddie across the face. The blow left a red mark on his cheek. The Pelican then jammed the elongated barrel into Eddie's soft gut.

"You wanna make more fun of my jaw now, ash-hole?" His face showed a controlled rage, the dark eyes full of hate.

Eddie raised his hands, saying, "Okay, okay. I didn't mean anything about your underbite. I was only trying to offer some professional advice."

"Shaddup," Fabian said, cocking his arm back again. Eddie cringed but no blow came. Fabian turned to Vanderberg. "You get their keys. I think we'll use this dude's Lexus. It's time to go start another one of them wild-fires."

"Roland, what's this all about?" I asked.

He compressed his lips and looked down at the floor as he went through Eddie's pockets.

"What about my family?"

"They're fine." He swallowed hard. "It was just a ruse. I'm sorry."

A ruse? Suddenly it all came together in my head. Good old venal Roland. I should have seen this coming. "Montoya. He bought you off, didn't he?" Vanderberg seemed to wither under my stare. "You Judas."

"Look, I didn't have any choice," he said. "They made me do it. I owe them a lot of money. This'll get me out from under." His eyes met mine for a fleeting second and I suddenly knew how this little train wreck was going to play out. A nice, convenient accident in the desert somewhere, with drunken Eddie strategically placed behind the wheel. We'd both be conveniently killed, I'd miss testifying before the Grand Jury to obtain the search warrant for the original plaster mold, which was probably already being destroyed, and Montoya's trial date would never arrive. Vanderberg fished the keys out of Eddie's pocket and handed them to Fabian. He shook his head and tossed two plastic flex-cuffs on the bed.

"You're gonna drive that one," he said. "Now tie their hands."

He looked hesitant, and the Pelican barked a repeat of the order. "Do it! Do it now!"

As Vanderberg grabbed my hands he muttered, "Sorry, Doctor."

"What makes you think they'll let you off the hook, Roland?" The moment they took us out of the room, we were as good as dead. "Once you're in this, you're a liability."

My words had little or no effect. He tightened the plastic band around my wrists so I couldn't move my hands. Fabian fingered Eddie's keys, then handed them to Vanderberg.

"You drive this one," he started to say, then his dark eyes flashed at the sound of a knocking on the door. "Go see who it is. Use the peephole." He turned to us and pointed the barrel of the pistol at Eddie's forehead. "Not a sound."

Vandenberg moved to the door, then scampered back. "It's two bimbos."

"They alone?"

"Looks like it."

Fabian considered this for a moment, then tapped the long barrel on Eddie's forehead. "Who are they? Hookers?"

"They're not hookers, they're just strippers," Eddie said. Tears rolled down his swollen cheek. "It's my bachelor party tonight."

Fabian stared at him intently. Another knock, more persistent this time, caused him to smirk. Turning to Vanderberg, he said, "This might work out better than I figured. Go answer the door. Tell them things ain't ready yet and take 'em downstairs for a drink."

Vanderberg blanched. "I wasn't supposed to get this involved. Montoya promised—"

Fabian whirled and grabbed him by his shirt, doubling it up inside his fist. "You do what I tell ya! Now go take 'em downstairs. When I call your cell, take 'em to the Lexus."

"How am I going to do that?"

Fabian pulled Vanderberg's face close to his. His voice was low, guttural. "Tell 'em you got some weed in the trunk. I don't care, just do it."

He released Vanderberg with a rough shove and I almost wished he would have shot him. I know I wanted to.

Straightening his collar, Vanderberg moved to the door, opened it slightly, and began to step out. I could already hear him exuding that unctuous, artificial charm. The son of a bitch.

Fabian waggled the long barrel at us. "Come on, we're taking the stairs. And if either of you tries anything, I'll shoot you both and leave you laying there."

My mind raced. I'd been an airborne ranger before I'd entered dental school, and had seen a little action in Operation Urgent Fury. I'd learned that escape was best accomplished before your enemy was totally set up, using the element of surprise. But with my hands tied behind me, I also knew I'd be dead before I could do anything. We went to the door and Fabian opened it, glancing up and down the hallway, then motioning us out. He draped a jacket over the long-barreled pistol and carried it down by his side. "Go down that way to the stairs," he said. "Real slow."

We walked single file, with me in the lead. I thought about the chances of making a break for it on the stairs or when we got to the lobby, but either way I'd be abandoning drunken Eddie and leaving myself open for a lethal shot. I had to wait for my chance.

Fabian had obviously spent some time on planning. He directed us down the stairway and through the back hallways to the parking area. It looked as deserted as a pauper's funeral. Pulling a set of keys and a remote from his pocket, he pressed the button and a black van next to a pillar flashed its lights. Fabian cocked his head toward it. When we got there, he pulled open the side door and ordered us in. The rear windows were darkly tinted and all of the seats had been removed from the rear portion. As we struggled to get inside, Eddie slipped and fell sideways. Fabian reached down and pulled him up, pushed him inside, and then punched him twice on the side of the face.

"Leave him alone," I said. "Can't you see he's defenseless?"

My rebuke inflamed Fabian more, and he pushed me to the floor. Stepping into the space, he closed the side door after him and kicked me hard in the stomach. I curled into a ball and fought for breath.

"You want some more?" he asked.

All I could do was struggle to breathe.

Fabian stood crouching over us for a few more seconds, then plopped down in the driver's seat. He shoved the keys into the ignition, started the van, and backed out of the parking spot. He drove about twenty feet and stopped, taking out his cell phone. I listened to the one-sided conversation as he spoke.

"Yeah, Vanderberg? You got the broads with you? Okay, I'm by the ash-hole's Lexus. You know where it's parked? Okay, bring them down here and we'll club 'em and stick 'em in the van."

He turned to us and grinned malevolently, his prognathic jaw making him look like a caricature. "This will look real neat. Two middle-aged ash-holes in a car with two hookers, and they all die in a fiery crash."

"Why are you doing this?" Eddie said, his voice cracking. "What did I ever do to you?"

Fabian smirked, then said, "Shut up. Be a man."

Eddie began to sob and Fabian turned away with a laugh. I rolled onto my side and edged closer to Eddie, reaching my hands down toward his back pockets. If I could get his dual-purpose mouth mirror there was a chance, albeit a slim one, that I could free myself. He rolled away at my touch and I worked closer to him, not daring to whisper. Fabian turned toward us.

"What are you two doing?"

"These damn plastic bands are cutting into our wrists," I said, managing to tap Eddie's behind with my fingers. I hoped he would realize what I was trying to do. "Can't you loosen them?"

Fabian emitted a low chuckle, the air whistling through his gaping cross-bite. "Don't worry, you won't have to suffer much longer."

My fingers caressed the cheek of Eddie's large posterior, walking their way up the flat edge of his back pocket. He stiffened, but stayed put. I worked my index finger and thumb down into the pocket, my hands feeling numb from the lack of circulation. Eddie held fast, even moving up slightly trying to assist me. I felt the circular edge of the mouth mirror and moved my finger down along the beveled metal, curling around it, twisting, working my thumb around to secure the grip, then lifting, pulling.

I had it. My fingers were nimble and strong from years of working in small oral cavities with minute movements. This was proving even more challenging. I twisted the mirrored end off and felt the sharp blade between my fingers. Working it up toward the tight band that was securing my wrists, I readjusted my grip and began a sawing motion, hoping Fabian wouldn't choose that moment to turn around.

His cell phone rang, and I heard him say, "Yeah, I see ya. Keep coming." He chucked again. "Nice-looking broads. Too bad we ain't got time to have some fun with 'em."

I continued the sawing. The blade slipped off a few times, and the pressure on my wrists was constant. Fabian shifted in his seat, then opened the driver's door. I heard him speaking, then a loud female voice of protest, followed by a truncated scream. Noises of someone colliding with the side of the van, then moving toward the rear quickened my pace. It was now or never. I pressed the blade against the plastic band again, pressing and sawing, pressing and sawing.

It gave way with a click. My hands were free, but so numb and tingling that I doubted I could use them. Struggling to my knees, I grabbed the small metal instrument with my left hand, and worked the fingers of my right, flexing and shaking. The rear door opened and I saw Fabian holding the pistol against the head of a young blond girl with a terrified look on her face. His protruding jaw rubbed against the girl's temple.

"Get in there, bitch," he said.

I took this moment to jump forward, reaching with my left hand to grab the elongated barrel of the pistol, and plunging the sharpened point of the mouth mirror into Fabian's left carotid. The gun popped, sending a round whizzing by my head and into the roof of the van. I threw my weight forward and we both were on the hard cement, rolling, punching, and kicking. Suddenly his resistance evaporated and he began to go limp. I pushed myself up on my hands and knees and saw the pelican man's lips twisting back over the huge jaw in a deadly grimace, bright arterial blood gushing like a broken pipe onto the gray floor.

I secured my grip on the pistol and saw one of the girls staring at me in terror.

"Find his cell phone," I said. "Call nine-one-one."

Vanderberg was standing a few feet away and began talking as I straightened up and walked toward him.

"Doctor Link, I can explain everything," he said, his voice quavering. "They forced me to tell, to cooperate. Forced me to tell them where you were. I had no idea—"

He stopped talking when my left fist collided with the front of his mouth. The punch, one of the first I'd thrown in anger in many, many years, knocked him backwards, sending him down to the concrete floor. His head made a popping sound as it hit the ground, which gave me an almost sadistic sense of satisfaction. His eyes rolled back into his head, exposing the white scalera momentarily, then the irises snapped back into place. He rolled onto his side and began coughing, spitting out a pool of blood with at least three broken porcelain crowns from his front incisors.

"They're coming," Eddie said.

"Good," I said. Vanderberg was up on his elbow but still spitting out bloody saliva. "It looks like you're going to need a good dentist. I'll see if I can convince my buddy Eddie to squeeze you in sometime." That is, if I can convince him to start doing prison work pro bono."

OCCAM'S RAZOR

BY MAYNARD F. THOMSON

The reporter, a large, middle-aged woman with an expression of perpetual concern, looked up from her notebook. "When I was on the crime beat I watched all your trials, you know. The Roberts kidnapping, the Hailsham Farm murders, Lonnie Burke, the Cannibal killings—all of them. I remember them vividly."

Dr. Stork lifted his chin just enough to allow him to spread his tented fingers in a gesture of acknowledgment. "That was all a long time ago," he said. His voice, which in court had held a rich, persuasive timbre, was high and cracked.

"People like reading about them, which is why I want to do a feature on you. Victor Marino said Lester Stork's the dean, simply the man who invented the modern criminalist."

"That's very kind, but he exaggerates."

Susan Bruce was increasingly frustrated; the old man seemed immune to flattery, and getting material was proving an ordeal. She wondered again if he'd slipped into senility.

"I was thinking about the Menendez case on my way over. I thought for sure his alibi witnesses would get him off, but you made it so clear he did it."

She wondered if he'd remember but Stork, his face half hidden in the fading late afternoon light, nodded. "Those two—Perkins and ... Seymour, wasn't it? Not very credible, really."

Christ, as though she remembered. Nothing wrong with the old man's memory, then, it was more as though he found the topic of his career boring. His manner, too, was so far from what she remembered in the courtroom.

There, he'd been everyone's favorite uncle, imperturbably explaining the evidence until any verdict save "guilty" would have been absurd. Now he was just a tired old man.

Still, Ms. Bruce was not easily put off a story. "Enough for reasonable doubt, I thought, until you testified."

"We had overwhelming physical evidence. The blood alone would have been sufficient. When an alibi conflicts with the physical evidence . . ." A wave of his thin hand completed the thought.

The reporter jotted a note. "And you made Dr. Danziger sound so—" she looked around, as though the word she wanted was on one of Stork's bookshelves "—forced. You know, as though he was just reciting lines from a bad script."

Stork nodded. "He was."

"And you weren't?" Perhaps she could needle him into becoming engaged.

Stork shrugged his thin shoulders. "The evidence pointed incontrovertibly to Mr. Menendez's guilt. All I had to do was lay it out, as simply as possible. Danziger had to account for that which couldn't be denied—the blood, for instance—while trying to supply a scenario that exculpated his client. Foolish to challenge Occam's Razor."

"Occam's Razor?" Susan Bruce's passage through journalism school hadn't included medieval English scholasticism.

Stork looked at the woman, with her blank, expectant air of impenetrable ignorance, and sighed. He thought again how glad he was that he could measure the remainder of his life in months, if that.

"A philosophical concept. In essence, it says that the simplest explanation that fits all the known data is most likely to be correct. Sy Danziger challenged Occam every time he testified. Occam usually won."

Ms. Bruce thought about this, wondering at the turn things had taken, then looked up abruptly. "Would you mind talking about how you got started?"

"How I got started?" He blinked uncertainly at the sudden shift in topic.

"Hmm. I know you became ME here in—" she flipped back through her notes "—fifty-nine, and that before that you were in Chicago, but I don't have anything on your background. I mean, how does someone become the country's leading medical examiner? When you were a little boy, did you say 'When I grow up, I want to be a forensic pathologist'?"

The old man gave a wheezy sniff. "Hardly."

"They do today, you know. Everybody wants to be a criminalist. Look," she made a sweeping gesture, as though the little office were filled with applicants, "there's a whole department here at the university."

Stork shook his head. "They're in for a disappointment. The glamour's on television. Squalor and lies, that's the reality. There's rarely any mystery, you know. The obvious person did the crime, and a six-year-old could solve it."

"Oh, that Occam thing." The reporter was momentarily flummoxed, then decided to approach it from a different direction. "Won't you tell me about your first case? I'm sure that would be interesting."

"My first case? That would be—" he pointed at her notepad "—the Barton matter. Didn't we already talk about that?"

"No, not your first case here, your first case ever."

"Well, I had cases as an assistant, in Chicago, but that was a long time ago. Let's see …"

"No. I mean, the case that got you started. Back in Minnesota, I think it was."

"Minnesota." He stopped, seeming struck by the name. "Yes, but there was nothing interesting, really. Just one thing led to another, I suppose." That was the way it had always seemed to him, anyway, when he thought about it. Which he hadn't, for years.

"Isn't that where you began your career? I was sure I read somewhere …"

"Maddie."

Ms. Bruce stopped, unsure whether Stork had said something, or if it had been a noise out in the hall. "Were you speaking to me, Dr. Stork?"

Now the yellow light from the window fell on his white head, and she saw him in profile. "Maddie, that was her name. Madelaine Birney, but I called her Maddie."

"What about her, Dr. Stork? Was she involved in your first case?" He suddenly seemed very, very far away.

"Involved." He turned to face her. "Yes, she was involved in my first case."

Something in his manner made her hesitate. "Would you like to talk about it?"

He looked away again. "You won't have heard of her, of course. Of her murder."

"I'm sorry, no."

"I haven't thought about the case in many years. I used to, but not for a long while. Odd." He blinked uncertainly. "I used to be able to see her. See her, lying there. But now . . ."

"Maybe it would be better if . . ." The reporter leaned forward, as though to rise, but Stork held his hand up and she sank back into the chair.

"She was what got me started, what you wanted to hear about. My career as 'the dean of American criminologists' started with Maddie Birney, in Sioux Junction, Minnesota, in nineteen fifty-four. I thought you wanted to hear how I got started?"

"I did, but . . . are you sure you want to tell me?"

There was a long pause, and she thought he was going to withdraw again, but then he said, "If you would be kind enough to pour us some more tea, I'll get the file."

"I never wanted to be a doctor. I wanted to be a singer, if you can imagine that. But my father was a doctor, and his father before him, and he made it clear there'd be no money for anything as 'useless,' as he put it, as music school. He also told me I wasn't good enough to even think of it, and I daresay he was right. In any case, I wasn't one to defy him. So I went to medical school, and at first it wasn't so bad. I found I rather enjoyed the technical side of it, the lab work, anatomy, that sort of thing. And I had a good memory, and enjoyed learning all the obscure names and facts, then regurgitating them on exams. It was only when I got into my third year and had to start dealing with living people, the part my classmates couldn't wait for, that I knew how big a mistake I was making."

He looked away. "I didn't care for it, not a bit. It seemed to me a dreadful responsibility, and there was the, the . . ."

She thought he seemed embarrassed as he sought the words. "It wasn't just seeing people the way I wasn't used to seeing them, but having them tell me the most private things. It made me extremely uncomfortable."

He swiveled in his chair and looked straight at her. "I've always been shy, you see. Psychiatrists would say I have a fear of intimacy. God knows my parents did nothing to make me welcome it."

She felt unaccustomedly uncomfortable in the presence of this old man's emotional exposure. "I wouldn't have guessed. In the courtroom . . ."

"That's different. When I got into the courtroom the first time, in the case I'm telling you about, I felt comfortable. I knew then I wanted to be there, doing my utmost to win justice for the victims, to see the guilty punished. I know what I've seen, and what it means, and to me it's the most important thing in the world. But actually . . . caring . . . for living people . . ."

His voice trailed off and she wondered if he had lost his thread. She was about to prompt him when he resumed.

"So I didn't do so well in my final years in medical school, and when I graduated the only internship I was offered was in a community hospital in Hibbing, Minnesota, where I had to deal with sick people twenty-four hours a day. That was a miserable experience for me and quite unsatisfactory to the hospital, but it led me to accepting a job as medical officer for the Taconite Mining Company, in Sioux Junction, in the iron ore belt north of Hibbing. My father wanted me to return to Minneapolis and join him, but I had just enough spine to stand up to the old man this time, and the Taconite post was the only other thing on offer."

He shook his head. "Sioux Junction, Minnesota, the back of the beyond. Just a huge crater a mile deep, and ten thousand people, most of them miners and their families, living on the edge of it. And it suited me just fine."

"It sounds rather bleak."

"You can't imagine. But as soon as I interviewed, I saw that they'd only created the position as a sop to the union. They wanted a medic on the payroll, to patch up any bumps and scrapes, and keep the more seriously injured miners alive long enough to send them to the hospital in Hibbing. Glorified school nurse was what I was. But it left me plenty of time to collect and analyze data on mining-related disease, which had come to interest me, and God knows the men weren't looking to me to share their life's secrets. I had a paycheck, my record collection, and a decent apartment. And as long as I had the title 'Doctor' my father couldn't complain too much. So all in all, I was content enough. For eighteen months I was reasonably happy, happier than I'd ever expected to be, at least as a doctor. And then it happened.

"The call came at about four in the afternoon, while I was in the company dispensary. October seventeen, nineteen fifty-four, a fine, crisp day. I should have been reviewing the results of the blood drive, but I had a record player there, and I remember I was listening to Schubert's String Quartet Number Fourteen as I picked up the receiver."

Stork's eyes lost their focus and he was gone in thought for a moment, before making a soft, wondering noise. "Strange, how a stray fact like that stays with you, all these years later. 'Death And The Maiden,' the piece is called. Ironic. Anyway," he brought his attention back to her, "at first it simply didn't register. It was the sheriff's office, but I couldn't understand why they were calling me.

"Then my mind cleared and of course it made perfect sense. Shortly after I'd arrived in Sioux Junction the local GP who served as county medical examiner, Dr. Latham, had retired and moved away. The other physicians in town had family practices and neither the time nor the taste for the job, so I'd agreed to take it on. The call was from the dispatcher, saying the sheriff wanted me to get over to Lakota Street right away, there'd been an accident. That was his term, 'an accident,' but I remember I felt a strange foreboding as I arrived.

"It was a two-family house, one unit above another, and a patrolman was just coming out of a side door. He saw me and pointed to the second floor. On the front porch of the house next door I saw a large, gray-haired woman standing with her arms crossed and a disapproving scowl on her red face, and on the sidewalk another patrolman was holding half a dozen gawking neighbors at bay. I was glad to slip through the screen door and hasten up the stairs, bag in hand, steeling myself for what I might find.

"Sheriff Coomer was a large, florid man. I suspected he drank more than was good for him. He was standing in the corner of the sitting room, watching as Harold Elkins, the town photographer, snapped pictures of the small figure lying on the floor. A deputy sheriff named Tongren had his back to us, staring out the window. I just had time to take it in before a flash bulb went off and I was momentarily blind.

"'That's it, Sheriff,' I heard Elkins say, as my vision cleared. Sheriff Coomer nodded to me. 'Then she's all yours, Doc.' He walked over and stood looking down at the body. 'Place downstairs is vacant, and the windows were closed, so nobody heard nothing, but the nosy old battleax next door got to wondering, saw the girl's car still here. Thought she might be sick, so when she didn't answer, came up and found her.'

"The sheriff pursed his lips. 'My take, she tripped and hit her head on that table.' His big chin indicated the marble-topped coffee table a foot from the body. It had been pushed askew from the settee behind it. 'Accident, I'd say. Sad, girl that age.'

"I felt horror as I stared at the still figure. This gave way to outrage as I digested the Sheriff's words, but I forced myself to remain calm. Any fool could see this had been no 'accident,' but that could wait. 'I'll look at her,' was all I said.

"'You do that, Doc,' the Sheriff said. 'I'm going down to call for the meat wagon.'

"Coomer and Elkins went out, and I waited until I heard the screen door slam to let out my pent-up breath. 'Some "accident," eh, Doc?' Deputy Tongren was standing next to me, looking down at the broken figure. I noticed dark blood had pooled next to her head, soaking the carpet. I felt myself sway, and forced myself not to think about anything but the job I had to do.

"'He's an idiot,' I said, stepping forward and sinking to my knees. 'This was murder.'

"'Think so?' Tongren, a big Swede, didn't sound the least surprised. 'Nothing to trip on, her housecoat's come loose, and she didn't just bump her head, push that heavy table back like that. Figure she was shoved, and hard. Course I could be wrong.'

"I looked up. There was nothing to betray Tongren's thoughts on that impassive face, but it occured to me that he was no fool. I'd missed the significance of the knotted robe, open enough to reveal her nakedness underneath it. I nodded and turned my full attention back to the pathetic form, lying just inches before me.

"I'd seen my share of dead bodies, but never one that affected me like this one. She was lying on her side, so that her right cheek was on the carpet, sightless eyes staring down her extended right arm, the fingers curled in a cadaveric spasm. Her lilac robe splayed on either side of her, like butterfly wings, her skin white except where her body pressed the floor and internal blood had pooled in a ghastly lividity. Tongren was right, the sash on the robe was still knotted, so she hadn't come into the room with it hanging open. It had been wrenched, probably when she was pushed. And even as my fingers touched the ringlets of light brown hair turned black with congealed blood, I knew that only a brutal force could have driven her head into the marble table-top hard enough to have produced the awful concavity they found.

"I completed my examination swiftly, repressing all extraneous thought as I jotted my findings in a notebook. There was no pulse, obviously, and her temperature was that of the ambient air. From that, the lividity, and the state of rigor mortis, I began to think about the time of death.

"While I was examining the body I was relatively calm, but as soon as I completed my initial examination the fact that she was lying that way, exposed and naked, horrified me, and I tried to draw the folds of her robe over her. As I did, my eye caught a scrap of paper wedged beneath her leg. I looked around for the deputy, but he'd disappeared, and I picked up the scrap, an irregularly-shaped piece of cream linen stationery perhaps two inches by three.

"I looked at it just long enough to see that it was covered with several lines of script in blue ink before thrusting it in my suit pocket. Perhaps I'd already formed a concern that the sheriff had no intention of handling this hideous crime seriously, and wanted to be sure the evidence was properly treated. My impression was only reinforced when the sheriff returned a minute later, as I was putting away my instruments.

"'Well, what do you think, Doc?' He stood, hands on hips, staring down at me with a look of dumb hope on his face. 'Fell and hit her head?'

"I glared up at him. 'It was no accident, I can tell you that. She was murdered. Some time last night, I'd say, though I can't be sure until the autopsy.'

"The sheriff screwed up his lips in a perplexed scowl. 'You sure about that?'

"'Absolutely. In my opinion, there is no possibility it was anything else. She was thrown into that table top with enough force to collapse her skull. No fall could have done that, even if there were anything to cause it, which there wasn't.'

"The sheriff grunted, then nodded resignedly. 'Coulda been a client, then. Happens. Didn't want to pay for it, most likely.'

"It took a second to sink in, then I sprang to my feet, overcome with sudden, murderous rage at this insensate fool's impenetrable stupidity. I must have appeared genuinely threatening, because Deputy Tongren, who'd returned with the sheriff, interposed a restraining arm between us. 'Easy,' he muttered.

"I had to fight to control my voice, and my fury. 'Her name is Madelaine Birney, and she teaches at the Indian school. She did, I mean.' Then, my emotions still gyrating wildly, I added: 'She was a lady.' It sounded ridiculous, even as I said it.

"The sheriff gaped at me. 'You knew her?'

"'Of course I knew her.' In fact, I was surprised the sheriff didn't. People knew each other in Sioux Junction. 'She played the organ at Faith Lutheran, where I sing in the choir. And you're not going to be able to pass this off as some Saturday night brothel killing, Sheriff. The community won't stand for it.'

"I wasn't sure what I meant by that, but I could see the sheriff weighing it in his little, pig eyes. Finally, he nodded. 'Just you finish your report and get it to me pronto. I'll decide what we do next. Probably some intruder, came in to rob the place, and she surprised him.'

"I was about to point out that there was apparently no evidence of forced entry, and she would hardly have opened the door to a strange man late at night, but I thought better of it and said nothing until the sheriff, scratching his chin, added, 'May have to call the fucking state in. Meantime, nobody talks to anybody, hear? Anybody asks, Doc, you got a girl here, died of unknown causes, that's all.' He pointed his big forefinger at me. 'Got it?'

"I nodded as two men carrying a gurney came through the door. The sheriff looked at me again, told Deputy Tongren to lock up, and stomped out, muttering a loud, disgusted 'Shit' as he went.

"Tongren stood next to me, watching as the attendants lifted the body onto the gurney for transport to Birdwell's funeral parlor, which let the county use the preparation room for postmortems. He didn't break into my silence until they were gone, for which I was grateful.

"'Nice girl, eh?'

"I nodded, fighting for control. 'A wonderful girl. I guess I didn't know her very well.' As I was to soon learn, even less well than I imagined.

"I put my hand over my eyes, hoping it would block the ghastly image, but of course that was burned into my brain. 'Sorry,' I muttered.

"Tongren made a soft, commiserative sound. 'Hell of a shock, you know someone gets done like that.'

"'Yes,' I said.

"'Sheriff isn't a bad type.' Tongren had the slow, quiet speech of the

Swedes in those parts. 'He'll get the state in, and do his best to get to the bottom of this. He just hoped it was something else. Gonna be a lot of frightened people, this gets about. Got an election coming up, helluva time to have somebody doing something like that.'

"'There aren't any good times for it, are there?' I knew he meant well, but my insides were leaden. The horror of what I'd experienced had left me feeling as though I was in a dream state.

"As we were descending the stairs I had a thought. 'How long before the state people arrive?'

"'Well, my guess is Sheriff'll wait as long as he can, see if he can turn anything up. He'd sure rather not have them bigfooting in his backyard, making it look like we aren't doing our job. Hell, maybe the man who did it'll get religion and turn himself in.' Tongren stopped and scratched his head. 'Two, three days, though, he'll have to make the call. We aren't set up for serious investigating. Can't even dust the place for prints.' He locked the door, pocketing the key as he turned his open, earnest eyes on me. 'But believe me, Doc, we'll get the bastard responsible for this.'

"I wanted to believe him, but I could envision the police settling on some loser, some miserable career criminal who'd confess to anything, just to close the case. This was a thought I could not abide, not then, not ever, and as I look back, I think it was then that I vowed that never, if I had any power to prevent it, would the kind of person responsible for Maddie Birney's death escape judgment.

"When I'd taken over as county medical examiner, old Dr. Latham had passed on to me his library of forensic medicine texts, which I'd supplemented with a few purchases of my own. The job, so alien to most physicians, whose passion is for the living, was congenial to the detached, cerebral curiosity that was all that bound me to my profession. I had studied the materials avidly, determined to be, whatever my limitations as a clinician, the best ME Lakota County had ever had. That night, as I reviewed protocols for the proper procedures for a forensic investigation, I felt curiously confident, as I never was in my dealings with patients.

"Of course, my duties as local medical examiner didn't relieve me of my responsibilities as the Taconite Company staff physician, however distracted I felt. So the next morning, a Wednesday, I went by Ralph Parker's office to discuss the results of the blood drive and my plans for TB screening. I could hardly bear the thought of seeing him, but there was no way to avoid it.

"From the outset I'd despised Parker, known inevitably as 'Ace.' I'd known we weren't compatible as soon as I interviewed with him in Minneapolis, before I even got the job. Parker was the mine superintendent, Taconite's top man in Sioux Junction, and the embodiment of everything I've always detested: loud, vulgar, facile in his dealings with others, glibly charming when he wanted to be, ever the glad-hander and coarse jokester. The kind of man who was always touching people. A big hand grasping your bicep, a squeeze to the secretaries' shoulders, a little pat or too-long kiss for the wives.

"He was popular, of course; such men usually are. He wasn't particularly handsome, but he had a sort of animal virility that women seem to find irresistible, without making men feel threatened. He wasn't a large man, no more than five-ten, but he had a good physique and was bull strong, liked to pitch in from time to time on some job at the mine requiring muscle, which endeared him to the workers. I'd seen him leave a group of miners with eighth-grade educations laughing like he was their best friend, while he hosted touring groups of steel company executives with the bluff self-assurance of a man utterly in command of his domain. The secretaries found his boorish innuendo vastly amusing, while the younger men in management thought Parker the ideal boss. They'd traipse off with him to Hibbing, and a few times a year to Minneapolis or Chicago, and when they'd return I'd have to suffer through raucous accounts of the drunken revels, the women they picked up, the idiotic references to 'ore houses,' followed by gales of laughter.

"Mrs. Parker was a meek, washed-out blonde with smeared, crimson lipstick. I'd met her when they'd had me over for huge slabs of burned meat shortly after I arrived. She seemed cowed by him, following him with her eyes, the first to laugh at his jokes, hanging on his blather.

"There was a group of us that night in the Parkers' back yard: loud, tipsy laughter and everybody kissing someone else's spouse. I'd turned down the next invitation and they stopped asking. I'd heard remarks, sickening remarks, that implied Parker might have struck his wife on occasion, but it was a measure of the degraded standards by which men like that are measured that these stories seemed to have done nothing to diminish his standing, even with the women. Perhaps, especially with the women.

"Men like Parker, who seemed to go through life as though it existed solely for their gratification, had always disgusted me. By the time I came to his office that morning, I loathed the man. But there was business to be done.

"Parker started each day with a visit to the pit, and hadn't arrived when I got to his office, so I availed myself of his bathroom, noting with disgust the bottles of aftershave and hair pomade. Then I settled in a chair and tried to distract myself by flipping through Parker's copy of *Mine Journal*, but nothing would keep the image of that poor girl's broken body out of my mind.

"For the fact was, Madelaine Birney had occupied a far larger role in my life than my account to the sheriff had implied. I had, in fact, been in love with her, the first woman for whom I'd ever held this feeling. Indeed, the only woman for whom I ever would.

"I'd met her at the church, as I'd said. What I hadn't told them, because it seemed ... pathetic ... in light of events, was that I had been wildly, insanely smitten from the first I laid eyes on her. I knew it would eventually come out that we'd been seen together, but under the circumstances I'd been in no mood to share my shattered dreams with strangers.

"I'd approached her after choir practice, that first night. I'd nervously praised her playing, stumbling awkwardly and feeling the fool, but she'd at once put me at my ease, as no girl had before her. She had blue eyes that looked right into mine, and freckles on her nose, and a quiet self-assurance that wasn't at all like the brassy familiarity of the other single women I'd encountered.

"Somehow I found myself having coffee with her that night. Then, a few days later, dinner, then a drive in the country, a tour of the reservation, once a deliriously perfect picnic in the woods on a hot August day. She had even had me over for dinner. She burned the chicken. I thought it ambrosial. I fixed her lamp, and felt so . . . manly.

"She punctured my pomposity, but in such a kind, gentle way that I simply felt better for it, and I was quite convinced that she was my destiny. I had never even worked up the courage to kiss her, yet for a few perfect months my every waking moment had been filled with visions of a life with her, with Mrs. Lester Stork. She would play the piano and I would sing. I would come home to perfect meals and perfect children, and we would lie in front of the fire and listen to records. I could even see the house, a perfect little cottage down a country lane. Maddie would soften my father, then humanize him. There would never be a word of reproach or anger between us.

"It was a married life such as can only exist in the mind of a man or woman who has never married, and for whom the other is an unrealizable ideal. I know that now. Maddie was sweet, and gentle, and pretty in the way of clean, wholesome young women scarcely out of girlhood, but she was no more ready or able to carry the weight of my fantasies than any other real person would have been. In the days just before her death I think I'd begun to realize that Maddie had never held the feelings for me I'd harbored for her, that in my inexperience I had mistaken her natural kindness and warmth for something more. Had there been time, had she lived, I expect I would have come to see her as I gather so many men see their first loves, as warm and amusing memories. But evil robbed us of that time.

"Parker blew away my thoughts with his sudden arrival, the random, animal energy so at odds with the clinical detachment I'd forced myself to adopt in my dealings with him. I literally flinched under the heavy weight of his hand as it fell on my shoulder, had to clench my teeth at the unfeeling jocularity of his 'How ya doin' Doc,' that on previous occasions had set my teeth on edge.

"I was relieved, actually, by his manner, which was normal for him. I'd had some concern that the sheriff would have spoken to him of Maddie's death, simply because nothing went on in Sioux Junction that wasn't thought to be properly the business of the Taconite Company's representative. I'd even feared a crude remark about Maddie, some foul irreverence that would have put me at his throat, but the sheriff had evidently followed his own orders, and the news had not spread. After Parker had kept me waiting long enough to remind me of my insignificance, and I'd gotten his signature on a requisition, I left, pleased, and at the same time rather shocked, that I'd been able to comport myself as though it was simply another day, as though Madelaine's body wasn't awaiting me at the mortuary.

"You ask how I became a criminalist? Well, it was that night, after a day of obsessing about Maddie, a day that had included the single most difficult thing I have ever done, her autopsy. No doubt I could have left it to the state medical examiner. Perhaps I should have. It never occurred to me. I conducted the procedure in a thoroughly professional manner, with an icy dispassion. And I doubt the most experienced pathologist in the country could have done more than I did.

"There is a popular belief that the time of death can be fixed, almost to the minute, but this is a myth. There is an almost infinite number of variables that can affect the indicia, and the truth is, lacking an eyewitness any estimate of time of death is at best a skilled guess. Nonetheless, when I finished I was prepared to say, with reasonable medical certainty, that Maddie had been killed some time between ten and midnight the previous Monday, October sixteenth. I won't go into the clinical details, but I recorded them in my notes, and was confident any other competent pathologist would concur with my conclusion. I called the sheriff's office and left this information with Deputy Tongren.

"I recorded only one other thing of significance, that even now, after having given it no thought these many years, leaves me feeling hollow. I determined that she had had intercourse, apparently consensual, shortly before she was murdered.

"Now, it seemed to me, the man responsible for her death had first robbed her of her innocence, that quality that had drawn me like nectar, and I was more determined than ever that he should pay, and at my hands. DNA testing didn't exist then, so I went back to her apartment to find the evidence that would attach a name to her killer. I was sure I'd find it.

"It wasn't difficult. Afterwards, people said I'd 'broken the case' through 'painstaking detective work.' The local paper made me sound like a latter-day Sherlock Holmes, and that was indeed why I got the offer in Chicago, but it was nonsense. I was motivated, certainly, far more motivated than a police investigator for whom this would have been just another murder, but I have worked on vastly more difficult cases since.

"I made no effort to conceal my presence. I was the authorized county medical examiner, and if anyone challenged me, I felt I had every right to make any reasonable investigation into the circumstances of Madelaine Birney's death. The sheriff, I knew, would not be pleased, but I really didn't care.

"I knew, from dropping Maddie off, that she kept a spare key under a flower box. I found it, unlocked the door, and went up the stairs.

"I had only a moment's hesitation, when I stood on the threshold of the apartment, and the smell of dried blood and the sight of that ghastly brown stain on the carpet made my knees buckle. But I forced myself to proceed. Maddie had mentioned once that she was a devoted diarist, and I had a notion that her journal, if I could find it, would help me destroy her destroyer. So I pressed on.

"I had never been in a woman's bedroom. Under other circumstances I probably would have been overwhelmed by the assault on my senses, but my purpose took me straight to the bedside table, and in the drawer, just as I had guessed, I found the diary, bound in red leather. I opened it at random.

"The malicious fate so active that week had taken me to the entry for August seventh, in her fine, even, light-blue script: 'Picnic and walk in woods with funny old L.'

"'Funny old L.' My stomach heaved and I flipped back to read sequentially, from the beginning. And gradually, sickeningly, it became clear.

"'April 4—Flat tire. Nice man stopped to help.' 'April 5—Man who changed tire called to see if OK.' 'April 8—Crazy! Drink with tire hero—sweet man.'

"Flipping ahead: 'May 18—Oh, God—think I'm falling in love. But he's married!'

"'May 23—Dinner in Hibbing. Kisses, such a yearning. He wanted to go to a hotel, I said no. Such a yearning, how can it be wrong? Oh, God!'

"'May 27—Am I evil? I don't care he's married! His wife is a horror. Father rolling in grave, and I don't care!'

"And then: 'May 30—I did it! Did it, did it, did it! I am a wanton WHORE, and I love it!!! And HE loves ME!!!'

"Sick, numb, turning the pages mechanically: 'June 17—Ralph's wife is a bitch, he's never loved her, but he can't leave her.'

"'Ralph.' The name swam before my eyes, but there it was again: 'June 23—"Mrs. Ralph Parker"—Oh, God, can it ever be? We love each other so. When I am in his arms, when I feel him in me, I . . .'

"I read on, every sickening word, more and more graphic. Now it was clear, now I could see why she hadn't responded to me.

"You must understand, this was nineteen fifty-four, and I knew nothing of women's inner lives. In my sheltered fantasy world, women, especially a woman I could care for, were pure, vestal, unsullied by anything base or animalistic. For me, then . . . well, to say I was horrified wouldn't begin to describe what I felt toward Parker. Revulsion, disgust, and most of all, blind, unreasoning hatred. I felt only pity for her, and love.

"I came to the last entry, October fourteenth, the previous Saturday. 'I can stand it no longer, I must have Ralph. I told him we had to tell his wife, that if he wouldn't, I would. We quarreled horribly, he says it would cost his job. Is this the end? I have never been more miserable, I think I shall die.'

"And so a man I had already despised had robbed me of the chance for love. I left then, seeing my course clearly.

"I was busy that night. First, I went to the office. It was late, and no one was there. I often worked late, on my research, so I went in quite openly, and did my business. And then . . .

"Well, the next morning I went to the sheriff's office. He was out but over a cup of coffee Deputy Tongren told me they'd had a break. 'The nosy neighbor called this morning. Just remembered she'd seen someone, from the size she thinks it was a man, leaving the girl's apartment Monday night. Ten-thirty sharp, she knows 'cause she waited' til her show ended to let the cat out.'

"My heart jumped. Parker! 'Could she identify him?' I asked.

"'Too dark, but it confirms your time of death estimate.'

"I nodded, pleased at that. The sheriff arrived and I gave them the diary, quickly summarizing the contents and the conclusion: 'Ralph Parker killed her. She was going to tell his wife, and he killed her.'

"The sheriff was aghast. 'God, man—you can't be . . .' He broke off as he thought about the insult to his authority. 'You went in there? You had no right—'

"I had no time for his posturing. 'I don't think you'll be complaining about that when you bring in the man who did this, since you'll get the credit. Now, suppose we conduct the search that should have been conducted two days ago?'

"He wasn't happy with me, but had no choice, and soon we were back in the apartment. This time I felt none of the dislocation that had afflicted me before, and very much in charge. 'Sheriff, why don't you and I search the bedroom, while Deputy Tongren searches out here?' I didn't wait for his concurrence.

"The bed clothes were in disarray and under the musty odor I imagined I smelled the thick musk of their love-making, but I forced myself to search the sheets, and was soon rewarded with the sight of a dark hair. I was just pointing it out to the sheriff when Tongren came in, smiling grimly. 'Found this in the rack by the chair. He was here that night, all right.' In his hand he held a copy of *Mine Journal*, bearing a label addressed to Ralph Parker. The company mailroom had stamped it in: October sixteenth, nineteen fifty-four.

"The sheriff was gaping at it when Tongren completed the picture. 'The bastard must have brought it with him. Then, like Doc says, they had another fight over telling the missus, he killed her, then panicked and forgot the magazine in his hurry to get out.'

"'Jesus.' The sheriff stood, scratching his head. I pressed the case home: 'That'll be Parker's hair we just found. Get one from him, it'll match.' Spotting a bottle on the dresser, I pulled out a handkerchief and picked it up. 'Wildroot. His hair tonic. And if his prints aren't on it, I'll be very surprised.'

"Tongren and I looked at the sheriff while he decided what to do. I could tell what he was thinking: 'Ralph Parker's Taconite's man. If I'm wrong . . .' Finally, he sighed. 'Okay, we'll pick him up.'"

"I gave them two hours, then went to the jail. I admit it, I wanted to see him behind bars, wanted to revel in the fear, the humiliation, the wreckage of his ugly, sordid life. But when I walked in the sheriff shot me a look of pure malice. He didn't mince words: 'He has an alibi. An absolutely ironclad alibi.'

"'That can't be. Who—?'

"'His wife.' Tongren looked at me unhappily. 'She puts him at home from a little after eight. She was with him every minute. They had a late dinner in front of the TV, then went to bed. Parker don't work, Doc.'

"'But . . .' I was completely at a loss, so certain had I been that the evidence convicted Parker. 'Where was he until eight?'

"The Sheriff spoke through clenched teeth. 'He says he stopped at a bar for a drink on the way home, but he's a bad liar. We know where he really was, but what the fuck difference does it make, eh? You're the smart guy, fixed the time of death no earlier than ten, you tell me why it matters what he was doing at eight.'

"'There has to be something wrong. I—'

"'Yeah, there's something wrong,' the sheriff growled. 'You. Got a hard-on for Parker 'cause you was sweet on the girl, and she was putting out for him. Thought you was a fairy, way I read things.'

"I ignored his taunt. 'Since you read her diary, you saw the last entry. They had a fight. They must have had another, and he killed her. It's obvious.' I felt it all slipping away.

"'What's obvious is the guy I got back in holding, Indian we caught breaking into a liquor store, got a list of assaults on his sheet a mile long. Figure he saw her at the reservation, figured she'd be an easy mark, and followed her home. And you know what? I got a feeling we'll have a full confession by morning.' He smiled a big, ugly smile.

"I forced myself to remain calm. 'His wife's lying, Sheriff, covering for him. Did you tell her he was having an affair with Miss Birney?'

"The grin faded, replaced by something even uglier. 'No, I did not. Man's getting some on the side, don't make him a killer, and how a man and his old lady make their marriage work, what they notice and what they don't, that's their business. I don't say Parker's some model husband, but he's a good man, plenty well liked around here, and it ain't for me to go wrecking his marriage. Or you, either, hear?'

"I rested my hands on the desk and put my face in his. 'Did you show her the diary?'

"He looked at me with bland disdain. 'What diary?'

"I think Tongren sensed I was going to go for the sheriff, because I suddenly found myself being escorted, none too gently, out the door. There was no resisting the big Swede, but I tried to reason with him. 'He can't just pretend it doesn't exist!'

"Tongren stopped in the doorway and let me go. 'Fraid he can.' Seeing my look, he added, 'Sheriff means well. Spreading that around wouldn't do Miss Birney or anyone else any good. Listen, I was there, and Mrs. Parker, she's telling the truth. Parker was with her. I'm not saying he didn't stop by the girl's on the way home, but he wasn't who killed her, not at ten o'clock. He was home then, for certain. Now, don't make trouble, okay?'"

* * *

Stork sat, staring into the gloom. The room was almost dark, and the hall outside had grown quiet. Finally, the reporter could stand the silence no longer. "But what happened. Wasn't the crime solved?"

He was so slow to answer that she feared he hadn't heard, but then, ever so slowly, he turned to face her. "Oh, yes, it was solved. Ralph Parker went to the electric chair. Back then we still believed in the death penalty for murder."

"But . . ." She felt she must have missed something, and she was a careful reporter who didn't like to miss things. "I thought he had an alibi."

"Mrs. Parker recanted. Went in that evening and said he hadn't gotten home until almost midnight."

"Oh." Ms. Bruce's mind raced. "What did Parker say?"

"Oh, he denied it to the end, that's why he got the chair. But the fact that he'd lied before, said he'd been at a bar when we could prove he'd been at her place, and that he claimed he'd been at home when he hadn't, the neighbor's testimony about a man leaving, and Mrs. Parker explaining she'd lied because she was afraid he'd kill her if she didn't—it didn't take the jury long."

She felt nauseous and wanted to get out, but her reportorial instincts were strong and she had a sudden intuition. "You put the magazine and hair cream in the apartment, didn't you? That was too convenient."

He looked at her with something like admiration. "Sometimes Occam's Razor needs a little help. I knew he was guilty, but the sheriff needed a road map."

Ms. Bruce gathered up her things, eager to find a drink, but there was one thing that puzzled her, and as she reached the door she turned back. "But why had Mrs. Parker lied for him in the first place?"

He didn't answer at first, just cocked his head and looked at her. She was turning the knob when he said, in the quiet, confident, courtroom voice she remembered, "She didn't. She lied for me."

Ms. Bruce felt her knees give and grasped the doorjam. "What . . . what do you mean?"

"He *had* been home by eight."

"But how did you get her . . . Why would she . . ."

"I persuaded her that her husband had been planning to leave her. Oddly enough, that affected her as his affairs and fists never had."

Stork shook his head. "You know, she wouldn't divorce him, even after he was convicted and was awaiting execution. She wanted next of kin privileges in the front row of the execution chamber. She sat next to me."

"But then, who . . ."

He turned his hands palms up. "My estimate of the time of death must have been off, don't you think? He killed her before he went home. As I said, it's not an exact science." Seeing the look on her face he added, "We all make mistakes, you know."

After she left, he realized he hadn't consulted the file at all. It had been so many years. He switched on his desk light and opened the folder. All it held were some notes, and a scrap of yellowed paper. The handwriting on the scrap was faded, but he knew it by heart, and just wanted to touch the lines she had written, those many years before. All that was left, after he'd torn her letter to shreds and thrown it in her face, after he'd done the monstrous thing that couldn't be undone, after he'd gathered the shreds and flushed them away, all but this one, pinned under her poor, broken body.

> *. . . so when we meet again,*
> *I will be Mrs. Ralph Parker,*
> *but still your friend.*
> *Affectionately, Maddie.*

No one but he, and she and Mrs. Parker had ever seen it, or ever would.

ON THE EVIDENCE
A LIAM CAMPBELL SHORT STORY

BY DANA STABENOW

WEDNESDAY AFTERNOON

IT WAS TWELVE BELOW ZERO, the high for the day, and if Millie Godden hadn't chosen to go into labor with a breech delivery during a first birth, it wouldn't have been Larry Bartman's first choice to be in the air that January afternoon. But when Millie Godden's frantic husband had raised dispatch on the marine band, Larry's name had been first on the Civil Air Patrol volunteer list.

When the phone rang he'd been curled up on his warm, wide couch, submitting happily to an enthusiastic and comprehensive ravishment by Alice Sampson, a pert young barista of nineteen, to whom Larry had given some thought to proposing. In this small town on stilts twenty-five miles north of the Arctic Circle the ratio of men to women was such that if you missed your turn you lost your place in line and were out of luck until summer when the park ranger interns showed up. Even then, if you did get lucky, three months later your luck went south again.

Still, Kotzebue was why God invented bush pilots, and there was nowhere else Larry was going to rack up the hours he needed to gain his commercial pilot's license as fast as he would here. This quick turnaround to Kiana would add another hour, hour and a half to an already impressive total.

And Alice had promised to wait for him.

They slipped over the edge of the mainland, leaving the frozen expanse of Kotzebue Sound behind them. Black spruce marched through snow up to their ears up across the Kobuk River Delta and right up the sides of the

Baird Mountains on the northern horizon. A movement caught Larry's eye and he looked down to see a timber wolf as it melted into the edge of the trees. A moment later he saw what had caught the wolf's attention, a cow moose with a calf, curled up together in a small clearing, conserving energy through the cold snap.

Howie Callahan nudged Larry with his elbow. "Hey," he said over his headset, and pointed down at the white surface of the Kobuk River. "What's that?"

Larry put the right wing down and the plane went into a wide, descending circle with the moving object on the river's surface below in its center.

"It's a man," Callahan said. "What's he doing on foot way the hell out here?"

Below them the man raised his face in their direction and waved his hands over his head.

"Must have been thrown by his snowgo," Larry said. He brought the plane around again, a slow, smooth glide ten feet off the deck, neck craned to check the surface of the river. He didn't spot anything to worry him, no open leads and a mostly smooth surface after Monday's snowfall, and came around a third time, setting down gently, the airplane rolling out to a graceful stop.

Larry opened his door and said, "You need a ride?"

The man started toward them, stumbled, got up, and came forward in a shambling run. As he got closer, they could see his eyes, wide, reddened, a little wild in a face that was burned red by sun and wind and cold. "They're all dead!" he yelled. "They're all dead, I'm the only one left!"

THURSDAY MORNING

The phone rang right next to Liam's ear. He snatched it up before it could ring again. "It's supposed to be my day off."

"Yes, sir," Corporal Prince replied amiably, ignoring the snarl in her superior officer's voice.

Next to him, Wy muttered and burrowed beneath the covers. Corporal

Prince was not so lacking in a sense of self-preservation that she either chuckled evilly over his irritation or commented on the company he was keeping. "You've got an urgent call from Kotzebue, sir. I thought you'd want to take it."

"Who?"

"Johnny Nageak."

Johnny Nageak had been a village public safety officer in training when Liam had taught a semester at the trooper academy. "What's he want?" he said, with marginally less truculence.

"He says he's got a situation he needs help with."

Liam gave up trying to scrub his brain awake through his scalp. "What's the Kotz trooper post say?"

"They're shorthanded."

Liam snorted. "Who isn't."

"Yes, sir, but they've got an attempted murder of a schoolteacher in Kivalina, and a bootlegger in Buckland, and—"

"Save it, I get the picture. What's Johnny's deal?"

"There's been a shooting. Four men down, one survivor the only eyewitness." Prince paused. "One of the dead men is named Nageak, sir. He didn't say, but I'm guessing that's why Officer Nageak wants you up there pronto. I've taken the liberty of booking you a seat on the first flight out."

"Hold on a minute," he said, and switched on the light. "Wy."

She rolled over and glared at him through a tangle of bronze curls. "What."

"I have to go to Kotzebue. How far is it?"

"About five hundred miles."

"Can we get there in your Cessna?"

She laughed.

"There's a murder scene out of Kotz I have to get to immediately."

She stopped laughing and threw off the covers to swing her feet to the floor. Over her shoulder she said, "I'll call around, see what I can find. This time of year everybody's grounded except for Alaska Airlines."

He watched her ass as she walked into the bathroom. She knew he was watching, and she was putting a little extra into it.

"Sir?" Prince said in his ear.

"Huh? Oh. Hold off on confirming the seat on the jet," he said, "Wy's going to try to rustle something up that might be a little more direct."

"I'll just bet she is," Prince said, but by then Liam had put down the receiver and joined Wy in the shower.

THURSDAY EVENING

Kurt Fraad was white, which surprised Liam when he walked into the interview room.

He found Fraad's story almost credible, which surprised him even more.

But what really knocked him off his balance was finding Kurt's father sitting next to him.

He looked at Johnny Nageak. Johnny's expression gave nothing away, but then he was Inupiaq and they medalled in poker face.

Liam turned to Karl Fraad. "Sir, could I ask you to step out? I need to speak to Kurt alone."

Karl, burly arms folded, massive, low-slung brow furrowed, eyes glaring, sat where he was.

Liam could force the issue but it would require fuss and bother, not to mention a large amount of physical exertion, and Liam had always preferred guile to brawn. He pulled out a chair. "I wanted to ask you some questions, Kurt."

"I already gave my statement to Officer Nageak," Kurt said. He clasped thin, almost frail hands on the table in front of him, peering out at Liam beneath hair growing untidily over the shelf of a brow he shared with his father. He was nineteen, according to Johnny Nageak, although he looked an undernourished twelve. "I don't know what more I can tell you." He dropped his head. "I ran," he said, his voice muffled. "I ran and hid. That's the only reason I'm here." He looked up, his eyes wet. "Maybe if I hadn't run—"

"Sometimes," Liam said, steering Kurt briskly away from the emotional shoal he was headed for all ahead full, "we remember more about events we've witnessed when we talk about them a little bit. They kept you in the hospital overnight, didn't they?"

"Yes," Kurt said in a low voice. "They were really nice to me, too. And I even told them that I ran, I—"

"Well, Kurt, shock from what you witnessed, followed immediately by exposure—" Liam shook his head. "I wouldn't be surprised if your memory of events was more than a little fuzzy." He smiled. No women were immune to Liam's smile, and for that matter very few men. "Could we just go through it? Only once more, I promise."

Kurt looked from Liam to his father. "Is it okay, Dad?"

There was a long pause. Liam kept his face as bland as possible beneath the burning stare. Kurt might be soothed, but Karl wasn't buying Liam's act for a moment. Still, a low growl rumbled up out of Karl's barrel chest that might have been assent.

"Good," Liam said. "Let's start with why you were in Kiana to begin with."

Karl was a construction manager for the Arctic Housing Authority. He lived in Anchorage, but was at present working from Kotzebue, surveying the outlying villages to assess each community's housing needs. Kurt had come with him, Liam gathered, because he didn't have much else going on at the time. Delicate inquiry as to Kurt's present employment came up with a reply of "business consultant," offered by his father, which was about the best description of someone who'd never held down a real job that Liam had ever heard.

While Kurt and Karl were in Kiana—the alliteration alone on this case was going to drive Liam insane—the village elders, always happy to see someone who was going to build them more housing, offered to take Kurt on a caribou hunt while Karl was busy in the village. Kurt accepted, Karl agreed, and Kurt left the following day, January 22, on the back of Noah Adams's snow machine, carrying the new .30-30 Winchester his father had given him for his birthday the week before. At three o'clock that afternoon they arrived at the camp Ray Nageak and Ben Amunson had set up the day before. That evening, Lars Kayuqtuq of Ambler, returning home from a hunting trip of his own, stopped by and stayed for dinner. Afterward, Kayuqtuq continued up the river.

At about ten o'clock, after Kurt had gone into the tent, he heard another snow machine approach. "It was cold," Kurt said, shivering at the memory. "There was ice on the inside of the tent. I didn't want to get out of my sleeping bag. I heard Noah and the other guys talking to a fourth guy whose voice I didn't recognize."

"Could you make out what they were saying?"

"I could hear them fine, but they were talking Eskimo," Kurt said. "They sounded mad, though."

Liam wondered if the new arrival had been drinking. "Was there alcohol in camp?" he said.

Kurt looked shocked. "Oh no, nothing like that. I don't think any of those guys drank. At least they didn't in front of me."

Liam nodded and motioned Kurt to continue.

The next day the four men went hunting for caribou. Or three of them did.

"I fell off the snogo," Kurt said. He didn't look at his father. "I had to follow on foot. By the time I caught up to them, they had already shot twelve caribou. I helped butcher them out, and we made camp for the night. They fried up some caribou heart. First time I ever ate something like that. It was really good, I was surprised."

"How far did you have to walk?"

"I don't know. Miles. It took hours for me to catch up."

"Not much fun, postholing through the snow on a cold winter day," Liam said in a neutral voice, and waited for a reaction.

Kurt shrugged. "They were hunting for food for their families. I understood."

"Still. One of them could have swung around and picked you up."

Kurt looked Liam in the eye and said firmly, "It was my own fault,

Sergeant Campbell. I'm not used to riding on a snogo and I had on the wrong gloves and my hands were so cold I couldn't hang on. And they told me they were in a hurry, that the caribou herd could move on and it would take that much longer to find them. And we only had food for five days."

Liam nodded, keeping his expression interested and cordial, acutely aware of the solid bulk of parental wrath simmering away at Kurt's side. "You butchered out the caribou, you set up camp, you had dinner. What happened next?"

"I hit the rack," Kurt said. His smile was rueful. "It had been a long day for me, and I was tired." His smile faded, and his face took on a strained look. "The guy on the snogo came back."

"The same one who had been there the night before?"

"Yes."

He recognized the sound of the snow machine because it was running very roughly. Again there was conversation in raised voices. This time Kurt got up to look.

The new guy was another Eskimo. He was wearing a dark green parka with fur trim around the hood. He had on a dark blue headband with the word "Alaska" written in white across it. He had a beard. His snow machine looked old, the black seat worn through in spots, the maker's name chipped and rusted off to the point of illegibility.

Kurt got cold so he crawled back in his sleeping bag. The voices outside the tent got louder. The snow machine with the bad engine started up again and moved away. Noah Evans and Ray Nageak came into the tent and started to get into their sleeping bags.

"That's when we heard the shots," Kurt said. "We could hear Ben's voice shouting 'No, no!' And then we couldn't hear him anymore."

Noah and Ray grabbed for their clothes, and then the bullets started hitting the tent. Noah went down first, then Ray. "They were in the middle of the tent, and I was in my bag on the side. I think that's the only reason I didn't get hit. Noah's knife was on his belt, and I used it to cut a way out of the back of the tent and ran and hid behind a tree. I looked back and I could see the guy shooting." He swallowed hard. "And then he stopped."

The killer got back on his snow machine and headed out in the direction of what Kurt thought was Kiana.

It was a vivid and detailed description. Kurt's voice shook a little when he gave it, and his face was pale and strained. This guy was either telling the truth or he was the best liar Liam had ever met, and he'd met some pretty good ones in his years on the force.

Kurt sat back with a shaky sigh. "I went back to the tent to get my clothes. And then I just started walking."

"Why didn't you take one of the snow machines?"

Kurt flushed again. "I don't know how to drive one," he said, shooting his father an anxious look. "And I was scared the guy would come back. I wanted to get out of there before he came back. I just—I don't know, I guess I just panicked, and ran."

Johnny looked at Liam when he came out of the room. "Feelings are running pretty high, Liam. We need to get both of them out of town."

They were in the school cafeteria, commandeered for them by the town mayor. Two doors into hallways leading to classrooms were monitored by grim-faced adults, around which peeked curious faces. Wy was sitting at one of the tables, nursing a cup of coffee. "I'm good to go," she said.

They parked the Fraads, pére et fils, at the airport terminal in Kotzebue, notified the troopers in Anchorage that the Fraads were on their way in and told them to make sure they didn't immediately get on another plane headed even farther south, stopped briefly in Kiana to pick up Johnny Nageak, and flew out to the scene.

It was after 2 p.m. by the time they got there and that flat bright light peculiar to an arctic winter sun was beginning its inevitable slide into a softer lavender twilight. Shadows lengthened on the Kobuk River, a white swath making wide turns through a dark forest of black spruce. It was clear and cold and absolutely still when Johnny touched Wy's shoulder and pointed. She banked immediately, a turn so smooth it felt painted on the sky. Liam was concentrating so hard on keeping the plane up in the air by the grip he had on his seat that he didn't realize they had landed until he heard the snow passing beneath the skis with a sibilant hiss. They stopped and Wy pushed in the throttle and the engine died. Liam took a deep and he hoped unobtrusive breath and let it out with a long sigh.

When he got out the cold hit him like a blow. The inside of his nose felt frozen, and he could actually feel the frost forming around his mouth. He pulled the hood of his parka as far forward as it would go. "Stay with the plane," he told Wy.

"Like hell," she said.

Liam would have sighed but he was afraid his lungs would freeze on the inhale. "Fine, but don't step on any evidence."

The camp was in a clearing about fifty feet off the bend of the river. The tent was Army surplus olive green, a battered twelve-by-twelve with front and back flaps, pitched to face south. A snow machine track that had seen a lot of use ran the fifty yards between the river's edge and the front flap of the tent. Another, lesser used track led to the back of the tent and into the woods beyond. A single track broke off a few feet up the bank from the river and made a loop around the camp before joining the main trail again.

Two snow machines sat in front of the tent, both with sleds attached. Liam and Johnny took photographs of the tracks surrounding them, thawing out the cameras under their arms between shots, and then Liam straddled the Bearcat and opened the gas cap. Johnny produced a flashlight and they both peered inside.

"Half full," Johnny said.

Liam nodded and replaced the cap. He pressed the starter and the engine roared to life. He switched it off and looked at Johnny. "How cold was it last night?"

Johnny shrugged. "Forty below? Forty-five?"

The other snow machine, a Ski-Doo Mach Z, took a little more coaxing, but it, too, started eventually.

They went through the sleds, which were loaded with camping and hunting gear, including a Winchester .243 caliber rifle. Liam's nose was so cold he couldn't smell if it had been fired recently.

"Liam," Johnny said, pointing with the flashlight.

In front of the Bearcat, two brass casings gleamed. "Get a photo," Liam said, and when Johnny was done, picked up the casings. "A thirty-ought-six and a thirty-thirty," he said, and bagged them.

There was more camping gear and multiple caribou carcasses in various stages of butchering out in the snow around the camp. Johnny found another rifle, a Winchester Model 94 in a case. He held up a box of .30-30 ammunition.

Liam nodded, and turned his flashlight to the tent. He heard Wy's breath go out in a little sigh.

A man lay on his stomach next to the side of the tent facing the river. He was fully dressed in jeans, boots, and a plaid shirt, but no coat. Both hands were stretched out in front of him, holding a pine bough.

"Ben Amunson," Johnny said.

Amunson was stiff with cold and death. He'd been shot more than once, but by now it was too dark to count how many times. The snow was stained in a trail that led to the front flap of the tent.

Liam stepped around Amunson's body, his boots crunching into the top layer of fallen snow, and lifted the tent flap. It caught on something. He pulled, and it came away, revealing an overturned camp stove. Beyond the stove was a second body, also lying face down, also fully clothed.

"Ray Nageak," Johnny said.

Like Amunson, Nageak's body showed multiple gunshot wounds. The knife sheath on his belt was empty.

Against the rear wall of the tent was the third man, on his back, shirt on, hands grasping the waist of his pants, which were halfway up his legs.

"Noah Adams," Johnny said.

The tent was a mess, the stove and cots overturned, pots, dishes, utensils, duffle bags, parkas, mittens, boots scattered wall to wall. The tea kettle sat oddly upright in the center of the debris field, pierced dead center by a bullet hole. Brass winked up at Liam from wherever he turned the flashlight.

"They were going for their weapons," Wy said.

"They got off some shots," Johnny said.

Liam stepped outside to play the light from the flash over the front of the tent. "Bullet holes in the front of the tent about four feet off the ground," he said, and stepped back inside to run the light across the back of the tent. "Bullets holes on the back wall about a foot off the ground."

In the rapidly waning light they examined the snow machine tracks around the camp. Liam's feet were slowly going numb when he pointed at one track. "Last one in and out."

"Yeah," Johnny said. "Evinrude."

Liam squinted at the horizon, a deep plum fading to black. "Headed east?"

Johnny nodded. "Ambler, be my guess."

"How far?"

"Around seventy-five miles, but there'll be cabins along the way. Someone will have seen or heard something."

Liam, who by now could no longer feel his nose, couldn't imagine why anyone would stick theirs out before spring, but then this wasn't his part of the country.

A wolf howled. Another one answered, sounding closer. "We'd better get the bodies out of here."

They hauled them down the river to a long straight stretch and loaded them into the Skywagon Wy had acquired in Kotz. It took a while to get into the air, and they were almost to Kotz before the interior of the plane warmed up. Luckily, it wasn't enough time for the bodies to thaw out.

Johnny Nageak's wife Bertha served them caribou liver and onions, after which Liam and Wy retired to the town's lone hotel. The room was shabby but clean, and the bed had a rut down the middle of it that suited them both.

"Again?" she said drowsily sometime in the night, coming awake to the slow stroke of his hands. "Something about Kotzebue that turns you on?"

He didn't answer, concentrating on drowning out the memory of that awkward stack of frozen bodies in the back of the plane in the seductive taste of her flesh.

The next morning Liam sent the bodies to Anchorage for forensic autopsy on the 7 a.m. jet. At noon, Brill, the medical examiner, called to give it as his opinion that all three men had died of multiple gunshot wounds. He asked Liam if he'd recovered any of the bullets, and Liam replied that he'd be recovering same just as soon as the ground thawed out in the spring. "Ah yes, the joys of crime scene investigation in the Arctic," Brill said cheerfully, and hung up.

Liam, Johnny, and Wy returned to the camp. They picked up Kurt Fraad's tracks heading south and used the two snow machines to follow them to where he'd been rescued. "Pretty much supports his story," Liam said.

"But why the hell would he walk out?" Johnny said. "Both the snogoes started on the first try."

"He said he didn't know how to drive one." He met Johnny's eyes. "I know, sounds lame to me, too, but I've heard dumber from cheechakoes, and so have you." He looked at Wy. "Any thoughts?"

She was frowning. "I don't know. Something . . ." Her voice trailed away. "I don't know," she said finally.

Johnny, whose manners were too good to let him query Liam as to why he was asking his girlfriend what she thought, very carefully did not hear this conversation.

They went north again and picked up the tracks of the Evinrude and followed them upriver to a snug log cabin on the mouth of the Fish River.

They left the machines on the river and stopped as soon as they came in sight of the door. "Hello the house!" Liam shouted. He had to shout pretty loud to be heard over the dogs howling out back.

The door was already open. "Hello backatcha!" a voice came down the bank. "Who's that?"

"It's Johnny Nageak, Tom," Johnny said, "along with a couple of troopers." He looked at Wy. "No offense."

She grinned. "None taken."

"You here about the shooting?" the voice said.

"Yeah. We're following some tracks. Talk to you a minute?"

"Come on up."

The cabin was home to Tom Burnside, a white man from Ohio, his wife Rhonda, an Inupiaq from Kiana, and their two daughters, Susie and Billie Jo, who peeped out at the visitors from behind their mother, fists clenched in her kuspuk. "Yeah," Burnside said in response to their question, "I heard that Evinrude pass by about nine o'clock that night."

"They didn't stop?"

Burnside shook his head. He was a big man with a full head of black hair and a big black beard, both neatly trimmed, deliberate of speech and movement. His wife was a tiny slip of a thing with snapping black eyes. She nodded at Johnny and gave Liam a discreet but distinctly appreciative once-over. She looked at Wy and her eyes widened. She said something in Inupiaq.

Wy shook her head. "I'm sorry," she said. "I don't speak Inupiaq."

"But you've got some," Rhonda said.

"My grandfather is Yupik," Wy said. "Moses Alakuyak."

Rhonda looked at Burnside and let loose with a stream of Inupiaq. Burnside replied laboriously in the same tongue and added, "English, Rhonda. We have guests." But Wy noticed that Burnside never once met her eyes after that.

On their way back down to the river, Liam let Johnny Nageak draw a little ahead. "What was that about?" he said to Wy in a low voice.

"I don't know," Wy said woodenly, "I don't speak Inupiaq."

He saw her expression and shut up. It wasn't easy being the granddaughter of someone most of western Alaska knew as the Old Man. A shaman and a drunk, no one but Moses knew which had come first, and only he and Wy and Liam knew that he might have passed on something to Wy that was more than blood and bone.

They continued to follow the Evinrude tracks north, stopping at three more cabins along the way. All reported hearing the snow machine pass by. None could identify the driver.

After they left the last cabin, Wy said, "This is crap, Liam. I'd bet money folks here can tell who's driving what up and down the river the same way folks in Bristol Bay can tell who's flying what overhead without looking up."

"I know," Liam said, and caught up with Johnny as he prepared to mount his snow machine. "Who was driving the Evinrude?"

Johnny looked up the river. "Be dark soon. We should head for the barn."

Liam tapped the badge on the front of Johnny's hat. "That mean anything to you, Johnny?"

A tinge of color crept up into Johnny's face, and for a change it wasn't windburn. Liam waited, and was mildly surprised when the other man answered before Liam had lost all the feeling in his fingers and toes.

"Simon Adams owns an Evinrude something like this model," Johnny said.

"Simon Adams?"

Johnny nodded, and blew on his hands. It was another heartbreaker of a day, sky the color of glass and temperature a murderous forty-two below zero.

"Any relation to Noah Adams?" Liam said.

Johnny nodded again. "His brother."

Liam struggled with himself. Ray Nageak, and now Simon Adams. What were the odds? "Did they get along?"

Johnny met his yes. "Well, if you're asking, I'd have to say, not real well, no."

"I'm asking," Liam said. "What happened?"

"Noah married Simon's girl while Simon was doing his National Guard service last year. Didn't help that Bev was in the family way before Simon left for Iraq."

"Liam," Wy said.

"What," he said, grimly.

"This wasn't a Inupiaq guy going off on a bunch of other Inupiaq guys. If there was alcohol involved, maybe. Maybe," she repeated, emphasizing the word. "But even Kurt says there was no drinking in camp, and going berserker on your ass isn't something these people do without artificially induced inspiration. Besides, what reason did this Simon have to take out the other two guys?"

"Still got to talk to him," Liam said, looking at Johnny.

Johnny, impassive, swung his leg over the snow machine. "He'll be in Ambler. We can spend the night in the school there."

When they got to Ambler, Simon Adams was nowhere to be found.

They found his .30-30, though, leaning up against the wall of his shack, just inside the door.

Liam picked it up. "We find thirty-thirty shells inside the tent?" he said to Johnny, already knowing the answer.

"Liam," Wy said.

Johnny gave a slow nod, not meeting Liam's eyes.

"We'll be taking this with us," Liam told the elder who had led them to Adams's place.

"Liam," Wy said again.

"Not now," Liam said.

Wy set her teeth and followed him outside.

It was too dark to follow the Evinrude's tracks that afternoon, so they waited until morning. They were easy to find with the shallow morning sun casting long shadows, and it wasn't two hours before they caught up with Simon Adams.

He hadn't taken his .30-30 with him because he had his .357 with him instead. Sometime the night before, he'd put the barrel in his mouth and pulled the trigger.

He'd been sitting in the snow with his back up against a spruce tree, and he'd frozen solid in that position, what was left of his brains splattered across the outspread branches like Christmas tree flocking. It was hell getting the body into the plane, and torture getting the door closed on it.

They found Bev in Kivalina, where she told the village public safety officer that Noah and Simon had fought when Simon came home. Noah had put her on a plane to Kivalina to keep her out of harm's way. She told them that Simon had been drinking before the fight, and that Noah had tried not to hurt him but that Simon had forced Noah to put him down hard. This had happened in Ambler the previous week, and right after that Noah had headed for Kiana to go hunting with his cousins.

Johnny talked to the Ambler elders and they were persuaded to admit that Simon had been holed up in his shack, drinking up a good portion of the local bootlegger's inventory, ever since. The day of the massacre, he had left early, last seen heading down river on the Evinrude.

That seemed to be that. When they got back to Kotzebue, there was a message waiting from Brill, who had called to say that by some twist of malign fate all of the wounds in all three bodies were through and through, no bullets or pieces of bullets remaing. "A hell of a mess, though," Brill said on voice mail. "Looks like somebody used a Cuisinart on these guys, on the inside, anyway."

The next morning Wy and Liam took off at daybreak.

Liam was marginally more comfortable at cruising altitude than he was at takeoff or landing, which explained why he didn't immediately notice which direction they were headed. "Uh, Wy?"

"What?" Her voice over the headphones was remote.

"Aren't we going in the wrong direction?"

"No."

He looked at the control panel and located the compass. "North-northeast? Last time I looked on a map, Newenham was south-southeast of Kotz."

"I need to check out something. It'll just take an hour or so."

Liam thought about this for a minute. "Do we have to land to check it out?" he said, without much hope for a reply in the negative.

"Yes," she said.

"What I thought," he said, and focused on the horizon, trying to white out the fact that there was only a thousand feet of nothing but air between his ass and the nearest object with the most gravitational pull.

She set them down gently on the surface of the river in spite of gravity, almost exactly in the tracks of the plane that had rescued Kurt Fraad the week before. She pulled two pairs of snowshoes out of the back of the plane and Liam was so glad to be even temporarily in connection yet again with Mother Earth that he didn't whine about the fact that it was now forty-five below zero.

Instead, he followed Wy up the river as she backtracked Kurt's postholing footsteps. It was, among other things, a fine opportunity to watch Wy's ass in motion, and he became so absorbed in the pastime that he didn't notice at first when she veered off Kurt's trail and headed for the side of the river.

"Hey," he said, waking up to the fact. "What's going on?"

She kept going until she reached the bank, a high white wall of snow and ice sparkling in the sun. The wall curved inward, topped with bare, spare bones of leafless brush looking as if they'd been gelled in place by a giant hand. Wy, moving as if she knew where she was going, knelt down and crawled beneath the overhang. She brushed at the snow. Liam could hear the sound of her down mitten scraping at the ice. "Wy, what on earth—"

A part of the icy bank fell away, then more, revealing a long, narrow hole in the bank. Wy tugged, and the rifle came free easily.

They stood, staring down at it for a long time.

"A thirty-thirty," Liam said.

Wy nodded, and pointed at a stain on the stock. "Blood?"

"Yeah," Liam said, and pointed at another and said, unnecessarily, "and brains."

They carried it back to the plane in silence and climbed inside. The engine, mercifully, started at first try.

"How did you know it was here?" Liam said, raising his voice to be heard over the roar.

Her mouth twisted. "I'm Moses Alakuyak's granddaughter," she said.

"I was in my sleeping bag, listening to them talk," Kurt said. "They were talking in Eskimo. I couldn't understand what they were saying. I was scared. I had to pee so I got up and went outside and one of them grabbed his rifle and started shooting, and I grabbed my rifle and started shooting back." He began to weep. "It was awful, I was all alone, all the way out there in the middle of nowhere. I just knew I was going to die."

"All three of them were outside talking?" Liam said.

"Yes," Kurt said, wiping his eyes with the heel of his hand.

"Funny how we found two of the men inside the tent," Liam said.

Kurt looked around, probably for his father, who this time hadn't been allowed anywhere near the interview room. They were in Anchorage this time too, and Liam had backup. "I don't know how that happened," he said, faltering.

"Oh, I think you do," Liam said, but he'd been at it for eight hours, with Kurt changing his story on average once per hour, and he needed more coffee if he was going to stay awake.

On the other side of the door a district attorney in a three-piece suit with a miniskirt and four-inch heels cocked a hip, displaying her admittedly killer legs for his appreciation. "A nutcase, but he knew what he was doing and he knew it was wrong. Slam dunk."

At trial, the defense claimed that Kurt Fraad was suffering from a paranoid psychosis with delusions of persecution, exacerbated by being in the middle of a killing field, pieces of dead caribou and blood all around him, with three Natives who couldn't or wouldn't speak English to him. "Mr. Fraad was totally unprepared for this hunt," said the defense shrink. "He felt himself to be in danger of losing his life, and he shot these men in self-defense."

The jury didn't buy it, finding Kurt guilty on all three counts. After the trial, the foreman told a reporter that the testimony of Dr. Brill and the graphic description of the multiple gunshot wounds in all three victims were what had put the prosecution's case over. Liam had testified to finding the rifle and to tracing the registration back to Fraad senior, and jury members were warmly complimentary of the professionalism of the state's finest. Wy's name hadn't come up.

Outside the courtroom, Brill tapped Liam on the shoulder. "You going back up to the scene anytime?"

Liam shook his head and hooked a thumb over his shoulder. "No need to."

Brill raised an eyebrow. "You that sure you got the right thirty-thirty? There were two of them, Adams's and Nageak's. I'd like to have just one bullet from a test round, and be sure."

Liam thought about Wy that day, snowshoeing determinedly upriver, goaded by some force she feared to identify and that he would not, could not question. "There are more things in heaven and earth, Horatio," he said beneath his breath.

"What?" Brillo said.

Liam adjusted his cap and slapped Brill on the shoulder.

"Forensics isn't everything," he said.

ABOUT THE AUTHORS

N. J. AYRES has published three forensics-based novels and numerous short stories and poems. When not indulging in common writers' delusions, Ayres edits reports and proposals dealing with the cleanup of spent lead and cartridges at firing ranges in the Northeast, frequently going on-site to better document the challenges and processes. Of course, a story will emanate from these experiences as well as from special locales in each of the nine U.S. states in which she has lived.

A police officer with the Matteson, Illinois, Police Department for twenty-nine years, **SERGEANT MICHAEL A. BLACK** is the author of two different series: one featuring Chicago-based private investigator Ron Shade *(A Killing Frost, Windy City Knights, A Final Judgment)* and the other featuring the male/female police detectives Leal and Hart *(Random Victim and the upcoming Hostile Takeovers)*. This award-winning author has also written two nonfiction works for young adults, two stand-alone thrillers *(The Heist and Freeze Me, Tender)*, a pulp-era adventure *(Melody of Vengeance)* and a novel with a celebrity who shall at the moment remain nameless. In addition, Mike collaborated with his writing partner, Julie Hyzy, on the recently released *Dead Ringer* (Five Star) in which Mike's private eye, Ron Shade, and Julie's protagonist, Alex St. James, team up to solve a baffling conspiracy. Please visit: www.michaelablack.com

MAX ALLAN COLLINS is the author of the *New York Times* best-selling graphic novel *Road to Perdition*, made into the Academy Award–winning film starring Tom Hanks and Paul Newman. His other credits include such comics as *Batman, Dick Tracy,* and his own *Ms. Tree;* film scripts for HBO and Lifetime TV; and the Shamus Award–winning Nathan Heller detective

264 | AT THE SCENE OF THE CRIME

novels. His tie-in novels include the best-sellers *Saving Private Ryan, Air Force One,* and *American Gangster.* He lives in Muscatine, Iowa, with his wife, Barb, a writer.

MATTHEW V. CLEMENS has collaborated with Collins as forensics researcher and co-plotter on eight *USA Today* best-selling *CSI* novels, two *CSI: MIAMI* novels, and tie-in novels for the TV series *Dark Angel, Bones,* and *Criminal Minds.* He and Collins have published over a dozen short stories together (some gathered in their collection *My Lolita Complex*). He is the coauthor of the true-crime regional bestseller, *Dead Water.* He lives in Davenport, Iowa, with his wife, Pam, a teacher.

BRENDAN DUBOIS is an award-winning author of short stories and novels. His short fiction has appeared in various publications, including *Playboy, Ellery Queen's Mystery Magazine,* and *Alfred Hitchcock's Mystery Magazine,* as well as numerous anthologies, including *The Best Mystery Stories of the Century.* He has twice received a Shamus Award for his short fiction and has been nominated for three Edgar Allan Poe Awards. DuBois' long fiction includes six previous books in the Lewis Cole mystery series, as well as several other suspense thrillers. DuBois lives in New Hampshire with his wife, Mona.

LOREN D. ESTLEMAN is the author of more than sixty novels. He has earned five Spur Awards from the Western Writers of America, four Shamus Awards from the Private Eye Writers of America, and three Western Heritage Awards from the National Cowboy Hall of Fame. In 2007, the Library of Michigan named his twentieth Amos Walker, private detective, novel *American Detective,* a Notable Book of the Year, and *Publishers' Weekly* singled it out as one of only eight mysteries on its list of 100 Best Novels of 2007.

JEREMIAH HEALY, a graduate of Rutgers College and Harvard Law School, is the creator of the John Francis Cuddy private investigator series and (under the pseudonym "Terry Devane") the Mairead O'Clare legal thriller series, both set primarily in Boston. Jerry has written eighteen novels and over sixty short stories, sixteen of which works have won or been nominated for the Shamus Award. He served a four-year term as the president of the International Association of Crime Writers (IACW), and he was the American Guest of Honour at the 35th World Mystery Convention (or "Bouchercon" —phonetically: "BOUGH-shur-con") in Toronto during October 2004. Currently he serves on the National Board of Directors for the Mystery Writers of America.

EDWARD D. HOCH (1930-2008) was a past president of Mystery Writers of America and winner of its Edgar Award for best short story. In 2001 he received MWA's Grand Master Award. He had been the guest of honor at Bouchercon, twice winner of its Anthony Award, and recipient of its Lifetime Achievement Award. The Private Eye Writers of America honored him with its Life Achievement Award as well. Author of some 950 published stories, his fiction appeared in every issue of *Ellery Queen's Mystery Magazine* for the past thirty-five years.

JULIE HYZY'S newest series debuted last January with *State of the Onion* featuring Olivia (Ollie) Paras, a White House chef who feeds the First Family and saves the world in her spare time. The second book in the series, tentatively titled *Hail to the Chef,* is due out soon. Julie has also written two books in her other series featuring Chicago news researcher and amateur sleuth Alex St. James, *Deadly Blessings* and *Deadly Interest,* which won the 2007 Lovey Award for best traditional mystery. Julie's short story, "Strictly Business," in the Bleak House anthology, *These Guns for Hire,* won a 2007 Derringer Award from the Short Mystery Fiction Society. In addition, Julie collaborated with her writing partner, Michael A. Black, on the recently released *Dead Ringer* (Five Star) where Julie's Chicago news reporter, Alex St. James, works with Mike's private eye, Ron Shade, to uncover a shocking mystery.

JOHN LUTZ is the author of more than forty novels and approximately 250 short stories and articles. He authored the book that was made into the hit movie *Single White Female,* and coauthored the screenplay for the HBO movie *The Ex,* adapted from his novel of the same title. He has won both the Edgar and Shamus awards, the Golden Derringer Lifetime Achievement Award for mystery short fiction, and the Shamus Lifetime Achievement Award. He has been president of both the Mystery Writers of America and Private Eye Writers of America. His latest novel is the *New York Times* bestseller *In for the Kill.*

KRISTINE KATHRYN RUSCH is an award-winning mystery, science fiction, romance, and mainstream author. Her latest mystery novel, written as Kris Nelscott, is *Days of Rage.* Her latest science fiction novel is a science fiction mystery called *The Recovery Man.* To find out more about her, look at her website, www.kristinekathrynrusch.com.

DANA STABENOW was born in Anchorage and raised on a seventy-five-foot fish tender in the Gulf of Alaska. She knew there was a warmer, drier job out there and she found it in writing. Her first science fiction novel, *Second Star* sank without a trace, her first crime fiction novel, *A Cold Day for Murder* won an Edgar award, her first thriller, *Blindfold Game* hit the *New York Times* bestseller list, and her twenty-fifth novel and sixteenth Kate Shugak novel, *Whisper to the Blood*, comes out in February 2009. No, she doesn't believe it either

JEANNE C. STEIN was raised in San Diego, the setting for her Anna Strong Vampire series. She now lives with her husband outside Denver, Colorado. where besides working on her books and short stories, she edits a newsletter for a beer importer and takes kick boxing classes to stay in shape.

MAYNARD F. THOMSON is the author of numerous novels, short stories, and articles. A lawyer, he was for many years a partner in one of America's leading law firms, specializing in litigation on behalf of large, well-heeled corporations hoping to shield their plunder from the red horde. Today he lives with his wife, Laura, and Airedale, Abby, in northern New Hampshire, where he plots crimes and climbs rocks.